SHAKESPEARE
FOR EVERY
NIGHT
OF THE YEAR

SHAKESPEARE
FOR EVERY
NIGHT
OF THE YEAR

EDITED BY COLIN SALTER

–

ILLUSTRATED BY DÁNIEL SZINVAI

BATSFORD

First published in the United Kingdom
in 2024 by
Batsford
43 Great Ormond Street
London WC1N 3HZ

An imprint of B. T. Batsford Holdings Limited

ISBN 9781849948241

A CIP catalogue record for this book is available from the British Library.

10 9 8 7 6 5 4 3 2

Reproduction by Rival Colour Ltd, UK
Printed by Dreamcolour, China

This book can be ordered direct from the publisher at www.batsfordbooks.com, or try your local bookshop

MIX
Paper | Supporting
responsible forestry
FSC® C188448
FSC
www.fsc.org

CONTENTS

INTRODUCTION

No other author has had such an impact on the cultural life of a nation, or indeed the world, as William Shakespeare. His plays remain staples of the theatrical repertoire, in English and in translation and have inspired works in other media, from paintings of beloved characters to entire operas. His 154 sonnets, most written to an unidentified 'fair youth' or a 'dark lady', are bywords for the poetic expression of love. Turns of phrase coined by him are so embedded in the English language that most of us don't even realise that he invented them. The course of true love never did run smooth. Neither a borrower nor a lender be. All the world's a stage. All that glitters is not gold.

What's so great about Shakespeare? First of all, we still speak the language Shakespeare wrote in. Some of his vocabulary is a little unfamiliar to twenty-first century readers, and some of his grammar can be a bit upside down and back to front, as he shoehorns his dialogue into strict lines of iambic pentameter. Essentially however, he writes in an English that is still comprehensible today. Compare him with Geoffrey Chaucer, author of the celebrated *Canterbury Tales*, who was living and working two hundred years before Shakespeare; those Tales are foundational works of English Literature, but quite difficult to read in the original medieval text.

Shakespeare shaped the way that the English see themselves, and the way the world sees England. He is still a central attraction for tourists visiting Great Britain. He also has much to say about England's relationship with the other countries that are now part of the British Isles. By the time Shakespeare was born Wales had long been a principality of England; and Wales and Welshmen are frequently a source of comedy in his plays (1 March).

Ireland had historically been an enemy of England, and it is hard to find a good word about the Irish in the Shakespearean canon. Shakespeare lived to see the union of the English and Scottish crowns under James VI of Scotland and I of England,

and his tone towards 'north Britain' changes notably after the event. Scotland had always been an enemy of England – and worse than that, an ally of England's other old enemy France. But after James – who was of Scottish descent – ascended the throne, Shakespeare's tone softens. In *Macbeth*, written after James became king, the Scots are honourable warriors and only Macbeth himself is a villain.

A fine volley of words, gentlemen, and quickly shot off.

The Two Gentlemen of Verona | Act II, scene 4

It is still possible, not only to read Shakespeare, but to be dazzled by his virtuosity with words. He can be richly descriptive: many of his plays use introductory speeches or prologues to set the scene with such vivid imagery that the audience is transported to another place and time (23 March). This so-called 'suspension of disbelief' is vital for the performance of theatre; theatregoers to a production of Hamlet know perfectly well that they're not on the battlements of Elsinore Castle in Denmark, and that the characters they're watching are only actors, and that it's not really a ghost emerging from the fog. They pretend to believe it for the sake of being entertained; and Shakespeare makes it easy, even with the scenic limitations of theatrical production in Elizabethan England.

His descriptive powers are immense. But, more than description, he sees patterns of behaviour and parallels of circumstance. His imaginative development of metaphor and simile is unique. He suggests that inner beauty enhances outer beauty in the same way that the invisible scent of a rose adds to its pretty appearance (25 April) and compares Macbeth's ferocity in battle to that of eagles attacking their prey (2 October). He seamlessly elevates ideas and turns words into pictures.

All this verbal dexterity would be mere waffle if it weren't for Shakespeare's remarkable grasp of the human condition. Shakespeare knows what makes us tick, and in showing us what makes his characters act as they do, he holds up a mirror to our own vices and virtues. The lines he writes for his characters not only describe their intentions and emotions but illustrate their inner workings. Juliet's nurse, for example (6 November) is more than a plot device to deliver news and move the story on: her lines show that she is flustered, she is breathless, she is unhurried, she cares for Juliet, she is teasing. Macbeth and his wife (14 August), speaking just after he has killed the king, show by their fragmented speech how shaken they are by the act of murder, despite their earlier bravado. It is this capacity to understand humanity, and capture it, that make Shakespeare's works universal and timeless.

Nay, then, God be wi' you, an you talk in blank verse.

As You Like It | Act IV, scene 1

Shakespeare writes using the conventional format of the time, in lines of iambic pentameter – a five-beat rhythm of 'da-DAH da-DAH da-DAH da-DAH da-DAH' – for example, 'If music be the food of love, play on' (28 March). A sonnet consists of fourteen rhyming lines of this rhythm, and although it is not a naturalistic way of speaking, he uses it in his plays to great effect. It is more useful than a four-beat rhythm, which is too musical and rigid. Five beats are flexible: the fifth beat often contains the important word of a line and Shakespeare will regularly conclude a scene or a significant speech with a rhyming couplet – two rhyming lines of iambic pentameter – to indicate the end.

Shakespeare exploits iambic pentameter to the full. An audience accustomed to the convention can be deliberately caught off-guard by a change in the rhythm; for example, in the line 'To be, or not to be, *that* is the question' (26 July). Breaking the rhythm draws attention to a line. Interrupting the rhythm, by dividing a line between two speakers (30 June), has a similar effect. And just to keep an audience on its toes, every now and then Shakespeare will slip in a short line, forcing a pause (19 July).

Not all of Shakespeare's speeches are in iambic pentameter. He makes a distinction between high-born characters (kings and queens and nobles) and low-born ones (tradespeople and figures of fun). For the latter, who are usually played for laughs, comic timing is more important than adherence to convention and their scenes are often written in straightforward prose (8 November).

The restricted format of iambic pentameter gives Shakespeare challenges in getting his message across. It sometimes forces him into unconventional grammatical constructions, the most frequent source of complaint among students trying to understand him. It's often the case that hearing actors speak the lines, or reading them aloud for oneself, can clarify their meaning. The same constraints sometimes force Shakespeare into his most imaginative and dextrous use of language.

My library was dukedom large enough.

The Tempest | Act I, scene 2

Shakespeare's preeminence is assisted by the large number of publications of his work during, and of course after, his life. Many of his plays were printed while he was still alive, and seven years after his death two actor friends of his drew together a compendium of most of them, now known as the First Folio. There are variations between the First Folio and other editions of his works, but it is considered the most authoritative single text, being based on either shorthand transcriptions of actual performances or on the stage manager's books of each script.

It's four hundred years since the First Folio was printed. It contains thirty-six of his plays, only nineteen of which had been previously published. A further three – *Pericles, The Two Noble*

Kinsmen and *Edward III* – are derived from other sources, while two more – *The History of Cardenio* and *Love's Labours Won* – are lost, their existence known only from contemporary references to their performance. Seven hundred and fifty copies of the First Folio were printed, and 235 survive, eighty-two of them in the highly respected research facility of the Folger Shakespeare Library in Washington, DC. Further copies of the First Folio are still discovered in dusty corners of libraries from time to time.

Shakespeare's sonnets were collected during his lifetime and first published in 1609, in a volume which includes the longer poem *A Lover's Complaint*. Shakespeare's published career began with two other long poems, *Venus and Adonis* and *The Rape of Lucrece* – works were written out of necessity when epidemics forced the closure of London's theatres in 1593–4. *The Passionate Pilgrim* appeared in an unauthorized anthology of his poetry in 1599, and there are doubts about its status as an authentic work of Shakespeare. I've included one or two examples here from which readers can make their own minds up. His last extended verse work, *The Phoenix and the Turtle*, was published in 1601.

So full-replete with choice of all delights.

Henry VI, Part 1 | Act V, scene 5

I hope that I've captured some of Shakespeare's infinite dexterity in this book. It includes sonnets, verses from the long poems, and extracts from plays. Famous soliloquies are interspersed with less well-known speeches and sections of dialogue which convey either the comedy or the tragedy of the scene. Purists may be upset to find that some of the material from the plays has been shortened for brevity. This is certainly a liberty; but the purpose of this book is to give its readers a taste of Shakespeare on every night of the year, not to tell all his stories in full. I hope I may be forgiven.

How does one choose a mere 366 examples from such a vast body of work? Shakespeare's sonnets alone could fill almost half the book. I have used daily anniversaries as prompts for the selections. This approach works most obviously on dates which are mentioned in the works – 1 August and 10 August for example. But on most days of the year I have cast my net a little wider: births and deaths of great Shakespeareans, dates of great events, Saints' Days, annual festivals – and on one occasion the invention of sliced bread. If some of the excuses for quoting Shakespeare seem a little flippant or obscure, the important thing is that it has led to the quotation in question. Nevertheless, I urge you to learn more about some of the events which caught my eye. They're all interesting in their own right.

There's no one quite like Shakespeare. You probably use many original Shakespearisms already and if, after a year of reading this book, you are working a few more into your daily conversations, then my work is done.

The poet's eye, in fine frenzy rolling,
Doth glance from heaven to earth, from earth to heaven;
And as imagination bodies forth
The forms of things unknown, the poet's pen
Turns them to shapes and gives to airy nothing
A local habitation and a name.

A Midsummer Night's Dream | Act V, scene 1

JANUARY

Methought the souls of all that I had murder'd
Came to my tent; and every one did threat
To-morrow's vengeance on the head of Richard.

Richard III | Act V, scene 3

1 JANUARY

King Ferdinand and three of his noblemen make a pact to give up the distracting company of women for three years, in favour of academic study. One has doubts.

LONGAVILLE
I am resolved; 'tis but a three years' fast:
The mind shall banquet, though the body pine:
Fat paunches have lean pates, and dainty bits
Make rich the ribs, but bankrupt quite the wits.

DUMAINE
My loving lord, Dumaine is mortified:
The grosser manner of these world's delights
He throws upon the gross world's baser slaves:
To love, to wealth, to pomp, I pine and die;
With all these living in philosophy.

BEROWNE
I can but say their protestation over;
So much, dear liege, I have already sworn,
That is, to live and study here three years.
But there are other strict observances;
As, not to see a woman in that term,
Which I hope well is not enrolled there;
And one day in a week to touch no food
And but one meal on every day beside,
The which I hope is not enrolled there;
And then, to sleep but three hours in the night,

And not be seen to wink of all the day –
When I was wont to think no harm all night
And make a dark night too of half the day –
Which I hope well is not enrolled there:
O, these are barren tasks, too hard to keep,
Not to see ladies, study, fast, not sleep!

Love's Labour's Lost | **Act I, scene 1**

2 JANUARY

The birthday in 1713 of French actress Marie Dumesnil, whose performance in Voltaire's tragedy Mérope had the audience in tears for the last three acts, according to the playwright

Juliet is in tears because her father wishes her to marry Count Paris. Her mother refers the matter upwards.

LADY CAPULET
Here comes your father; tell him so yourself,
And see how he will take it at your hands.
[Enter Capulet]

CAPULET
When the sun sets, the air doth drizzle dew;
But for the sunset of my brother's son
It rains downright.
How now! a conduit, girl? what, still in tears?
Evermore showering? In one little body
Thou counterfeit'st a bark, a sea, a wind;
For still thy eyes, which I may call the sea,
Do ebb and flow with tears; the bark thy body is,
Sailing in this salt flood; the winds, thy sighs;
Who, raging with thy tears, and they with them,
Without a sudden calm, will overset
Thy tempest-tossed body. How now, wife!
Have you deliver'd to her our decree?

LADY CAPULET
Ay, sir; but she will none, she gives you thanks.
I would the fool were married to her grave!

Romeo and Juliet | **Act III, scene 5**

3 JANUARY

The birthday in 1892 of J.R.R. Tolkien, whose Lord of the Rings *is the foundation stone of modern fantasy literature*

Mercutio has let his imagination run away with him.

ROMEO
Peace, peace, Mercutio, peace!
Thou talk'st of nothing.

MERCUTIO
True, I talk of dreams,
Which are the children of an idle brain,
Begot of nothing but vain fantasy,
Which is as thin of substance as the air
And more inconstant than the wind, who wooes
Even now the frozen bosom of the north,
And, being anger'd, puffs away from thence,
Turning his face to the dew-dropping south.

Romeo and Juliet | **Act I, scene 4**

4 JANUARY

The death in 1961 of Austrian scientist Erwin Schrödinger, famous for his thought experiment that a cat held unobserved in a box may be considered both alive and dead before the box is opened

The poet is alive only to his lover, and dead to everyone else.   .

SONNET 112

Your love and pity doth the impression fill
Which vulgar scandal stamp'd upon my brow;
For what care I who calls me well or ill,
So you o'er-green my bad, my good allow?
You are my all the world, and I must strive
To know my shames and praises from your tongue:
None else to me, nor I to none alive,
That my steel'd sense or changes right or wrong.
In so profound abysm I throw all care
Of others' voices, that my adder's sense
To critic and to flatterer stopped are.
Mark how with my neglect I do dispense:
You are so strongly in my purpose bred
That all the world besides methinks are dead.

5 JANUARY

The USA's National Bird Day

Birdsong lifts the heart.

TAMORA
My lovely Aaron, wherefore look'st thou sad,
When every thing doth make a gleeful boast?
The birds chant melody on every bush,
The snake lies rolled in the cheerful sun,
The green leaves quiver with the cooling wind
And make a chequer'd shadow on the ground:
Under their sweet shade, Aaron, let us sit,
And, whilst the babbling echo mocks the hounds,
Replying shrilly to the well-tuned horns,
As if a double hunt were heard at once,
Let us sit down and mark their yelping noise;
And, after conflict such as was supposed
The wandering prince and Dido once enjoy'd,
When with a happy storm they were surprised
And curtain'd with a counsel-keeping cave,
We may, each wreathed in the other's arms,
Our pastimes done, possess a golden slumber;
Whiles hounds and horns and sweet melodious birds
Be unto us as is a nurse's song
Of lullaby to bring her babe asleep.

Titus Andronicus | **Act II, scene 3**

6 JANUARY

The day in 2021 when supporters of President Trump attacked the Capitol

Richard of York claims that he is fitter to be king than Henry VI, whom he had promised to protect and serve if the Earl of Somerset were imprisoned.

RICHARD OF YORK
How now! is Somerset at liberty?
Then, York, unloose thy long-imprison'd thoughts,
And let thy tongue be equal with thy heart.
Shall I endure the sight of Somerset?
False king! why hast thou broken faith with me,
Knowing how hardly I can brook abuse?
King did I call thee? no, thou art not king,
Not fit to govern and rule multitudes,
Which darest not, no, nor canst not rule a traitor.
That head of thine doth not become a crown;
Thy hand is made to grasp a palmer's staff,
And not to grace an awful princely sceptre.
That gold must round engirt these brows of mine,
Whose smile and frown, like to Achilles' spear,
Is able with the change to kill and cure.
Here is a hand to hold a sceptre up
And with the same to act controlling laws.
Give place: by heaven, thou shalt rule no more
O'er him whom heaven created for thy ruler.

EARL OF SOMERSET
O monstrous traitor! I arrest thee, York,
Of capital treason 'gainst the king and crown;
Obey, audacious traitor; kneel for grace.

Henry VI, Part 2 | Act V, scene 1

7 JANUARY

Feast Day of St André of Montreal, whose preserved heart – kept in a reliquary in the church which he helped to build – was stolen in 1973

Lysander and Hermia love each other; but under a spell Lysander has fallen in love with Helena.

HERMIA
What, can you do me greater harm than hate?
Hate me? Wherefore? O me! What news, my love?
Am not I Hermia? are not you Lysander?
I am as fair now as I was erewhile.
Since night you loved me; yet since night you left me:
Why, then you left me -- O, the gods forbid! –
In earnest, shall I say?

LYSANDER
Ay, by my life;
And never did desire to see thee more.
Therefore be out of hope, of question, of doubt;
Be certain, nothing truer; 'tis no jest
That I do hate thee and love Helena.

HERMIA
[To Helena] O me! you juggler! you canker-blossom!
You thief of love! what, have you come by night
And stolen my love's heart from him?

A Midsummer Night's Dream | **Act III, scene 2**

8 JANUARY

The birthday in 1865 of socialite Winnaretta Singer, Princesse Edmond de Polignac, heiress to the Singer Sewing Machine family fortune

The ability to sew was considered a virtue in women, and it is one of the items in an assessment of one woman's good points.

LAUNCE
[Pulling out a paper] Here is the cate-log of her condition. 'Imprimis: She can fetch and carry.' Why, a horse can do no more: nay, a horse cannot fetch, but only carry; therefore is she better than a jade. 'Item: She can milk;' look you, a sweet virtue in a maid with clean hands.
[Enter Speed]

SPEED
How now, Signior Launce! What news with your mastership?
[...]

LAUNCE
The blackest news that ever thou heardest.

SPEED
Why, man, how black?

LAUNCE
Why, as black as ink.

SPEED
Let me read them.

LAUNCE
Fie on thee, jolt-head! thou canst not read.

SPEED
Thou liest; I can ... Come, fool, come; try me in thy paper.
[...]

LAUNCE
There; and St. Nicholas be thy speed!

SPEED
[Reads] 'Item: She can sew.'

LAUNCE
That's as much as to say, Can she so?

SPEED.
'Item: She can knit.'

LAUNCE
What need a man care for a stock with a wench, when
she can knit him a stock?

SPEED
'Item: She can wash and scour.'

LAUNCE
A special virtue: for then she need not be washed
and scoured.

SPEED
'Item: She can spin.'

LAUNCE
Then may I set the world on wheels, when she can spin
for her living.

SPEED
'Item: She hath many nameless virtues.'

LAUNCE
That's as much as to say, bastard virtues; that, indeed,
know not their fathers and therefore have no names.

SPEED
'Here follow her vices.'

LAUNCE
Close at the heels of her virtues.

SPEED
'Item: She is not to be kissed fasting in respect of
her breath.'

LAUNCE
Well, that fault may be mended with a breakfast. Read on.

SPEED
'Item: She hath a sweet mouth.'

LAUNCE
That makes amends for her sour breath.

SPEED
'Item: She doth talk in her sleep.'

LAUNCE
It's no matter for that, so she sleep not in her talk.

SPEED
'Item: She is slow in words.'

LAUNCE

O villain, that set this down among her vices! To be slow in words is a woman's only virtue: I pray thee, out with't, and place it for her chief virtue.

[...]

SPEED

'Item: She will often praise her liquor.'

LAUNCE

If her liquor be good, she shall: if she will not, I will; for good things should be praised.

SPEED

'Item: She hath more hair than wit,'—

LAUNCE

More hair than wit? It may be; I'll prove it. The cover of the salt hides the salt, and therefore it is more than the salt; the hair that covers the wit is more than the wit, for the greater hides the less. What's next?

SPEED

'And more faults than hairs,'—

[...] 'And more wealth than faults.'

LAUNCE

Why, that word makes the faults gracious. Well, I'll have her...

The Two Gentlemen of Verona | Act III, scene 1

9 JANUARY

The death in 1598 of Jasper Heywood, a contemporary of Shakespeare who translated the plays of Roman playwright Seneca

Polonius praises the talents of a visiting theatre company for their versatility.

POLONIUS
The best actors in the world, either for tragedy, comedy, history, pastoral, pastoral-comical, historical-pastoral, tragical-historical, tragical-comical-historical-pastoral; scene individable, or poem unlimited. Seneca cannot be too heavy, nor Plautus too light. For the law of writ and the liberty, these are the only men.

Hamlet | Act II, scene 2

10 JANUARY

The death in 1971 of Coco Chanel, designer of high fashion and expensive perfumes

Venus muses on the role of the senses in invoking passions.

'Had I no eyes but ears, my ears would love
That inward beauty and invisible;
Or were I deaf, thy outward parts would move
Each part in me that were but sensible:
Though neither eyes nor ears, to hear nor see,
Yet should I be in love by touching thee.

'Say, that the sense of feeling were bereft me,
And that I could not see, nor hear, nor touch,
And nothing but the very smell were left me,
Yet would my love to thee be still as much;
For from the stillitory of thy face excelling
Comes breath perfumed that breedeth love by smelling.

'But, O, what banquet wert thou to the taste,
Being nurse and feeder of the other four!
Would they not wish the feast might ever last,
And bid Suspicion double-lock the door,
Lest Jealousy, that sour unwelcome guest,
Should, by his stealing in, disturb the feast?'

From Venus and Adonis

11 JANUARY

The Feast Day of St Vitalis of Gaza, patron saint of labourers and prostitutes

Falstaff is unhappy, having made what he considers virtuous, abstemious lifestyle choices. Compass can mean a sense of direction or the measurement of an outline.

FALSTAFF
Bardolph, am I not fallen away vilely since this last action? do I not bate? do I not dwindle? Why my skin hangs about me like an old lady's loose gown; I am withered like an old apple-john. Well, I'll repent, and that suddenly, while I am in some liking; I shall be out of heart shortly, and then I shall have no strength to repent. [...] Company, villainous company, hath been the spoil of me.

LORD BARDOLPH
Sir John, you are so fretful, you cannot live long.

FALSTAFF
Why, there is it: come sing me a bawdy song; make me merry. I was as virtuously given as a gentleman need to be; virtuous enough; swore little; diced not above seven times a week; went to a bawdy-house once in a quarter – of an hour; paid money that I borrowed, three of four times; lived well and in good compass: and now I live out of all order, out of all compass.

LORD BARDOLPH
Why, you are so fat, Sir John, that you must needs be out of all compass, out of all reasonable compass, Sir John.

Henry IV, Part 1 | Act III, scene 3

12 JANUARY

The birthday in 1628 of Charles Perrault, whose retellings of old folk tales were the first modern fairy stories

Puck, also known as Robin Goodfellow or Hobgoblin, is Shakespeare's foremost mischief-maker, but in folklore the character predates the Bard by many centuries.

FAIRY
Either I mistake your shape and making quite,
Or else you are that shrewd and knavish sprite
Call'd Robin Goodfellow: are not you he
That frights the maidens of the villagery;
Skim milk, and sometimes labour in the quern
And bootless make the breathless housewife churn;
And sometime make the drink to bear no barm;
Mislead night-wanderers, laughing at their harm?
Those that Hobgoblin call you and sweet Puck,
You do their work, and they shall have good luck:
Are not you he?

PUCK
Thou speak'st aright;
I am that merry wanderer of the night.
I jest to Oberon and make him smile
When I a fat and bean-fed horse beguile,
Neighing in likeness of a filly foal:
And sometime lurk I in a gossip's bowl,
In very likeness of a roasted crab,
And when she drinks, against her lips I bob
And on her wither'd dewlap pour the ale.
The wisest aunt, telling the saddest tale,
Sometime for three-foot stool mistaketh me;

Then slip I from her bum, down topples she,
And 'tailor' cries, and falls into a cough;
And then the whole quire hold their hips and laugh,
And waxen in their mirth and neeze and swear
A merrier hour was never wasted there.
But room, fairy! Here comes Oberon.

A Midsummer Night's Dream | **Act II, scene 1**

13 JANUARY

In 1941 Henry Ford patents a project car made of soybeans and flax, and powered by hemp oil

Flax yarn was once used to make wicks for oil lamps, which Clifford refers to after seeing his dead father.

YOUNG CLIFFORD
O, let the vile world end,
And the premised flames of the last day
Knit earth and heaven together!
Now let the general trumpet blow his blast,
Particularities and petty sounds
To cease! Wast thou ordain'd, dear father,
To lose thy youth in peace, and to achieve
The silver livery of advised age,
And, in thy reverence and thy chair-days, thus
To die in ruffian battle? Even at this sight
My heart is turn'd to stone: and while 'tis mine,
It shall be stony. York not our old men spares;
No more will I their babes: tears virginal
Shall be to me even as the dew to fire,
And beauty that the tyrant oft reclaims
Shall to my flaming wrath be oil and flax.
Henceforth I will not have to do with pity:
Meet I an infant of the house of York,
Into as many gobbets will I cut it
As wild Medea young Absyrtus did:
In cruelty will I seek out my fame.
Come, thou new ruin of old Clifford's house:
As did Aeneas old Anchises bear,
So bear I thee upon my manly shoulders;
But then Aeneas bare a living load,
Nothing so heavy as these woes of mine.

Henry VI, Part 2 | Act V, scene 2

14 JANUARY

The Feast of the Ass in Medieval Christianity

Welsh warrior Fluellen teaches a lesson that every parent has tried to pass on – just because someone else does it, doesn't mean that you should too.

GOWER
[shouting] Captain Fluellen!

FLUELLEN
So! in the name of Jesu Christ, speak lower. It is the greatest admiration of the universal world, when the true and aunchient prerogatifes and laws of the wars is not kept: if you would take the pains but to examine the wars of Pompey the Great, you shall find, I warrant you, that there is no tiddle toddle nor pibble pabble in Pompey's camp; I warrant you, you shall find the ceremonies of the wars, and the cares of it, and the forms of it, and the sobriety of it, and the modesty of it, to be otherwise.

GOWER
Why, the enemy is loud; you hear him all night.

FLUELLEN
If the enemy is an ass and a fool and a prating coxcomb, is it meet, think you, that we should also, look you, be an ass and a fool and a prating coxcomb? in your own conscience, now?

GOWER
I will speak lower.

Henry V | Act IV, scene 1

15 JANUARY

In 1936 the first building to be entirely encased in glass is completed in Toledo, Ohio, for the Owens-Illinois Glass Company – which still makes half of all the world's glass containers today

The poet considers the passing of the seasons, which nurture the seeds of the future but also destroy beauty. Yet beauty's essence can be preserved in a bottle.

SONNET 5

Those hours, that with gentle work did frame
The lovely gaze where every eye doth dwell,
Will play the tyrants to the very same
And that unfair which fairly doth excel:
For never-resting time leads summer on
To hideous winter and confounds him there;
Sap cheque'd with frost and lusty leaves quite gone,
Beauty o'ersnow'd and bareness every where:
Then, were not summer's distillation left,
A liquid prisoner pent in walls of glass,
Beauty's effect with beauty were bereft,
Nor it nor no remembrance what it was:
But flowers distill'd though they with winter meet,
Leese but their show; their substance still lives sweet.

16 JANUARY

In 1362 a tidal surge in the North Sea drowns some 25,000 people in England and northern Europe, and destroys whole towns, including Ravenser Odd in the Humber estuary

Henry IV landed at nearby Ravenspurgh, now also under the sea, in 1399 when he came to challenge Richard II. Henry doubts his son Prince Hal's pledge to join him in the fight against Hotspur (Percy).

PRINCE HAL
I shall hereafter, my thrice gracious lord,
Be more myself.

HENRY BOLINGBROKE
For all the world
As thou art to this hour was Richard then
When I from France set foot at Ravenspurgh,
And even as I was then is Percy now.
Now, by my sceptre and my soul to boot,
He hath more worthy interest to the state
Than thou the shadow of succession;
For of no right, nor colour like to right,
He doth fill fields with harness in the realm,
Turns head against the lion's armed jaws,
And, being no more in debt to years than thou,
Leads ancient lords and reverend bishops on
To bloody battles and to bruising arms.
What never-dying honour hath he got
Against renowned Douglas! whose high deeds,
Whose hot incursions and great name in arms
Holds from all soldiers chief majority
And military title capital
Through all the kingdoms that acknowledge Christ:
Thrice hath this Hotspur, Mars in swathling clothes,

This infant warrior, in his enterprises
Discomfited great Douglas, ta'en him once,
Enlarged him and made a friend of him,
To fill the mouth of deep defiance up
And shake the peace and safety of our throne.
And what say you to this? Percy, Northumberland,
The Archbishop's grace of York, Douglas, Mortimer,
Capitulate against us and are up.
But wherefore do I tell these news to thee?
Why, Harry, do I tell thee of my foes,
Which art my near'st and dearest enemy?
Thou that art like enough, through vassal fear,
Base inclination and the start of spleen
To fight against me under Percy's pay,
To dog his heels and curtsy at his frowns,
To show how much thou art degenerate.

PRINCE HAL
Do not think so; you shall not find it so:
And God forgive them that so much have sway'd
Your majesty's good thoughts away from me!

Henry IV, Part 1 | Act III, scene 2

17 JANUARY

The death in 1456 of early German novelist Elisabeth of Lorraine-Vaudémont, who also translated French romances for her German readership

Although Shakespeare has nothing to say about German women, it seems that French men had no words for 'No, thank you' when it came to Italian signorinas.

KING OF FRANCE
Those girls of Italy, take heed of them:
They say, our French lack language to deny,
If they demand: beware of being captives,
Before you serve.

All's Well That Ends Well | **Act II, scene 1**

18 JANUARY

The birthday in 1882 of author A.A. Milne, who created Winnie the Pooh, the self-confessed 'bear of very little brain'

Thersites has a very low opinion of the warriors Achilles and Patroclus.

THERSITES
With too much blood and too little brain, these two may run mad; but, if with too much brain and too little blood they do, I'll be a curer of madmen. Here's Agamemnon, an honest fellow enough and one that loves quails; but he has not so much brain as earwax: and the goodly transformation of Jupiter there, his brother, the bull – the primitive statue, and oblique memorial of cuckolds; a thrifty shoeing-horn in a chain, hanging at his brother's leg – to what form but that he is, should wit larded with malice and malice forced with wit turn him to? To an ass, were nothing; he is both ass and ox: to an ox, were nothing; he is both ox and ass. To be a dog, a mule, a cat, a fitchew, a toad, a lizard, an owl, a puttock, or a herring without a roe, I would not care; but to be Menelaus, I would conspire against destiny. Ask me not, what I would be, if I were not Thersites; for I care not to be the louse of a lazar, so I were not Menelaus! Hey-day! spirits and fires!

Troilus and Cressida | Act V, scene 1

19 JANUARY

Husbands Day in Iceland

What if wives acted like their husbands?

EMILIA

But I do think it is their husbands' faults
If wives do fall: say that they slack their duties,
And pour our treasures into foreign laps,
Or else break out in peevish jealousies,
Throwing restraint upon us; or say they strike us,
Or scant our former having in despite;
Why, we have galls, and though we have some grace,
Yet have we some revenge. Let husbands know
Their wives have sense like them: they see and smell
And have their palates both for sweet and sour,
As husbands have. What is it that they do
When they change us for others? Is it sport?
I think it is: and doth affection breed it?
I think it doth: is't frailty that thus errs?
It is so too: and have not we affections,
Desires for sport, and frailty, as men have?
Then let them use us well: else let them know,
The ills we do, their ills instruct us so.

Othello | Act IV, scene 3

20 JANUARY

The death in 1779 of David Garrick, actor and theatre manager, who did much to revive public interest in Shakespeare

Garrick's breakthrough role was Shakespeare's Richard III, for whom the end is close at hand.

RICHARD III

Give me another horse: bind up my wounds.
Have mercy, Jesu! – Soft! I did but dream.
O coward conscience, how dost thou afflict me!
The lights burn blue. It is now dead midnight.
Cold fearful drops stand on my trembling flesh.
What do I fear? myself? there's none else by:
Richard loves Richard; that is, I am I.
Is there a murderer here? No. Yes, I am:
Then fly. What, from myself? Great reason why:
Lest I revenge. What, myself upon myself?
Alack. I love myself. Wherefore? for any good
That I myself have done unto myself?
O, no! alas, I rather hate myself
For hateful deeds committed by myself!
I am a villain: yet I lie. I am not.
Fool, of thyself speak well: fool, do not flatter.
My conscience hath a thousand several tongues,
And every tongue brings in a several tale,
And every tale condemns me for a villain.
Perjury, perjury, in the high'st degree
Murder, stern murder, in the direst degree;
All several sins, all used in each degree,
Throng to the bar, crying all, Guilty! guilty!

I shall despair. There is no creature loves me;
And if I die, no soul shall pity me:
Nay, wherefore should they, since that I myself
Find in myself no pity to myself?
Methought the souls of all that I had murder'd
Came to my tent; and every one did threat
To-morrow's vengeance on the head of Richard.

Richard III | Act V, scene 3

21 JANUARY

Grandmothers Day in Poland

Pythagoras believed in reincarnation. Feste disguised
as Sir Topas is pretending that Malvolio is mad.

MALVOLIO
Sir Topas, never was man thus wronged: good Sir Topas,
do not think i am mad: they have laid me here in hideous
darkness.

FESTE
Fie, thou dishonest Satan! I call thee by the most modest
terms; for I am one of those gentle ones that will use the
devil himself with courtest: sayest thou that house is dark?

MALVOLIO
As hell, Sir Topas.

FESTE
Why it hath bay windows transparent as barricadoes, and
the clearstores toward the south north are as lustrous as
ebony; and yet complainest thou of obstruction?

MALVOLIO
I am not mad, Sir Topas: I say to you, this house is dark.

FESTE
Madman, thou errest: I say, there is no darkness but
igorance; in which thou art more puzzled than the
Eqyptians in their fog.

MALVOLIO
I say, this house is as dark as ignorance, though ignorance
were as dark as hell; and I say, there was never man thus

abused. I am no more mad than you are: make the trial
of it in any constant question.

FESTE
What is the opinion of Pythagoras concerning wild fowl?

MALVOLIO
That the soul of our grandam might haply inhabit a bird.

FESTE
What thinkest thou of his opinion?

MALVOLIO
I think nobly of the soul, and no way approve his opinion.

FESTE
Fare thee well. Remain thou still in darkness: thou shalt
hold the opinion of Pythagoras ere I will allow of thy
wits, and fear to kill a woodcock, lest thou dispossess the
soul of thy grandam. Fare thee well.

Twelfth Night | Act IV, scene 2

22 JANUARY

Grandfathers Day in Poland

Shakespeare comments succinctly on nature versus nurture; on inheritance versus ability; and on passing the buck. The Duke of Gloucester is the Duke of York's son.

DUKE OF GLOUCESTER
Will you we show our title to the crown?
If not, our swords shall plead it in the field.

HENRY VI
What title hast thou, traitor, to the crown?
Thy father was, as thou art, Duke of York;
Thy grandfather, Roger Mortimer, Earl of March:
I am the son of Henry the Fifth,
Who made the Dauphin and the French to stoop
And seized upon their towns and provinces.

EARL OF WARWICK
Talk not of France, sith thou hast lost it all.

HENRY VI
The lord protector lost it, and not I:
When I was crown'd I was but nine months old.

DUKE OF YORK
You are old enough now, and yet, methinks, you lose.
Father, tear the crown from the usurper's head.

Henry VI, Part 3 | Act I, scene 1

23 JANUARY

The birthday in 1918 of pharmacologist Gertrude 'Trudy' Elion, whose work on targeted drugs paved the way for AZT, the first treatment used widely in the fight against AIDS

Shakespeare often characterizes love as a disease, here made worse by his cruel treatment by the so-called Dark Lady who is the object of several of his sonnets.

SONNET 147

My love is as a fever, longing still
For that which longer nurseth the disease,
Feeding on that which doth preserve the ill,
The uncertain sickly appetite to please.
My reason, the physician to my love,
Angry that his prescriptions are not kept,
Hath left me, and I desperate now approve
Desire is death, which physic did except.
Past cure I am, now reason is past care,
And frantic-mad with evermore unrest;
My thoughts and my discourse as madmen's are,
At random from the truth vainly express'd;
For I have sworn thee fair and thought thee bright,
Who art as black as hell, as dark as night.

24 JANUARY

The discovery in 1972 of Sgt Shoichi Yokoi, a soldier who had remained in hiding on Guam since World War Two, believing that surrender and capture were more dishonourable than death

Claudio and Isabella discuss death and dishonour.

CLAUDIO
Death is a fearful thing.

ISABELLA
And shamed life a hateful.

CLAUDIO
Ay, but to die, and go we know not where;
To lie in cold obstruction and to rot;
This sensible warm motion to become
A kneaded clod; and the delighted spirit
To bathe in fiery floods, or to reside
In thrilling region of thick-ribbed ice;
To be imprison'd in the viewless winds,
And blown with restless violence round about
The pendent world; or to be worse than worst
Of those that lawless and incertain thought
Imagine howling: 'tis too horrible!
The weariest and most loathed worldly life
That age, ache, penury and imprisonment
Can lay on nature is a paradise
To what we fear of death.

Measure for Measure | Act III, scene 1

25 JANUARY

Burns Night, when the Scottish poet Robert Burns is honoured at
haggis dinners throughout the world

Touchstone is in love with simple goat-girl Audrey and
wishes that she had a lover's interest in poetry.

TOUCHSTONE
When a man's verses cannot be understood, nor a
man's good wit seconded with the forward child
understanding, it strikes a man more dead than a great
reckoning in a little room. Truly, I would the gods had
made thee poetical.

AUDREY
I do not know what 'poetical' is. Is it honest in deed and
word? Is it a true thing?

TOUCHSTONE
No, truly; for the truest poetry is the most feigning, and
lovers are given to poetry; and what they swear in poetry
may be said as lovers they do feign.

AUDREY
Do you wish, then, that the gods had made me poetical?

TOUCHSTONE
I do, truly, for thou swear'st to me thou art honest;
now, if thou wert a poet, I might have some hope thou
didst feign.

As You Like It | Act III, scene 3

26 JANUARY

In 1905 the world's largest diamond, the Cullinan, is found in a South African mine

Diamonds may be a girl's best friend, but not necessarily a king's.

HENRY VI
My crown is in my heart, not on my head;
Not decked with diamonds and Indian stones,
Nor to be seen: my crown is called content:
A crown it is that seldom kings enjoy.

Henry VI, Part 3 | Act III, scene 1

27 JANUARY

The death in 1922 of pioneering investigative journalist Nellie Bly, whose Ten Days in a Madhouse *exposed the ill-treatment of women suffering from mental illness*

Hamlet, having killed Laertes' father, excuses himself on the grounds of temporary insanity.

HAMLET
Give me your pardon, sir. I have done you wrong;
But pardon't, as you are a gentleman.
This presence knows,
And you must needs have heard, how I am punish'd
With sore distraction. What I have done
That might your nature, honour, and exception
Roughly awake, I here proclaim was madness.
Was't Hamlet wrong'd Laertes? Never Hamlet.
If Hamlet from himself be taken away,
And when he's not himself does wrong Laertes,
Then Hamlet does it not, Hamlet denies it.
Who does it, then? His madness. If't be so,
Hamlet is of the faction that is wrong'd;
His madness is poor Hamlet's enemy.
Sir, in this audience,
Let my disclaiming from a purpos'd evil
Free me so far in your most generous thoughts
That I have shot my arrow o'er the house
And hurt my brother.

Hamlet | Act V, scene 2

28 JANUARY

In 1591, Agnes Sampson is hung as a witch in North Berwick, Scotland

Resentful Hamlet resolves never to approve his mother's marriage to his uncle.

HAMLET
'Tis now the very witching time of night,
When churchyards yawn, and hell itself breathes out
Contagion to this world. Now could I drink hot blood
And do such bitter business as the day
Would quake to look on. Soft! now to my mother!
O heart, lose not thy nature; let not ever
The soul of Nero enter this firm bosom.
Let me be cruel, not unnatural;
I will speak daggers to her, but use none.
My tongue and soul in this be hypocrites –
How in my words somever she be shent,
To give them seals never, my soul, consent!

Hamlet | Act III, scene 2

29 JANUARY

The death in 1961 of novelist Angela Thirkell, who declared after two marriages that 'it's very peaceful with no husbands'

Katherina takes the same view, when her husband-to-be has yet to arrive on her wedding day.

KATHERINA

No shame but mine; I must, forsooth, be forc'd
To give my hand, oppos'd against my heart,
Unto a mad-brain rudesby, full of spleen,
Who woo'd in haste and means to wed at leisure.
I told you, I, he was a frantic fool,
Hiding his bitter jests in blunt behaviour;
And, to be noted for a merry man,
He'll woo a thousand, 'point the day of marriage,
Make friends invited, and proclaim the banns;
Yet never means to wed where he hath woo'd.
Now must the world point at poor Katherine,
And say 'Lo, there is mad Petruchio's wife,
If it would please him come and marry her!'

The Taming of the Shrew | Act III, scene 2

30 JANUARY

The day in 1649 when Charles I of England was beheaded

Queen Margaret mocks her prisoner Richard Plantagenet, Duke of York, a man who would be king.

QUEEN MARGARET
[...] York cannot speak, unless he wear a crown.
A crown for York! and, lords, bow low to him:
Hold you his hands, whilst I do set it on.
[Putting a paper crown on his head]
Ay, marry, sir, now looks he like a king!
Ay, this is he that took King Henry's chair,
And this is he was his adopted heir.
But how is it that great Plantagenet
Is crown'd so soon, and broke his solemn oath?
As I bethink me, you should not be king
Till our King Henry had shook hands with death.
And will you pale your head in Henry's glory,
And rob his temples of the diadem,
Now in his life, against your holy oath?
O, 'tis a fault too too unpardonable!
Off with the crown, and with the crown his head;
And, whilst we breathe, take time to do him dead.

Henry VI, Part 3 | Act I, scene 4

31 JANUARY

Anton Chekhov's play The Three Sisters *premieres in Moscow in 1901*

Chekhov was not the first person to write a play about three sisters. King Lear's favourite daughter, now Queen of France, hears news in a letter of the treachery of her two siblings towards their father.

EARL OF KENT
Did your letters pierce the Queen to any demonstration
of grief?

GENTLEMAN
Ay, sir. She took them, read them in my presence,
And now and then an ample tear trill'd down
Her delicate cheek. It seem'd she was a queen
Over her passion, who, most rebel-like,
Sought to be king o'er her.

EARL OF KENT
O, then it mov'd her?

GENTLEMAN
Not to a rage. Patience and sorrow strove
Who should express her goodliest. You have seen
Sunshine and rain at once: her smiles and tears
Were like, a better way. Those happy smilets
That play'd on her ripe lip seem'd not to know
What guests were in her eyes, which parted thence
As pearls from diamonds dropp'd. In brief,
Sorrow would be a rarity most belov'd,
If all could so become it.

EARL OF KENT
Made she no verbal question?

GENTLEMAN
Faith, once or twice she heav'd the name of father
Pantingly forth, as if it press'd her heart;
Cried 'Sisters, sisters! Shame of ladies! Sisters!
Kent! father! sisters! What, i' th' storm? i' th' night?
Let pity not be believ'd!' There she shook
The holy water from her heavenly eyes,
And clamour moisten'd. Then away she started
To deal with grief alone.

King Lear | **Act IV, scene 3**

FEBRUARY

Come, let's away to prison.
We two alone will sing like birds i' th' cage.

King Lear | Act V, scene 3

1 FEBRUARY

The month's name in Poland and Ukraine is derived from the word for ice or hard frost

In Slovenian the name refers to icicles, while in Old English it was Solmonath – Mud Month.

DON PEDRO
Good morrow, Benedick. Why, what's the matter,
That you have such a February face,
So full of frost, of storm and cloudiness?

Much Ado about Nothing | Act V, scene 4

2 FEBRUARY

Groundhog Day in Punxsutawney, Pennsylvania, since 1887, when a rodent's remarks are said to predict the weather

Some turn to groundhogs, some to the stars, for their information.

SONNET 14

Not from the stars do I my judgment pluck;
And yet methinks I have astronomy,
But not to tell of good or evil luck,
Of plagues, of dearths, or seasons' quality;
Nor can I fortune to brief minutes tell,
Pointing to each his thunder, rain and wind,
Or say with princes if it shall go well,
By oft predict that I in heaven find:
But from thine eyes my knowledge I derive,
And, constant stars, in them I read such art
As truth and beauty shall together thrive,
If from thyself to store thou wouldst convert;
Or else of thee this I prognosticate:
Thy end is truth's and beauty's doom and date.

3 FEBRUARY

*The Day the Music Died – in 1959, rock'n'roll stars Buddy Holly,
Ritchie Valens and The Big Bopper are killed in a plane crash*

*Holly's first posthumous release was the song 'True
Love Ways'.*

BEROWNE
A lover's eyes will gaze an eagle blind;
A lover's ear will hear the lowest sound,
When the suspicious head of theft is stopp'd:
Love's feeling is more soft and sensible
Than are the tender horns of cockl'd snails;
Love's tongue proves dainty Bacchus gross in taste:
For valour, is not Love a Hercules,
Still climbing trees in the Hesperides?
Subtle as Sphinx; as sweet and musical
As bright Apollo's lute, strung with his hair:
And when Love speaks, the voice of all the gods
Makes heaven drowsy with the harmony.
Never durst poet touch a pen to write
Until his ink were temper'd with Love's sighs;
O, then his lines would ravish savage ears
And plant in tyrants mild humility.
From women's eyes this doctrine I derive:
They sparkle still the right Promethean fire;
They are the books, the arts, the academes,
That show, contain and nourish all the world:
Else none at all in ought proves excellent.
Then fools you were these women to forswear,
Or keeping what is sworn, you will prove fools.
For wisdom's sake, a word that all men love,

Or for love's sake, a word that loves all men,
Or for men's sake, the authors of these women,
Or women's sake, by whom we men are men,
Let us once lose our oaths to find ourselves,
Or else we lose ourselves to keep our oaths.
It is religion to be thus forsworn,
For charity itself fulfills the law,
And who can sever love from charity?

Love's Labour's Lost | Act IV, scene 3

4 FEBRUARY

The birthday in 1818 of Joshua Norton, self-proclaimed Emperor of the United States and Protector of Mexico, Norton the First

After the death of Emperor Titus, his son Emperor Lucius moves decisively to restore order and punish trouble-makers Aaron the Moor and Empress Tamora.

ALL
Lucius, all hail, Rome's royal emperor!

MARCUS ANDRONICUS
Go, go into old Titus' sorrowful house,
And hither hale that misbelieving Moor,
To be adjudged some direful slaughtering death,
As punishment for his most wicked life.

ALL
Lucius, all hail, Rome's gracious governor!

LUCIUS
Thanks, gentle Romans: may I govern so,
To heal Rome's harms, and wipe away her woe!
[Enter Attendants with Aaron]
[...]

LUCIUS
Set him breast-deep in earth, and famish him;
There let him stand, and rave, and cry for food;
If any one relieves or pities him,
For the offence he dies. This is our doom:
Some stay to see him fasten'd in the earth.

AARON

O, why should wrath be mute, and fury dumb?
I am no baby, I, that with base prayers
I should repent the evils I have done:
Ten thousand worse than ever yet I did
Would I perform, if I might have my will;
If one good deed in all my life I did,
I do repent it from my very soul.

LUCIUS

Some loving friends convey the emperor hence,
And give him burial in his father's grave:
As for that heinous tiger, Tamora,
No funeral rite, nor man in mourning weeds,
No mournful bell shall ring her burial;
But throw her forth to beasts and birds of prey:
Her life was beast-like, and devoid of pity;
And, being so, shall have like want of pity.
See justice done on Aaron, that damn'd Moor,
By whom our heavy haps had their beginning:
Then, afterwards, to order well the state,
That like events may ne'er it ruinate.

Titus Andronicus | Act V, scene 3

5 FEBRUARY

The death in 1922 of Croatian engineer Eduard Penkala, whose inventions include the mechanical pencil, a hot water bottle, Croatia's first airplane and a solid-ink fountain pen

Olivia loves Cesario. Sir Andrew loves Olivia. Sir Toby encourages Sir Andrew to challenge Cesario, 'the count's youth', to a duel in order to impress Olivia.

SIR TOBY BELCH
Why, then, build me thy fortunes upon the basis of valour. Challenge me the count's youth to fight with him; hurt him in eleven places: my niece shall take note of it; and assure thyself, there is no love-broker in the world can more prevail in man's commendation with woman than report of valour.

FABIAN
There is no way but this, Sir Andrew.

SIR ANDREW AGUECHEEK
Will either of you bear me a challenge to him?

SIR TOBY BELCH
Go, write it in a martial hand; be curst and brief; it is no matter how witty, so it be eloquent and full of invention: taunt him with the licence of ink: if thou thou'st him some thrice, it shall not be amiss; and as many lies as will lie in thy sheet of paper, although the sheet were big enough for the bed of Ware in England, set 'em down: go, about it. Let there be gall enough in thy ink, though thou write with a goose-pen, no matter: about it.

Twelfth Night | Act III, scene 2

6 FEBRUARY

The Feast Day of Saint Relindis, eighth-century Belgian abbess and skilled embroiderer – her vestments are the oldest surviving Anglo-Saxon examples of the craft

School friends Helena and Hermia have fallen out over a man.

HELENA
[...] O, is it all forgot?
All school-days' friendship, childhood innocence?
We, Hermia, like two artificial gods,
Have with our needles created both one flower,
Both on one sampler, sitting on one cushion,
Both warbling of one song, both in one key,
As if our hands, our sides, voices and minds,
Had been incorporate. So we grow together,
Like to a double cherry, seeming parted,
But yet a union in partition;
Two lovely berries moulded on one stem;
So, with two seeming bodies, but one heart;
Two of the first, like coats in heraldry,
Due but to one and crowned with one crest.
And will you rent our ancient love asunder,
To join with men in scorning your poor friend?
It is not friendly, 'tis not maidenly:
Our sex, as well as I, may chide you for it,
Though I alone do feel the injury.

A Midsummer Night's Dream | Act III, scene 2

7 FEBRUARY

The birthday in 1923 of comic actress Dora Bryan, who played a celebrated Mistress Quickly in The Merry Wives of Windsor

Ms Quickly acts as a go-between in Falstaff's efforts to woo not one but two women. First she has a message for him from Mistress Ford.

FALSTAFF
But what says she to me? be brief, my good she-Mercury.

HOSTESS QUICKLY
Marry, she hath received your letter, for the which she thanks you a thousand times; and she gives you to notify that her husband will be absence from his house between ten and eleven.

FALSTAFF
Ten and eleven?

HOSTESS QUICKLY
Ay, forsooth; and then you may come and see the picture, she says, that you wot of: Master Ford, her husband, will be from home. Alas! the sweet woman leads an ill life with him: he's a very jealousy man: she leads a very frampold life with him, good heart.

FALSTAFF
Ten and eleven. Woman, commend me to her; I will not fail her.

HOSTESS QUICKLY

Why, you say well. But I have another messenger to your worship. Mistress Page hath her hearty commendations to you too: and let me tell you in your ear, she's as fartuous a civil modest wife, and one, I tell you, that will not miss you morning nor evening prayer, as any is in Windsor, whoe'er be the other: and she bade me tell your worship that her husband is seldom from home; but she hopes there will come a time. I never knew a woman so dote upon a man: surely I think you have charms, la; yes, in truth.

The Merry Wives of Windsor | Act II, scene 2

8 FEBRUARY

The birthday in 1876 of German Expressionist painter Paula Modersohn-Becker, the first woman to paint female nudes, whose art the Nazi regime denounced as degenerate

Becker was noted for her 'blunt, unapologetic humanity', and broke ground by painting herself naked and pregnant. Nazis considered her unfeminine.

SONNET 24

Mine eye hath play'd the painter and hath stell'd
Thy beauty's form in table of my heart;
My body is the frame wherein 'tis held,
And perspective it is the painter's art.
For through the painter must you see his skill,
To find where your true image pictured lies;
Which in my bosom's shop is hanging still,
That hath his windows glazed with thine eyes.
Now see what good turns eyes for eyes have done:
Mine eyes have drawn thy shape, and thine for me
Are windows to my breast, where-through the sun
Delights to peep, to gaze therein on thee;
Yet eyes this cunning want to grace their art;
They draw but what they see, know not the heart.

9 FEBRUARY

In 1907, 3000 suffragettes make a protest march through London which became known as the Mud March because of the wet weather

Katherina offers a far-from-feminist point of view as she tries to pursuade her fellow wives to obey their husbands.

KATHERINA

[...] A woman mov'd is like a fountain troubled –
Muddy, ill-seeming, thick, bereft of beauty;
And while it is so, none so dry or thirsty
Will deign to sip or touch one drop of it.
Thy husband is thy lord, thy life, thy keeper,
Thy head, thy sovereign; one that cares for thee,
And for thy maintenance commits his body
To painful labour both by sea and land,
To watch the night in storms, the day in cold,
Whilst thou liest warm at home, secure and safe;
And craves no other tribute at thy hands
But love, fair looks, and true obedience –
Too little payment for so great a debt.
Such duty as the subject owes the prince,
Even such a woman oweth to her husband;
And when she is froward, peevish, sullen, sour,
And not obedient to his honest will,
What is she but a foul contending rebel
And graceless traitor to her loving lord?
I am asham'd that women are so simple
To offer war where they should kneel for peace;
Or seek for rule, supremacy, and sway,
When they are bound to serve, love, and obey.

Why are our bodies soft and weak and smooth,
Unapt to toil and trouble in the world,
But that our soft conditions and our hearts
Should well agree with our external parts?

The Taming of the Shrew | Act V, scene 2

10 FEBRUARY

In 1355 a complaint by students about bad wine in Oxford's Swindlestock Tavern becomes a brawl, then a riot between townspeople and university members which leaves a hundred dead

Cassio, an officer serving under Othello, is embarrassed, having got into a fight while drunk.

CASSIO
Reputation, reputation, reputation! O, I have lost my reputation! I have lost the immortal part of myself, and what remains is bestial. My reputation, Iago, my reputation!

IAGO
As I am an honest man, I thought you had received some bodily wound; there is more sense in that than in reputation. Reputation is an idle and most false imposition: oft got without merit, and lost without deserving.
[...]

CASSIO
I will rather sue to be despised than to deceive so good a commander with so slight, so drunken, and so indiscreet an officer. Drunk? and speak parrot? and squabble? swagger? swear? and discourse fustian with one's own shadow? O thou invisible spirit of wine, if thou hast no name to be known by, let us call thee devil!

IAGO
What was he that you followed with your sword?
What had he done to you?

CASSIO
I know not.

IAGO
Is't possible?

CASSIO
I remember a mass of things, but nothing distinctly; a quarrel, but nothing wherefore. O God, that men should put an enemy in their mouths to steal away their brains! that we should, with joy, pleasance revel and applause, transform ourselves into beasts!

IAGO
Why, but you are now well enough: how came you thus recovered?

CASSIO
It hath pleased the devil drunkenness to give place to the devil wrath; one unperfectness shows me another, to make me frankly despise myself.

Othello | Act II, scene 3

11 FEBRUARY

The death in 1862 of Elizabeth Siddal, muse to the Pre-Raphaelites and the model for John Everett Millais' famous painting of Ophelia

Ophelia is distressed by Hamlet's descent into madness.

OPHELIA
O, what a noble mind is here o'erthrown!
The courtier's, scholar's, soldier's, eye, tongue, sword,
Th' expectancy and rose of the fair state,
The glass of fashion and the mould of form,
Th' observ'd of all observers – quite, quite down!
And I, of ladies most deject and wretched,
That suck'd the honey of his music vows,
Now see that noble and most sovereign reason,
Like sweet bells jangled, out of tune and harsh;
That unmatch'd form and feature of blown youth
Blasted with ecstasy. O, woe is me
T' have seen what I have seen, see what I see!

Hamlet | Act III, scene 1

12 FEBRUARY

Red Hand Day, part of the United Nations' campaign against child soldiers

Macbeth's hands are red with the blood of his victim, King Duncan, and he is agitated.

LADY MACBETH
[...] Why did you bring these daggers from the place?
They must lie there: go carry them; and smear
The sleepy grooms with blood.

MACBETH
I'll go no more:
I am afraid to think what I have done;
Look on't again I dare not.

LADY MACBETH
Infirm of purpose!
Give me the daggers: the sleeping and the dead
Are but as pictures: 'tis the eye of childhood
That fears a painted devil. If he do bleed,
I'll gild the faces of the grooms withal;
For it must seem their guilt.
[Exit. Knocking within]

MACBETH
Whence is that knocking?
How is't with me, when every noise appals me?
What hands are here? ha! they pluck out mine eyes.
Will all great Neptune's ocean wash this blood
Clean from my hand? No, this my hand will rather
The multitudinous seas in incarnadine,
Making the green one red.
[Re-enter Lady Macbeth]

LADY MACBETH

My hands are of your colour; but I shame
To wear a heart so white.
[Knocking within]
I hear a knocking
At the south entry: retire we to our chamber;
A little water clears us of this deed:
How easy is it, then!

Macbeth | Act II, scene 2

13 FEBRUARY

In 2004 the white dwarf star BPM 37093 is discovered, with a crystalline composition like that of diamonds – it is named Lucy after the Beatles' song 'Lucy in the Sky with Diamonds'

In ancient Britain the Earl of Kent believe that destiny is shaped by the positions of the stars; but in ancient Rome Cassius thinks the stars may not be to blame.

EARL OF KENT
It is the stars,
The stars above us, govern our conditions...

King Lear | Act IV, scene 3

CASSIUS
Why, man, he doth bestride the narrow world
Like a Colossus, and we petty men
Walk under his huge legs and peep about
To find ourselves dishonourable graves.
Men at some time are masters of their fates:
The fault, dear Brutus, is not in our stars,
But in ourselves, that we are underlings.
Brutus and Caesar: what should be in that 'Caesar'?
Why should that name be sounded more than yours?
Write them together, yours is as fair a name;
Sound them, it doth become the mouth as well;
Weigh them, it is as heavy; conjure with 'em,
Brutus will start a spirit as soon as Caesar.
Now, in the names of all the gods at once,
Upon what meat doth this our Caesar feed,
That he is grown so great? Age, thou art shamed!
Rome, thou hast lost the breed of noble bloods!
When went there by an age, since the great flood,
But it was famed with more than with one man?

When could they say till now, that talk'd of Rome,
That her wide walls encompass'd but one man?
Now is it Rome indeed and room enough,
When there is in it but one only man.
O, you and I have heard our fathers say,
There was a Brutus once that would have brook'd
The eternal devil to keep his state in Rome
As easily as a king.

Julius Caesar | **Act I, scene 2**

14 FEBRUARY

St Valentine's Day, when lovers exchange tokens of love

Ophelia, having lost her heart to Hamlet,
has lost her mind.

OPHELIA
Pray let's have no words of this; but when they ask you
what it means, say you this:
> *[Sings] To-morrow is Saint Valentine's day,*
> *All in the morning bedtime,*
> *And I a maid at your window,*
> *To be your Valentine.*
> *Then up he rose and donn'd his clo'es*
> *And dupp'd the chamber door,*
> *Let in the maid, that out a maid*
> *Never departed more.*

CLAUDIUS
Pretty Ophelia!

OPHELIA
Indeed, la, without an oath, I'll make an end on't!
> *[Sings] By Gis and by Saint Charity,*
> *Alack, and fie for shame!*
> *Young men will do't if they come to't*
> *By Cock, they are to blame.*
> *Quoth she, 'Before you tumbled me,*
> *You promis'd me to wed.'*

He answers:
> *'So would I 'a done, by yonder sun,*
> *An thou hadst not come to my bed.'*

Hamlet | Act IV, scene 5

15 FEBRUARY

Decimal Day in 1971, when Britain and Ireland converted to a decimal currency

Pre-decimal measures were a source of humour even in Shakespeare's day. There were twenty shillings in a pound. A wether is a sheep, and eleven wethers yielded a tod of wool – 28lbs.

CLOWN
Let me see: every 'leven wether tods; every tod yields pound and odd shilling; fifteen hundred shorn. what comes the wool to? [...] I cannot do't without counters. Let me see; what am I to buy for our sheep-shearing feast? Three pound of sugar, five pound of currants, rice, – what will this sister of mine do with rice? But my father hath made her mistress of the feast, and she lays it on. She hath made me four and twenty nose-gays for the shearers, three-man-song-men all, and very good ones; but they are most of them means and bases; but one puritan amongst them, and he sings psalms to horn-pipes. I must have saffron to colour the warden pies; mace; dates? – none, that's out of my note; nutmegs, seven; a race or two of ginger, but that I may beg; four pound of prunes, and as many of raisins o' the sun.

The Winter's Tale | Act IV, scene 3

16 FEBRUARY

The birthday in 1893 of stage actress Katharine Cornell, who found success as Shakespeare's Juliet and Cleopatra, and as Mary Fitton in Clemence Dane's play Will Shakespeare

Dane's play speculates on the identity of the Dark Lady, the object of many of Shakespeare's sonnets, who may have been Mary Fitton, mistress of the Earl of Pembroke.

SONNET 127

In the old age black was not counted fair,
Or if it were, it bore not beauty's name;
But now is black beauty's successive heir,
And beauty slander'd with a bastard shame:
For since each hand hath put on nature's power,
Fairing the foul with art's false borrow'd face,
Sweet beauty hath no name, no holy bower,
But is profaned, if not lives in disgrace.
Therefore my mistress' brows are raven black,
Her eyes so suited, and they mourners seem
At such who, not born fair, no beauty lack,
Slandering creation with a false esteem:
Yet so they mourn, becoming of their woe,
That every tongue says beauty should look so.

17 FEBRUARY

The formation in 1863 of the International Committee for Relief to the Wounded, the organization which became the International Red Cross

Injuries in battle during the many wars of European history were the most important sources of knowledge for early surgeons and anatomists.

BATES

Ay, or more than we seek after; for we know enough, if we know we are the king's subjects: if his cause be wrong, our obedience to the king wipes the crime of it out of us.

WILLIAMS

But if the cause be not good, the king himself hath a heavy reckoning to make, when all those legs and arms and heads, chopped off in battle, shall join together at the latter day and cry all 'We died at such a place;' some swearing, some crying for a surgeon, some upon their wives left poor behind them, some upon the debts they owe, some upon their children rawly left. I am afeard there are few die well that die in a battle; for how can they charitably dispose of any thing, when blood is their argument? Now, if these men do not die well, it will be a black matter for the king that led them to it; whom to disobey were against all proportion of subjection.

Henry V | Act IV, scene 1

18 FEBRUARY

One of eighteen days on which the Virgin Mary appeared to Bernadette Soubirous in 1858 near Lourdes – this day she promises Bernadette happiness not in this life but in the next

Orlando, fleeing his brother, has fallen in love with Rosalind at first sight. She, daughter of 'the banish'd Duke', must leave the city, having angered her uncle, the new usurping Duke.

ORLANDO
I thank you, sir; and pray you tell me this:
Which of the two was daughter of the Duke
That here was at the wrestling?

LE BEAU
Neither his daughter, if we judge by manners;
But yet, indeed, the smaller is his daughter;
The other is daughter to the banish'd Duke,
And here detain'd by her usurping uncle,
To keep his daughter company; whose loves
Are dearer than the natural bond of sisters.
But I can tell you that of late this Duke
Hath ta'en displeasure 'gainst his gentle niece,
Grounded upon no other argument
But that the people praise her for her virtues
And pity her for her good father's sake;
And, on my life, his malice 'gainst the lady
Will suddenly break forth. Sir, fare you well.
Hereafter, in a better world than this,
I shall desire more love and knowledge of you.

ORLANDO

I rest much bounden to you; fare you well.

[Exit Le Beau]

Thus must I from the smoke into the smother;

From tyrant Duke unto a tyrant brother.

But heavenly Rosalind!

As You Like It | Act I, scene 2

19 FEBRUARY

In 1847 the first rescuers reach a group of travellers trapped over winter in the Sierra Nevada, who had resorted to cannibalism to survive

Richard Plantagenet, Duke of York, a prisoner after the Battle of Wakefield, has been shown a cloth dipped in the blood of his twelve-year-old son, who was killed by his captors.

RICHARD PLANTAGENET
That face of his the hungry cannibals
Would not have touch'd, would not have stain'd with blood:
But you are more inhuman, more inexorable,
O, ten times more, than tigers of Hyrcania.
See, ruthless queen, a hapless father's tears:
This cloth thou dip'dst in blood of my sweet boy,
And I with tears do wash the blood away.
Keep thou the napkin, and go boast of this:
And if thou tell'st the heavy story right,
Upon my soul, the hearers will shed tears;
Yea even my foes will shed fast-falling tears,
And say 'Alas, it was a piteous deed!'
There, take the crown, and, with the crown, my curse;
And in thy need such comfort come to thee
As now I reap at thy too cruel hand!
Hard-hearted Clifford, take me from the world:
My soul to heaven, my blood upon your heads!

Henry VI, Part 3 | Act I, scene 4

20 FEBRUARY

In 1792 the United States Post Office Department is established by the signature of George Washington

Malvolio is only too willing to believe that a forged letter comes from his adored Olivia, encouraging him to behave in outlandish ways to prove his love for her.

MALVOLIO
By my life, this is my lady's hand, these be her very C's, her U's and her T's and thus makes she her great P's. It is, in contempt of question, her hand.

SIR ANDREW AGUECHECK
Her C's, her U's and her T's: why that?

MALVOLIO
[Reads] To the unknown beloved, this, and my good wishes: – her very phrases! By your leave, wax. Soft! and the impressure her Lucrece, with which she uses to seal: 'tis my lady. To whom should this be?

FABIAN
This wins him, liver and all.

MALVOLIO
[Reads]
> *Jove knows I love: But who?*
> *Lips, do not move;*
> *No man must know.*

'No man must know.' What follows? the numbers altered! 'No man must know:' if this should be thee, Malvolio?

SIR TOBY BELCH
Marry, hang thee, brock!

MALVOLIO
[Reads]

> *I may command where I adore;*
> *But silence, like a Lucrece knife,*
> *With bloodless stroke my heart doth gore:*
> *M, O, A, I, doth sway my life.*

'M, O, A, I, doth sway my life.' Nay, but first, let me see,
let me see, let me see. 'I may command where I adore.'
Why, she may command me: I serve her; she is my lady.
Why, this is evident to any formal capacity; there is no
obstruction in this: and the end, – what should that
alphabetical position portend? If I could make that
resemble something in me, – Softly! M, O, A, I, – M,
– Malvolio; M, – why, that begins my name. M, – but
then there is no consonancy in the sequel; that suffers
under probation A should follow but O does. And then
I comes behind. M, O, A, I; this simulation is not as the
former: and yet, to crush this a little, it would bow to
me, for every one of these letters are in my name. Soft!
here follows prose. *[Reads]*

> *If this fall into thy hand, revolve. In my stars I am above*
> *thee; but be not afraid of greatness: some are born great,*
> *some achieve greatness, and some have greatness thrust*
> *upon 'em. Thy Fates open their hands; let thy blood and*
> *spirit embrace them; and, to inure thyself to what thou*
> *art like to be, cast thy humble slough and appear fresh.*
> *Be opposite with a kinsman, surly with servants; let thy*
> *tongue tang arguments of state; put thyself into the trick*
> *of singularity: she thus advises thee that sighs for thee.*
> *Remember who commended thy yellow stockings, and*
> *wished to see thee ever cross-gartered: I say, remember.*

Go to, thou art made, if thou desirest to be so; if not, let
me see thee a steward still, the fellow of servants, and not
worthy to touch Fortune's fingers. Farewell.
She that would alter services with thee,
THE FORTUNATE-UNHAPPY.

Daylight and champaign discovers not more: this is
open. I will be proud, I will read politic authors, I will
baffle Sir Toby, I will wash off gross acquaintance, I
will be point-devise the very man. I do not now fool
myself, to let imagination jade me; for every reason
excites to this, that my lady loves me. She did commend
my yellow stockings of late, she did praise my leg being
cross-gartered; and in this she manifests herself to my
love, and with a kind of injunction drives me to these
habits of her liking. I thank my stars I am happy. I will
be strange, stout, in yellow stockings, and cross-gartered,
even with the swiftness of putting on. Jove and my stars
be praised! Here is yet a postscript. *[Reads]*

Thou canst not choose but know who I am. If thou
entertainest my love, let it appear in thy smiling; thy
smiles become thee well; therefore in my presence still
smile, dear my sweet, I prithee.

Jove, I thank thee: I will smile; I will do everything that
thou wilt have me.

Twelfth Night | Act II, scene 5

21 FEBRUARY

The death of Catholic poet-priest Robert Southwell, who after years of torture was hanged, drawn and quartered – he was a distant cousin of Shakespeare's and a literary influence on the Bard

This speech by Lear, after he and his daughter Cordelia have been taken prisoner, makes reference to Southwell's poem 'Decease Release'.

CORDELIA
We are not the first
Who with best meaning have incurr'd the worst.
For thee, oppressed king, am I cast down;
Myself could else outfrown false Fortune's frown.
Shall we not see these daughters and these sisters?

LEAR
No, no, no, no! Come, let's away to prison.
We two alone will sing like birds i' th' cage.
When thou dost ask me blessing, I'll kneel down
And ask of thee forgiveness. So we'll live,
And pray, and sing, and tell old tales, and laugh
At gilded butterflies, and hear poor rogues
Talk of court news; and we'll talk with them too –
Who loses and who wins; who's in, who's out –
And take upon 's the mystery of things,
As if we were God's spies; and we'll wear out,
In a wall'd prison, packs and sects of great ones
That ebb and flow by th' moon.

EDMUND
Take them away.

King Lear | Act V, scene 3

22 FEBRUARY

In 1983 the play Moose Murders *becomes a byword for a Broadway flop when it opens and closes on the same night – one critic called it 'the worst play I've ever seen on a Broadway stage.'*

Several of Shakespeare's plays end with the hope that the audience liked it, and an encouragement to applaud.

DANCER

First my fear, then my curtsy, last my speech. My fear, is your displeasure; my curtsy, my duty; and my speech, to beg your pardons. If you look for a good speech now, you undo me; for what I have to say is of mine own making; and what, indeed, I should say will, I doubt, prove mine own marring. But to the purpose, and so to the venture.

Be it known to you, as it is very well, I was lately here in the end of a displeasing play, to pray your patience for it and to promise you a better. I meant, indeed, to pay you with this; which if like an ill venture it come unluckily home, I break, and you, my gentle creditors, lose. Here I promis'd you I would be, and here I commit my body to your mercies. Bate me some, and I will pay you some, and, as most debtors do, promise you infinitely; and so I kneel down before you – but, indeed, to pray for the Queen.

If my tongue cannot entreat you to acquit me, will you command me to use my legs? And yet that were but light payment – to dance out of your debt. But a good conscience will make any possible satisfaction, and so would I. All the gentlewomen here have forgiven me. If the gentlemen will not, then the gentlemen do not agree with the gentlewomen, which was never seen before in such an assembly.

One word more, I beseech you. If you be not too much
cloy'd with fat meat, our humble author will continue
the story, with Sir John in it, and make you merry with
fair Katherine of France; where, for anything I know,
Falstaff shall die of a sweat, unless already he be killed
with your hard opinions; for Oldcastle died a martyr and
this is not the man. My tongue is weary; when my legs
are too, I will bid you good night.

Henry IV, Part 2 | Epilogue

23 FEBRUARY

The Feast Day of fourth-century St Serenus the Gardener, who lived a self-sufficient life on his plot of land in Serbia

In the Duke of York's garden, similes and metaphors abound.

GARDENER
Go, bind thou up yon dangling apricocks,
Which, like unruly children, make their sire
Stoop with oppression of their prodigal weight:
Give some supportance to the bending twigs.
Go thou, and like an executioner,
Cut off the heads of too fast growing sprays,
That look too lofty in our commonwealth:
All must be even in our government.
You thus employ'd, I will go root away
The noisome weeds, which without profit suck
The soil's fertility from wholesome flowers.

SERVANT
Why should we in the compass of a pale
Keep law and form and due proportion,
Showing, as in a model, our firm estate,
When our sea-walled garden, the whole land,
Is full of weeds, her fairest flowers choked up,
Her fruit-trees all upturned, her hedges ruin'd,
Her knots disorder'd and her wholesome herbs
Swarming with caterpillars?

GARDENER
Hold thy peace:
He that hath suffer'd this disorder'd spring
Hath now himself met with the fall of leaf:
The weeds which his broad-spreading leaves did shelter,

That seem'd in eating him to hold him up,
Are pluck'd up root and all by Bolingbroke,
I mean the Earl of Wiltshire, Bushy, Green.

SERVANT
What, are they dead?

GARDENER
They are; and Bolingbroke
Hath seized the wasteful king. O, what pity is it
That he had not so trimm'd and dress'd his land
As we this garden! We at time of year
Do wound the bark, the skin of our fruit-trees,
Lest, being over-proud in sap and blood,
With too much riches it confound itself:
Had he done so to great and growing men,
They might have lived to bear and he to taste
Their fruits of duty: superfluous branches
We lop away, that bearing boughs may live:
Had he done so, himself had borne the crown,
Which waste of idle hours hath quite thrown down.

Richard II | Act III, scene 4

24 FEBRUARY

Dragobete, a traditional Romanian holiday celebrating love and the onset of spring, when the birds are said to be betrothed, and young woman collect snow from which to make love potions

Demetrius, under a spell cast by Puck, has transferred his affections from Hermia to Helena.

DEMETRIUS

My lord, fair Helen told me of their stealth,
Of this their purpose hither to this wood;
And I in fury hither follow'd them,
Fair Helena in fancy following me.
But, my good lord, I wot not by what power –
But by some power it is – my love to Hermia,
Melted as the snow, seems to me now
As the remembrance of an idle gaud
Which in my childhood I did dote upon;
And all the faith, the virtue of my heart,
The object and the pleasure of mine eye,
Is only Helena. To her, my lord,
Was I betroth'd ere I saw Hermia:
But, like in sickness, did I loathe this food;
But, as in health, come to my natural taste,
Now I do wish it, love it, long for it,
And will for evermore be true to it.

A Midsummer Night's Dream | Act IV, scene 1

25 FEBRUARY

The death in 1756 of actress, playwright and pioneering novelist Eliza Haywood, whose first stage appearance was in an adaptation of Timon of Athens *in Dublin*

Such adaptations were often greatly altered to reflect the tastes of the time. There are only two female characters, apart from dancers, in Shakespeare's original Timon – both prostitutes.

APEMANTUS
Hoy-day, what a sweep of vanity comes this way!
They dance! they are mad women.
Like madness is the glory of this life.
As this pomp shows to a little oil and root.
We make ourselves fools, to disport ourselves;
And spend our flatteries, to drink those men
Upon whose age we void it up again,
With poisonous spite and envy.
Who lives that's not depraved or depraves?
Who dies, that bears not one spurn to their graves
Of their friends' gift?
I should fear those that dance before me now
Would one day stamp upon me: 't has been done;
Men shut their doors against a setting sun.
[The Lords rise from table, with much adoring of Timon;
and to show their loves, each singles out an Amazon, and
all dance, men with women, a lofty strain or two to the
hautboys, and cease]

Timon of Athens | Act I, scene 2

26 FEBRUARY

The baptism in 1564 – the same year as Shakespeare – of playwright Christopher Marlowe, with whom Shakespeare may have collaborated on the three parts of Henry VI

As You Like It *has many references to Marlowe's work and death, allegedly in a brawl after an argument about a bill (or 'reckoning') in a little room in a tavern run by Eleanor Bull.*

TOUCHSTONE
When a man's verses cannot be understood, nor a man's good wit seconded with the forward child understanding, it strikes a man more dead than a great reckoning in a little room.

As You Like It | Act III, scene 3

27 FEBRUARY

The birthday in 1859 of Bertha Pappenheim who, as a patient of Josef Breuer, helped to lay the foundations of psychoanalysis

Pappenheim's physical symptoms resulted from mental anguish. Hamlet has asked the Player King to add a speech to a play, hoping to prompt a psychological reaction from his uncle in the audience.

PLAYER KING
I do believe you think what now you speak;
But what we do determine oft we break.
Purpose is but the slave to memory,
Of violent birth, but poor validity;
Which now, like fruit unripe, sticks on the tree,
But fall unshaken when they mellow be.
Most necessary 'tis that we forget
To pay ourselves what to ourselves is debt.
What to ourselves in passion we propose,
The passion ending, doth the purpose lose.
The violence of either grief or joy
Their own enactures with themselves destroy.
Where joy most revels, grief doth most lament;
Grief joys, joy grieves, on slender accident.
This world is not for aye, nor 'tis not strange
That even our loves should with our fortunes change;
For 'tis a question left us yet to prove,
Whether love lead fortune, or else fortune love.
The great man down, you mark his favourite flies,
The poor advanc'd makes friends of enemies;
And hitherto doth love on fortune tend,
For who not needs shall never lack a friend,
And who in want a hollow friend doth try,
Directly seasons him his enemy.
But, orderly to end where I begun,

Our wills and fates do so contrary run
That our devices still are overthrown;
Our thoughts are ours, their ends none of our own.
So think thou wilt no second husband wed;
But die thy thoughts when thy first lord is dead.

Hamlet | Act III, scene 2

28 FEBRUARY

In 1525 Spanish conquistador Hernán Cortés executes Cuauhtémoc,
the last emperor of the Aztecs

The emperor's name means 'descending eagle', invoking the bird's swoop on its prey.

SICILIUS LEONATUS
He came in thunder; his celestial breath
Was sulphurous to smell: the holy eagle
Stoop'd as to foot us: his ascension is
More sweet than our blest fields: his royal bird
Prunes the immortal wing and cloys his beak,
As when his god is pleased.

Cymbeline | Act V, scene 4

29 FEBRUARY

A day that comes only once every four years, on which traditionally women are allowed to propose marriage to their men

Petruchio is delighted that he and Katherine are to be wed. Spoiler alert – the course of true love, as Shakespeare once wrote, never did run smooth.

PETRUCHIO
Be patient, gentlemen. I choose her for myself;
If she and I be pleas'd, what's that to you?
'Tis bargain'd 'twixt us twain, being alone,
That she shall still be curst in company.
I tell you 'tis incredible to believe.
How much she loves me – O, the kindest Kate!
She hung about my neck, and kiss on kiss
She vied so fast, protesting oath on oath,
That in a twink she won me to her love.
O, you are novices! 'Tis a world to see,
How tame, when men and women are alone,
A meacock wretch can make the curstest shrew.
Give me thy hand, Kate; I will unto Venice,
To buy apparel 'gainst the wedding-day.
Provide the feast, father, and bid the guests;
I will be sure my Katherine shall be fine.

The Taming of the Shrew | Act II, scene 1

MARCH

For I have neither wit, nor words, nor worth,
Action, nor utterance, nor the power of speech,
To stir men's blood...

Julius Caesar | Act III, scene 2

1 MARCH

St David's Day

St David is the patron saint of Wales; the Welsh national plant is a leek; and Fluellen is a Welsh soldier in Henry V's army, from whom Shakespeare derives much humour about his accent.

FLUELLEN
Your majesty says very true: if your majesties is
remembered of it, the Welshmen did good service
in a garden where leeks did grow, wearing leeks
in their Monmouth caps; which, your majesty know,
to this hour is an honourable badge of the service;
and I do believe your majesty takes no scorn
to wear the leek upon Saint Tavy's day.

HENRY V
I wear it for a memorable honour;
For I am Welsh, you know, good countryman.

FLUELLEN
All the water in Wye cannot wash your majesty's
Welsh plood out of your pody, I can tell you that:
God pless it and preserve it, as long as it pleases
his grace, and his majesty too!

Henry V | Act IV, scene 7

2 MARCH

March is National Reading Month in the USA

There are advantages and disadvantages to seeing into the future.

HENRY IV

O God! that one might read the book of fate,
And see the revolution of the times
Make mountains level, and the continent,
Weary of solid firmness, melt itself
Into the sea; and other times to see
The beachy girdle of the ocean
Too wide for Neptune's hips; how chances mock,
And changes fill the cup of alteration
With divers liquors! O, if this were seen,
The happiest youth, viewing his progress through,
What perils past, what crosses to ensue,
Would shut the book and sit him down and die.

Henry IV, Part 2 | Act III, scene 1

3 MARCH

Hinamatsuri, celebrating daughters and marriage in Japan

The god Hymen enjoys his successful intervention in the lives of four couples.

HYMEN
Peace, ho! I bar confusion;
'Tis I must make conclusion
Of these most strange events.
Here's eight that must take hands
To join in Hymen's bands,
If truth holds true contents.
You and you no cross shall part;
You and you are heart in heart;
You to his love must accord,
Or have a woman to your lord;
You and you are sure together,
As the winter to foul weather.
Whiles a wedlock-hymn we sing,
Feed yourselves with questioning,
That reason wonder may diminish,
How thus we met, and these things finish.
[he sings]
 Wedding is great Juno's crown;
 O blessed bond of board and bed!
 'Tis Hymen peoples every town;
 High wedlock then be honoured.
 Honour, high honour, and renown,
 To Hymen, god of every town!

As You Like It | Act V, scene 4

4 MARCH

The anniversary of the end of the 1943 Battle of the Bismarck Sea

Shakespeare conjures an entire fleet of ships, sailors and soldiers with a few words.

THE CHORUS
Thus with imagined wing our swift scene flies
In motion of no less celerity
Than that of thought. Suppose that you have seen
The well-appointed king at Hampton pier
Embark his royalty; and his brave fleet
With silken streamers the young Phoebus fanning:
Play with your fancies, and in them behold
Upon the hempen tackle ship-boys climbing;
Hear the shrill whistle which doth order give
To sounds confused; behold the threaden sails,
Borne with the invisible and creeping wind,
Draw the huge bottoms through the furrow'd sea,
Breasting the lofty surge: O, do but think
You stand upon the ravage and behold
A city on the inconstant billows dancing;
For so appears this fleet majestical,
Holding due course to Harfleur. Follow, follow:
Grapple your minds to sternage of this navy,
And leave your England, as dead midnight still,
Guarded with grandsires, babies and old women,
Either past or not arrived to pith and puissance;
For who is he, whose chin is but enrich'd
With one appearing hair, that will not follow
These cull'd and choice-drawn cavaliers to France?

Henry V | Act III, prologue

5 MARCH

Feast day of St Ciarán of Saigir, a hermit of Ireland

A princess challenges her suitor to prove his love.

FERDINAND
Now, at the latest minute of the hour,
Grant us your loves.

PRINCESS OF FRANCE
[...] If for my love, as there is no such cause,
You will do aught, this shall you do for me:
Your oath I will not trust; but go with speed
To some forlorn and naked hermitage,
Remote from all the pleasures of the world;
There stay until the twelve celestial signs
Have brought about the annual reckoning.
If this austere insociable life
Change not your offer made in heat of blood;
If frosts and fasts, hard lodging and thin weeds
Nip not the gaudy blossoms of your love,
But that it bear this trial and last love;
Then, at the expiration of the year,
Come challenge me, challenge me by these deserts,
And, by this virgin palm now kissing thine
I will be thine; and till that instant shut
My woeful self up in a mourning house,
Raining the tears of lamentation
For the remembrance of my father's death.
If this thou do deny, let our hands part,
Neither entitled in the other's heart.

Love's Labour's Lost | Act V, scene 2

6 MARCH

Even when one knows what is righteous, the battle between conscience and temptation is fierce.

MACBETH

If it were done when 'tis done, then 'twere well
It were done quickly: if the assassination
Could trammel up the consequence, and catch
With his surcease success; that but this blow
Might be the be-all and the end-all here,
But here, upon this bank and shoal of time,
We'd jump the life to come. But in these cases
We still have judgment here; [...] this even-handed justice
Commends the ingredients of our poison'd chalice
To our own lips. He's here in double trust;
First, as I am his kinsman and his subject,
Strong both against the deed; then, as his host,
Who should against his murderer shut the door,
Not bear the knife myself. Besides, this Duncan
Hath borne his faculties so meek, hath been
So clear in his great office, that his virtues
Will plead like angels, trumpet-tongued, against
The deep damnation of his taking-off;
And pity, like a naked new-born babe,
Striding the blast, or heaven's cherubim, horsed
Upon the sightless couriers of the air,
Shall blow the horrid deed in every eye,
That tears shall drown the wind. I have no spur
To prick the sides of my intent, but only
Vaulting ambition, which o'erleaps itself
And falls on the other.

Macbeth | Act I, scene 7

7 MARCH

Anniversary, in 1876, of the award to Alexander Graham Bell of a patent for the telephone

Distance is no barrier to love.

SONNET 44

If the dull substance of my flesh were thought,
Injurious distance should not stop my way;
For then despite of space I would be brought,
From limits far remote where thou dost stay.
No matter then although my foot did stand
Upon the farthest earth removed from thee;
For nimble thought can jump both sea and land
As soon as think the place where he would be.
But ah! thought kills me that I am not thought,
To leap large lengths of miles when thou art gone,
But that so much of earth and water wrought
I must attend time's leisure with my moan,
Receiving nought by elements so slow
But heavy tears, badges of either's woe.

8 MARCH

International Women's Day

On a scholarly retreat, a nobleman regrets his oath to live without women.

BEROWNE
[...] From women's eyes this doctrine I derive:
They sparkle still the right Promethean fire;
They are the books, the arts, the academes,
That show, contain and nourish all the world:
Else none at all in ought proves excellent.
Then fools you were these women to forswear,
Or keeping what is sworn, you will prove fools.
For wisdom's sake, a word that all men love,
Or for love's sake, a word that loves all men,
Or for men's sake, the authors of these women,
Or women's sake, by whom we men are men,
Let us once lose our oaths to find ourselves,
Or else we lose ourselves to keep our oaths.
It is religion to be thus forsworn,
For charity itself fulfills the law,
And who can sever love from charity?

Love's Labour's Lost | Act IV, scene 3

9 MARCH

Teachers' Day in Lebanon

A day not always celebrated by pupils.

GREMIO
O this learning, what a thing it is!

The Taming of the Shrew | Act I, scene 2

10 MARCH

Feast day of St Attala, who restored books

In praise of a good read.

EARL OF WORCESTER
Peace, cousin, say no m ore:
And now I will unclasp a secret book,
And to your quick-conceiving discontents
I'll read you matter deep and dangerous,
As full of peril and adventurous spirit
As to o'er-walk a current roaring loud
On the unsteadfast footing of a spear.

Henry IV, Part 1 | Act I, scene 3

11 MARCH

The anniversary of the Great Blizzard of 1888 on America's eastern seaboard

Wizard Prospero has commanded the spirit Ariel to conjure up a storm.

PROSPERO
Hast thou, spirit,
Perform'd to point the tempest that I bade thee?

ARIEL
To every article.
I boarded the king's ship; now on the beak,
Now in the waist, the deck, in every cabin,
I flamed amazement: sometime I'd divide,
And burn in many places; on the topmast,
The yards and bowsprit, would I flame distinctly,
Then meet and join. Jove's lightnings, the precursors
O' the dreadful thunder-claps, more momentary
And sight-outrunning were not; the fire and cracks
Of sulphurous roaring the most mighty Neptune
Seem to besiege and make his bold waves tremble,
Yea, his dread trident shake.

PROSPERO
My brave spirit!
Who was so firm, so constant, that this coil
Would not infect his reason?

ARIEL

Not a soul
But felt a fever of the mad and play'd
Some tricks of desperation. All but mariners
Plunged in the foaming brine and quit the vessel,
Then all afire with me: the king's son, Ferdinand,
With hair up-staring – then like reeds, not hair –
Was the first man that leap'd; cried, 'Hell is empty
And all the devils are here.'

The Tempest | Act I, scene 2

12 MARCH

In 1930 Mahatma Gandhi leads the 200-mile Salt March, a protest against Imperial Britain's monopoly on salt production in India

Cressida is attracted to Achilles. Her uncle Pandarus thinks he lacks character, in the same way that food without seasoning lacks flavour. Cressida thinks seasoning is for mince.

CRESSIDA
There is among the Greeks Achilles, a better man
than Troilus.

PANDARUS
Achilles! a drayman, a porter, a very camel.

CRESSIDA
Well, well.

PANDARUS
'Well, well!' why, have you any discretion? Have you any
eyes? Do you know what a man is? Is not birth, beauty,
good shape, discourse, manhood, learning, gentleness,
virtue, youth, liberality, and such like, the spice and salt
that season a man?

CRESSIDA
Ay, a minced man: and then to be baked with no date in
the pie, for then the man's date's out.

Troilus and Cressida | Act I, scene 2

13 MARCH

Anniversary of the Battle of Badr between Muslims and the Quraysh, 624 CE

A court jester explains how arguments escalate.

TOUCHSTONE
[...] I did dislike the cut of a certain courtier's beard; he sent me word, if I said his beard was not cut well, he was in the mind it was. This is call'd the Retort Courteous. If I sent him word again it was not well cut, he would send me word he cut it to please himself. This is call'd the Quip Modest. If again it was not well cut, he disabled my judgment. This is call'd the Reply Churlish. If again it was not well cut, he would answer I spake not true. This is call'd the Reproof Valiant. If again it was not well cut, he would say I lie. This is call'd the Countercheck Quarrelsome. And so to the Lie Circumstantial and the Lie Direct.

JAQUES (LORD)
And how oft did you say his beard was not well cut?

TOUCHSTONE
I durst go no further than the Lie Circumstantial, nor he durst not give me the Lie Direct; and so we measur'd swords and parted.

JAQUES (LORD)
Can you nominate in order now the degrees of the lie?

TOUCHSTONE

O, sir, we quarrel in print by the book, as you have books
for good manners. I will name you the degrees. The first,
the Retort Courteous; the second, the Quip Modest;
the third, the Reply Churlish; the fourth, the Reproof
Valiant; the fifth, the Countercheck Quarrelsome; the
sixth, the Lie with Circumstance; the seventh, the Lie
Direct. All these you may avoid but the Lie Direct; and
you may avoid that too with an If. I knew when seven
justices could not take up a quarrel; but when the parties
were met themselves, one of them thought but of an If,
as: 'If you said so, then I said so.' And they shook hands,
and swore brothers. Your If is the only peace-maker;
much virtue in If.

As You Like It | Act V, scene 4

14 MARCH

The birthday in 1804 of Johann Strauss I, founder of the waltz dynasty

A sharp-witted heroine explains the course of love in a musical metaphor.

BEATRICE
The fault will be in the music, cousin, if you be
not wooed in good time: if the prince be too
important, tell him there is measure in every thing
and so dance out the answer. For, hear me, Hero:
wooing, wedding, and repenting, is as a Scotch jig,
a measure, and a cinque pace: the first suit is hot
and hasty, like a Scotch jig, and full as
fantastical; the wedding, mannerly-modest, as a
measure, full of state and ancientry; and then comes
repentance and, with his bad legs, falls into the
cinque pace faster and faster, till he sink into his grave.

Much Ado about Nothing | Act II, scene 1

15 MARCH

The Ides of March

Julius Caesar dismisses a fateful warning.

SOOTHSAYER
Caesar!

CAESAR
Ha! who calls?

CASCA
Bid every noise be still: peace yet again!

CAESAR
Who is it in the press that calls on me?
I hear a tongue, shriller than all the music,
Cry 'Caesar!' Speak; Caesar is turn'd to hear.

SOOTHSAYER
Beware the ides of March.

CAESAR
What man is that?

BRUTUS
A soothsayer bids you beware the ides of March.

CAESAR
Set him before me; let me see his face.

CASSIUS
Fellow, come from the throng; look upon Caesar.

CAESAR

What say'st thou to me now? speak once again.

SOOTHSAYER

Beware the ides of March.

CAESAR

He is a dreamer; let us leave him: pass.

Julius Caesar | Act I, scene 2

16 MARCH

Anniversary of the first ever FA Cup Final, won in 1872, by Wanderers FC

There are at least two references in the works of Shakespeare to the game of football.

ADRIANA
Hence, prating peasant! fetch thy master home.

DROMIO OF EPHESUS
Am I so round with you as you with me,
That like a football you do spurn me thus?
You spurn me hence, and he will spurn me hither:
If I last in this service, you must case me in leather.

The Comedy of Errors | Act II, scene 1

17 MARCH

St Patrick's Day

St Patrick was England's enemy in Shakespeare's time and he has few good words to say about its countrymen. But he frequently celebrates music and poetry, for which Ireland is famous.

JESSICA
I am never merry when I hear sweet music.

LORENZO
The reason is, your spirits are attentive:
For do but note a wild and wanton herd,
Or race of youthful and unhandled colts,
Fetching mad bounds, bellowing and neighing loud,
Which is the hot condition of their blood;
If they but hear perchance a trumpet sound,
Or any air of music touch their ears,
You shall perceive them make a mutual stand,
Their savage eyes turn'd to a modest gaze
By the sweet power of music: therefore the poet
Did feign that Orpheus drew trees, stones and floods;
Since nought so stockish, hard and full of rage,
But music for the time doth change his nature.
The man that hath no music in himself,
Nor is not moved with concord of sweet sounds,
Is fit for treasons, stratagems and spoils;
The motions of his spirit are dull as night
And his affections dark as Erebus:
Let no such man be trusted. Mark the music.

The Merchant of Venice | Act V, scene 1

18 MARCH

Anniversary of an earthquake in 1068 which shook the Arabian peninsula

Venus asks a disinterested Adonis if the earth moves for him.

Didst thou not mark my face? was it not white?
Saw'st thou not signs of fear lurk in mine eye?
Grew I not faint? and fell I not downright?
Within my bosom, whereon thou dost lie,
My boding heart pants, beats, and takes no rest,
But, like an earthquake, shakes thee on my breast.

From Venus and Adonis

19 MARCH

Anniversary of the establishment of standard time zones in US law by the US Senate in 1918

Imprisoned by Lord Bolingbroke, Richard II contemplates the passage of time.

RICHARD II
[...] Music do I hear?
Ha, ha! keep time: how sour sweet music is,
When time is broke and no proportion kept!
So is it in the music of men's lives.
And here have I the daintiness of ear
To cheque time broke in a disorder'd string;
But for the concord of my state and time
Had not an ear to hear my true time broke.
I wasted time, and now doth time waste me;
For now hath time made me his numbering clock:
My thoughts are minutes; and with sighs they jar
Their watches on unto mine eyes, the outward watch,
Whereto my finger, like a dial's point,
Is pointing still, in cleansing them from tears.
Now sir, the sound that tells what hour it is
Are clamorous groans, which strike upon my heart,
Which is the bell: so sighs and tears and groans
Show minutes, times, and hours: but my time
Runs posting on in Bolingbroke's proud joy,
While I stand fooling here, his Jack o' the clock.

Richard II | Act V, scene 5

20 MARCH

United Nations French Language Day

*Henry V, wooing the French king's daughter, displays
the usual English difficulty with foreign languages.*

HENRY V
Fair Katharine, and most fair,
Will you vouchsafe to teach a soldier terms
Such as will enter at a lady's ear
And plead his love-suit to her gentle heart?

KATHARINE
Your majesty shall mock at me; I cannot speak
your England.

HENRY V
O fair Katharine, if you will love me soundly with
your French heart, I will be glad to hear you confess it
brokenly with your English tongue. Do you like me, Kate?

KATHARINE
Pardonnez-moi, I cannot tell wat is 'like me.'

HENRY V
An angel is like you, Kate, and you are like an angel.

KATHARINE
[To Alice] Que dit-il? que je suis semblable a les anges?

ALICE
Oui, vraiment, sauf votre grace, ainsi dit-il.

HENRY V
I said so, dear Katharine; and I must not blush to affirm it.

KATHARINE

O bon Dieu! les langues des hommes sont pleines
de tromperies.

HENRY V

What says she, fair one? that the tongues of men are full
of deceits?

ALICE

Oui, dat de tongues of de mans is be full of deceits: dat is
de princess.
[...]

KATHARINE

Is it possible dat I sould love de enemy of France?

HENRY V

No; it is not possible you should love the enemy of
France, Kate: but, in loving me, you should love the
friend of France; for I love France so well that I will
not part with a village of it; I will have it all mine: and,
Kate, when France is mine and I am yours, then yours is
France and you are mine.

KATHARINE

I cannot tell wat is dat.

HENRY V

No, Kate? I will tell thee in French; which I am sure will
hang upon my tongue like a new-married wife about her
husband's neck, hardly to be shook off. Je quand sur le
possession de France, et quand vous avez le possession de
moi – let me see, what then? Saint Denis be my speed!
– donc votre est France et vous etes mienne. It is as easy

for me, Kate, to conquer the kingdom as to speak so
much more French: I shall never move thee in French,
unless it be to laugh at me.

KATHARINE
Sauf votre honneur, le Francois que vous parlez, il est
meilleur que l'Anglois lequel je parle.

HENRY V
No, faith, is't not, Kate: but thy speaking of my tongue,
and I thine, most truly-falsely, must needs be granted to
be much at one. But, Kate, dost thou understand thus
much English, canst thou love me?

KATHARINE
I cannot tell.

Henry V | Act V, scene 2

21 MARCH

The Spring Equinox

Traditionally the first day of spring, when the sap starts to rise.

PERICLES
See where she comes, apparell'd like the Spring,
Graces her subjects, and her thoughts the king
Of every virtue gives renown to men!
Her face the book of praises, where is read
Nothing but curious pleasures, as from thence
Sorrow were ever razed and testy wrath
Could never be her mild companion.
You gods that made me man, and sway in love,
That have inflamed desire in my breast
To taste the fruit of yon celestial tree,
Or die in the adventure, be my helps,
As I am son and servant to your will,
To compass such a boundless happiness!

Pericles | Act I, scene 1

22 MARCH

Anniversary of the Plymouth Colony's 1621 Peace Treaty with the Wampanoags

With news of an impending attack, three servants discuss the relative merits of peace and war.

SECOND SERVINGMAN
Why, then we shall have a stirring world again. This peace is nothing, but to rust iron, increase tailors, and breed ballad-makers.

FIRST SERVINGMAN
Let me have war, say I; it exceeds peace as far as day does night; it's spritely, waking, audible, and full of vent. Peace is a very apoplexy, lethargy; mulled, deaf, sleepy, insensible; a getter of more bastard children than war's a destroyer of men.

SECOND SERVINGMAN
'Tis so: and as war, in some sort, may be said to be a ravisher, so it cannot be denied but peace is a great maker of cuckolds.

FIRST SERVINGMAN
Ay, and it makes men hate one another.

THIRD SERVINGMAN
Reason; because they then less need one another. The wars for my money.

Coriolanus | Act IV, scene 5

23 MARCH

Friendship Day in Poland and Hungary, which celebrates the volatile
bonds between the two countries, expressed in the Hungarian couplet:
Pole and Hungarian – two great friends,
Fighting and drinking at the end.

You can choose your friends and lovers, but not
your family.

THE CHORUS
Two households, both alike in dignity,
In fair Verona, where we lay our scene,
From ancient grudge break to new mutiny,
Where civil blood makes civil hands unclean.
From forth the fatal loins of these two foes
A pair of star-cross'd lovers take their life;
Whose misadventured piteous overthrows
Do with their death bury their parents' strife.
The fearful passage of their death-mark'd love,
And the continuance of their parents' rage,
Which, but their children's end, nought could remove,
Is now the two hours' traffic of our stage;
The which if you with patient ears attend,
What here shall miss, our toil shall strive to mend.

Romeo and Juliet | **Act I, prologue**

24 MARCH

Accession of King James VI and I in 1603 after the death of Elizabeth I

The new king's fascination with witchcraft inspired
Shakespeare to write a famous opening scene.

[Thunder and lightning. Enter three Witches]

FIRST WITCH
When shall we three meet again
In thunder, lightning, or in rain?

SECOND WITCH
When the hurlyburly's done,
When the battle's lost and won.

THIRD WITCH
That will be ere the set of sun.

FIRST WITCH
Where the place?

SECOND WITCH
Upon the heath.

THIRD WITCH
There to meet with Macbeth.

FIRST WITCH
I come, Graymalkin!

SECOND WITCH
Paddock calls.

THIRD WITCH

Anon.

ALL

Fair is foul, and foul is fair:

Hover through the fog and filthy air.

[Exeunt]

Macbeth | Act I, scene 1

25 MARCH

The date in 1576 when land was leased on which to build one of the earliest Elizabethan theatres

The Newington Butts Theatre saw productions of Titus Andronicus *and an early version of* Hamlet.

HAMLET
Speak the speech, I pray you, as I pronounc'd it to you, trippingly on the tongue. But if you mouth it, as many of our players do, I had as live the town crier spoke my lines. Nor do not saw the air too much with your hand, thus, but use all gently; for in the very torrent, tempest, and (as I may say) whirlwind of your passion, you must acquire and beget a temperance that may give it smoothness. O, it offends me to the soul to hear a robustious periwig-pated fellow tear a passion to tatters, to very rags, to split the ears of the groundlings, who (for the most part) are capable of nothing but inexplicable dumb shows and noise.

Hamlet | Act III, scene 2

26 MARCH

The day in 1484 when William Caxton printed his translation of Aesop's Fables

The leader of a peasants' revolt berates his prisoner for investing in schools and books.

JACK CADE
[...] Thou hast most traitorously corrupted the youth of the realm in erecting a grammar school; and whereas, before, our forefathers had no other books but the score and the tally, thou hast caused printing to be used, and, contrary to the king, his crown and dignity, thou hast built a paper-mill. It will be proved to thy face that thou hast men about thee that usually talk of a noun and a verb, and such abominable words as no Christian ear can endure to hear.
[...]

LORD SAY
You men of Kent –

DICK THE BUTCHER
What say you of Kent?

LORD SAY
Nothing but this; 'tis 'bona terra, mala gens.'

JACK CADE
Away with him, away with him! he speaks Latin.

Henry VI, Part 2 | Act IV, scene 7

27 MARCH

World Theatre Day

Some performances are a hard act to follow. Richard II's predecessor Edward III had a long and stable reign, restoring royal authority and England's military reputation.

EDMUND OF LANGLEY
As in a theatre, the eyes of men,
After a well-graced actor leaves the stage,
Are idly bent on him that enters next,
Thinking his prattle to be tedious;
Even so, or with much more contempt, men's eyes
Did scowl on gentle Richard; no man cried 'God save him!'
No joyful tongue gave him his welcome home:
But dust was thrown upon his sacred head:
Which with such gentle sorrow he shook off,
His face still combating with tears and smiles,
The badges of his grief and patience,
That had not God, for some strong purpose, steel'd
The hearts of men, they must perforce have melted
And barbarism itself have pitied him.
But heaven hath a hand in these events,
To whose high will we bound our calm contents.
To Bolingbroke are we sworn subjects now,
Whose state and honour I for aye allow.

Richard II | Act V, scene 2

28 MARCH

The anniversary of the inaugural concert by the Vienna Philharmonic Orchestra in 1842

The program, conducted by Otto Nicolai, included works by Beethoven and Mozart.

ORSINO

If music be the food of love, play on;
Give me excess of it, that, surfeiting,
The appetite may sicken, and so die.
That strain again! it had a dying fall:
O, it came o'er my ear like the sweet sound,
That breathes upon a bank of violets,
Stealing and giving odour! Enough; no more:
'Tis not so sweet now as it was before.
O spirit of love! how quick and fresh art thou,
That, notwithstanding thy capacity
Receiveth as the sea, nought enters there,
Of what validity and pitch soe'er,
But falls into abatement and low price,
Even in a minute: so full of shapes is fancy
That it alone is high fantastical.

Twelfth Night | Act I, scene 1

29 MARCH

Anniversary of the Sunbeam 1000hp becoming, in 1927, the first car to travel at more than 200mph

Juliet awaits news of Romeo from her nurse, who does not seem to feel the need for speed.

JULIET

The clock struck nine when I did send the nurse;
In half an hour she promised to return.
Perchance she cannot meet him: that's not so.
O, she is lame! Love's heralds should be thoughts,
Which ten times faster glide than the sun's beams,
Driving back shadows over louring hills:
Therefore do nimble-pinion'd doves draw love,
And therefore hath the wind-swift Cupid wings.
Now is the sun upon the highmost hill
Of this day's journey, and from nine till twelve
Is three long hours, yet she is not come.
Had she affections and warm youthful blood,
She would be as swift in motion as a ball;
My words would bandy her to my sweet love,
And his to me:
But old folks, many feign as they were dead;
Unwieldy, slow, heavy and pale as lead.
O God, she comes! O honey nurse, what news?

Romeo and Juliet | Act II, scene 5

30 MARCH

National Doctors Day in the United States

Watched by a doctor and a gentlewoman, Lady Macbeth sleepwalks, haunted by her husband's victims.

LADY MACBETH

Out, damned spot! out, I say! – One: two: why, then, 'tis time to do't. – Hell is murky! – Fie, my lord, fie! a soldier, and afeard? What need we fear who knows it, when none can call our power to account? – Yet who would have thought the old man to have had so much blood in him.

DOCTOR

Do you mark that?

LADY MACBETH

The Thane of Fife had a wife: where is she now? – What, will these hands ne'er be clean? – No more o' that, my lord, no more o' that: you mar all with this starting. Here's the smell of the blood still: all the perfumes of Arabia will not sweeten this little hand. Oh, oh, oh!

DOCTOR

What a sigh is there! The heart is sorely charged.

GENTLEWOMAN

I would not have such a heart in my bosom for the dignity of the whole body.
[...]

DOCTOR

This disease is beyond my practise: yet I have known
those which have walked in their sleep who have died
holily in their beds.

LADY MACBETH

Wash your hands, put on your nightgown; look not so
pale. – I tell you yet again, Banquo's buried; he cannot
come out on's grave.

DOCTOR

Even so?

LADY MACBETH

To bed, to bed! there's knocking at the gate: come, come,
come, come, give me your hand. What's done cannot be
undone. – To bed, to bed, to bed!

DOCTOR

Will she go now to bed?

GENTLEWOMAN

Directly.

DOCTOR

Foul whisperings are abroad: unnatural deeds
Do breed unnatural troubles: infected minds
To their deaf pillows will discharge their secrets:
More needs she the divine than the physician.

Macbeth | **Act V, scene 1**

31 MARCH

Anniversary of the death in 1631 of the metaphysical poet John Donne

Whether Donne and Shakespeare met each other is unknown; but they were contemporaries.

THESEUS
[...] The lunatic, the lover and the poet
Are of imagination all compact:
One sees more devils than vast hell can hold,
That is, the madman: the lover, all as frantic,
Sees Helen's beauty in a brow of Egypt:
The poet's eye, in fine frenzy rolling,
Doth glance from heaven to earth, from earth to heaven;
And as imagination bodies forth
The forms of things unknown, the poet's pen
Turns them to shapes and gives to airy nothing
A local habitation and a name.
Such tricks hath strong imagination,
That if it would but apprehend some joy,
It comprehends some bringer of that joy;
Or in the night, imagining some fear,
How easy is a bush supposed a bear!

A Midsummer Night's Dream | **Act V, scene 1**

APRIL

Dishonour not your mothers; now attest
That those whom you call'd fathers did beget you.
Be copy now to men of grosser blood,
And teach them how to war.

Henry V | Act III, scene 1

1 APRIL

All Fools' Day

A fool muses on the nature of foolery. He invents Quinapalus to give his remark some credibility.

FESTE
Wit, an't be thy will, put me into good fooling!
Those wits, that think they have thee, do very oft
prove fools; and I, that am sure I lack thee, may
pass for a wise man: for what says Quinapalus?
'Better a witty fool, than a foolish wit.'

Twelfth Night | Act I, scene 5

2 APRIL

Anniversary of Spanish explorer Juan Ponce de León's landing in Florida in 1513

A double sonnet, with florid imagery, addressed to an unknown young man.

SONNET 98

From you have I been absent in the spring,
When proud-pied April dress'd in all his trim
Hath put a spirit of youth in every thing,
That heavy Saturn laugh'd and leap'd with him.
Yet nor the lays of birds nor the sweet smell
Of different flowers in odour and in hue
Could make me any summer's story tell,
Or from their proud lap pluck them where they grew;
Nor did I wonder at the lily's white,
Nor praise the deep vermilion in the rose;
They were but sweet, but figures of delight,
Drawn after you, you pattern of all those.
Yet seem'd it Winter still, and, you away,
As with your shadow I with these did play:

SONNET 99

The forward violet thus did I chide:
Sweet thief, whence didst thou steal thy sweet that smells,
If not from my love's breath? The purple pride
Which on thy soft cheek for complexion dwells
In my love's veins thou hast too grossly dy'd.
The lily I condemned for thy hand,
And buds of marjoram had stol'n thy hair;
The roses fearfully on thorns did stand,
One blushing shame, another white despair;

A third, nor red nor white, had stol'n of both,
And to his robbery had annexed thy breath;
But, for his theft, in pride of all his growth
A vengeful canker eat him up to death.
More flowers I noted, yet I none could see,
But sweet, or colour it had stol'n from thee.

3 APRIL

The day in 1860 when the first Pony Express service was launched, between Missouri and California

The ability to spread the news is also the ability to spread fake news.

RUMOUR

Open your ears; for which of you will stop
The vent of hearing when loud Rumour speaks?
I, from the orient to the drooping west,
Making the wind my post-horse, still unfold
The acts commenced on this ball of earth.
Upon my tongues continual slanders ride,
The which in every language I pronounce,
Stuffing the ears of men with false reports.
I speak of peace while covert emnity,
Under the smile of safety, wounds the world;
And who but Rumour, who but only I,
Make fearful musters and prepar'd defence,
Whiles the big year, swoln with some other grief,
Is thought with child by the stern tyrant war,
And no such matter? Rumour is a pipe
Blown by surmises, jealousies, conjectures,
And of so easy and so plain a stop
That the blunt monster with uncounted heads,
The still-discordant wav'ring multitude,
Can play upon it. But what need I thus
My well-known body to anatomize
Among my household? Why is Rumour here?
I run before King Harry's victory,
Who, in a bloody field by Shrewsbury,
Hath beaten down young Hotspur and his troops,
Quenching the flame of bold rebellion
Even with the rebels' blood. But what mean I

To speak so true at first? My office is
To noise abroad that Harry Monmouth fell
Under the wrath of noble Hotspur's sword,
And that the King before the Douglas' rage
Stoop'd his anointed head as low as death.
This have I rumour'd through the peasant towns
Between that royal field of Shrewsbury
And this worm-eaten hold of ragged stone,
Where Hotspur's father, old Northumberland,
Lies crafty-sick. The posts come tiring on,
And not a man of them brings other news
Than they have learnt of me. From Rumour's tongues
They bring smooth comforts false, worse than true wrongs.

Henry IV, Part 2 | Prologue

4 APRIL

Birthday in 1572 of the English writer William Strachey

Strachey's eye-witness account of a shipwreck inspired
The Tempest, *in which Prospero conjures a storm.*
Prospero's daughter Miranda begs him to stop the
suffering of those at sea.

MIRANDA
If by your art, my dearest father, you have
Put the wild waters in this roar, allay them.
The sky, it seems, would pour down stinking pitch,
But that the sea, mounting to the welkin's cheek,
Dashes the fire out. O, I have suffered
With those that I saw suffer: a brave vessel,
Who had, no doubt, some noble creature in her,
Dash'd all to pieces. O, the cry did knock
Against my very heart. Poor souls, they perish'd.
Had I been any god of power, I would
Have sunk the sea within the earth or ere
It should the good ship so have swallow'd and
The fraughting souls within her.

The Tempest | Act I, scene 2

5 APRIL

National Maritime Day in India

The king's butler, having survived a shipwreck, is drowning his sorrows.

[Enter Stephano, singing: a bottle in his hand]

STEPHANO
> *I shall no more to sea, to sea,*
> *Here shall I die ashore—*

This is a very scurvy tune to sing at a man's funeral: well, here's my comfort. *[Drinks]*
[Sings]
> *The master, the swabber, the boatswain and I,*
> *The gunner and his mate*
> *Loved Mall, Meg and Marian and Margery,*
> *But none of us cared for Kate;*
> *For she had a tongue with a tang,*
> *Would cry to a sailor, Go hang!*
> *She loved not the savour of tar nor of pitch,*
> *Yet a tailor might scratch her where'er she did itch:*
> *Then to sea, boys, and let her go hang!*

This is a scurvy tune too: but here's my comfort.
[Drinks]

The Tempest | Act II, scene 2

6 APRIL

In 1896, the first day of the first modern Olympic Games

Rallying after a defeat, the Yorkists prepare for the Battle of Townton in the Wars of the Roses.

GEORGE PLANTAGENET
Yet let us all together to our troops,
And give them leave to fly that will not stay;
And call them pillars that will stand to us;
And, if we thrive, promise them such rewards
As victors wear at the Olympian games:
This may plant courage in their quailing breasts;
For yet is hope of life and victory.
Forslow no longer, make we hence amain.

Henry VI, Part 3 | Act II, scene 3

7 APRIL

National Beer Day, celebrating the day in 1933 when America's prohibition on beer was lifted

Shakespeare plays to his audience with a drunk man singing the praises of English drinkers.

CASSIO
'Fore God, an excellent song.

IAGO
I learned it in England, where, indeed, they are most potent in potting: your Dane, your German, and your swag-bellied Hollander – Drink, ho! – are nothing to your English.

CASSIO
Is your Englishman so expert in his drinking?

IAGO
Why, he drinks you, with facility, your Dane dead drunk; he sweats not to overthrow your Almain; gives your Hollander a vomit, ere the next pottle can be filled.

CASSIO
To the health of our general!

Othello | Act II, scene 3

8 APRIL

Hermia swears by Venus, the goddess of love, that she loves Lysander.

HERMIA
My good Lysander!
I swear to thee, by Cupid's strongest bow,
By his best arrow with the golden head,
By the simplicity of Venus' doves,
By that which knitteth souls and prospers loves,
And by that fire which burn'd the Carthage queen,
When the false Troyan under sail was seen,
By all the vows that ever men have broke,
In number more than ever women spoke,
In that same place thou hast appointed me,
To-morrow truly will I meet with thee.

A Midsummer Night's Dream | Act I, scene 1

9 APRIL

The date in 1860 of the oldest known recording of the human voice

Édouard-Léon Scott de Martinville recorded 'Au Clair de la Lune' on his invention, the phonautograph.

SONNET 59

If there be nothing new, but that which is
Hath been before, how are our brains beguiled,
Which, labouring for invention, bear amiss
The second burden of a former child!
O, that record could with a backward look,
Even of five hundred courses of the sun,
Show me your image in some antique book,
Since mind at first in character was done!
That I might see what the old world could say
To this composed wonder of your frame;
Whether we are mended, or whether better they,
Or whether revolution be the same.
O, sure I am, the wits of former days
To subjects worse have given admiring praise.

10 APRIL

The Day of the Builder, celebrated in Azerbaijan

Two clowns indulge in some gallows humour.

FIRST CLOWN
What is he that builds stronger than either the mason,
the shipwright, or the carpenter?

SECOND CLOWN
The gallows-maker; for that frame outlives a thousand
tenants.

FIRST CLOWN
I like thy wit well, in good faith. The gallows does well.
But how does it well? It does well to those that do ill.
Now, thou dost ill to say the gallows is built stronger
than the church. Argal, the gallows may do well to thee.
To't again, come!

SECOND CLOWN
Who builds stronger than a mason, a shipwright, or
a carpenter?

FIRST CLOWN
Ay, tell me that, and unyoke.

SECOND CLOWN
Marry, now I can tell!

FIRST CLOWN
To't.

SECOND CLOWN
Mass, I cannot tell.

FIRST CLOWN

Cudgel thy brains no more about it, for your dull ass will not mend his pace with beating; and when you are ask'd this question next, say 'a grave-maker.' The houses he makes lasts till doomsday. Go, get thee to Yaughan; fetch me a stoup of liquor.

Hamlet | Act V, scene 1

11 APRIL

The Stone of Destiny, stolen by Scottish nationalists, is recovered, in 1951

Hecate, queen of the witches, berates the three witches for meddling in Macbeth's destiny.

FIRST WITCH

Why, how now, Hecate! you look angerly.

HECATE

Have I not reason, beldams as you are,
Saucy and overbold? How did you dare
To trade and traffic with Macbeth
In riddles and affairs of death;
And I, the mistress of your charms,
The close contriver of all harms,
Was never call'd to bear my part,
Or show the glory of our art?
And, which is worse, all you have done
Hath been but for a wayward son,
Spiteful and wrathful, who, as others do,
Loves for his own ends, not for you.
But make amends now: get you gone,
And at the pit of Acheron
Meet me i' the morning: thither he
Will come to know his destiny:
Your vessels and your spells provide,
Your charms and every thing beside.
I am for the air; this night I'll spend
Unto a dismal and a fatal end:
Great business must be wrought ere noon:
Upon the corner of the moon
There hangs a vaporous drop profound;
I'll catch it ere it come to ground:

And that distill'd by magic sleights
Shall raise such artificial sprites
As by the strength of their illusion
Shall draw him on to his confusion:
He shall spurn fate, scorn death, and bear
He hopes 'bove wisdom, grace and fear:
And you all know, security
Is mortals' chiefest enemy.
[Music and a song within: 'Come away, come away,' etc.
Hark! I am call'd; my little spirit, see,
Sits in a foggy cloud, and stays for me.
[Exit]

FIRST WITCH
Come, let's make haste; she'll soon be back again.

Macbeth | Act III, scene 5

12 APRIL

In 1961, the day on which Yuri Gagarin became the first man in space, exactly twenty years before the launch of the first Space Shuttle

As conspirators encircle Julius Caesar, their leader claims to have been steadfastly loyal to him.

CASSIUS
[...] But I am constant as the northern star,
Of whose true-fix'd and resting quality
There is no fellow in the firmament.
The skies are painted with unnumber'd sparks,
They are all fire and every one doth shine,
But there's but one in all doth hold his place:
So in the world; 'tis furnish'd well with men,
And men are flesh and blood, and apprehensive;
Yet in the number I do know but one
That unassailable holds on his rank,
Unshaked of motion: and that I am he,
Let me a little show it, even in this;
That I was constant Cimber should be banish'd,
And constant do remain to keep him so.
[...]

CASCA
Speak, hands for me!
[Casca first, then the other conspirators and Brutus stab Caesar]

CAESAR
Et tu, Brute! Then fall, Caesar.
[He dies]

Julius Caesar | Act III, scene 1

13 APRIL

Birthday in 1570 of Guy Fawkes, celebrated by bonfires for his failure to blow up the Houses of Parliament

In France, in 1429, bonfires are lit to celebrate the liberation of Orléans from English siege, by a French army led by Joan of Arc.

REIGNIER
Why ring not out the bells aloud throughout the town?
Dauphin, command the citizens make bonfires
And feast and banquet in the open streets,
To celebrate the joy that God hath given us.

DUKE OF ALENCON
All France will be replete with mirth and joy,
When they shall hear how we have play'd the men.

CHARLES, KING OF FRANCE
'Tis Joan, not we, by whom the day is won;
For which I will divide my crown with her,
And all the priests and friars in my realm
Shall in procession sing her endless praise.
[...] In memory of her when she is dead,
Her ashes, in an urn more precious
Than the rich-jewel'd of Darius,
Transported shall be at high festivals
Before the kings and queens of France.
No longer on Saint Denis will we cry,
But Joan la Pucelle shall be France's saint.
Come in, and let us banquet royally,
After this golden day of victory.

Henry VI, Part 1 | Act I, scene 6

14 APRIL

St Tiburtius' Day, traditionally when the first cuckoo of spring is heard

Because the cuckoo lays its eggs in another bird's nest, the cuckoo has come to represent the cuckold.

DON ADRIANO DE ARMADO
[...] But, most esteemed greatness, will you hear the dialogue that the two learned men have compiled in praise of the owl and the cuckoo? It should have followed in the end of our show.

FERDINAND
Call them forth quickly; we will do so.

DON ADRIANO DE ARMADO
Holla! approach.
[Re-enter Holofernes, Sir Nathaniel, Moth, Costard, and others]

[THE SONG]

SPRING
> *When daisies pied and violets blue*
> *And lady-smocks all silver-white*
> *And cuckoo-buds of yellow hue*
> *Do paint the meadows with delight,*
> *The cuckoo then, on every tree,*
> *Mocks married men; for thus sings he; Cuckoo;*
> *Cuckoo, cuckoo: O word of fear,*
> *Unpleasing to a married ear!*
> *When shepherds pipe on oaten straws*
> *And merry larks are ploughmen's clocks,*
> *When turtles tread, and rooks, and daws,*
> *And maidens bleach their summer smocks*

The cuckoo then, on every tree,
Mocks married men; for thus sings he; Cuckoo;
Cuckoo, cuckoo: O word of fear,
Unpleasing to a married ear!

Love's Labour's Lost | Act V, scene 2

15 APRIL

Tax Day in the United States

Money, Shakespeare argues, isn't everything.

SONNET 91

Some glory in their birth, some in their skill,
Some in their wealth, some in their bodies' force,
Some in their garments, though new-fangled ill,
Some in their hawks and hounds, some in their horse;
And every humour hath his adjunct pleasure,
Wherein it finds a joy above the rest:
But these particulars are not my measure;
All these I better in one general best.
Thy love is better than high birth to me,
Richer than wealth, prouder than garments' cost,
Of more delight than hawks or horses be;
And having thee, of all men's pride I boast:
Wretched in this alone, that thou mayst take
All this away and me most wretched make.

16 APRIL

Birthday in 1889 of the great clown of silent cinema Charlie Chaplin

Hamlet advises comedians not to improvise, milk the laughter or upstage the serious parts of a play.

HAMLET
O, reform it altogether! And let those that play your clowns speak no more than is set down for them. For there be of them that will themselves laugh, to set on some quantity of barren spectators to laugh too, though in the mean time some necessary question of the play be then to be considered. That's villainous and shows a most pitiful ambition in the fool that uses it. Go make you ready.

Hamlet | Act III, scene 2

17 APRIL

The start in 1797 of an unsuccessful uprising by the citizens of Verona against their French occupiers

In The Two Gentlemen of Verona, *Shakespeare's first romcom, the course of true love is never smooth.*

PROTEUS
[...] O, how this spring of love resembleth
The uncertain glory of an April day;
Which now shows all the beauty of the sun,
And by and by a cloud takes all away!

The Two Gentlemen of Verona | **Act I, scene 3**

18 APRIL

A day in 1930 when nothing happened, according to the BBC, whose radio news bulletin reported that 'there is no news'

In 1403, however, a dramatic news bulletin brings the audience up to date, in the first scene of a sequel.

MORTON

I am sorry I should force you to believe
That which I would to God I had not seen;
But these mine eyes saw him in bloody state,
Rend'ring faint quittance, wearied and out-breath'd,
To Harry Monmouth, whose swift wrath beat down
The never-daunted Percy to the earth,
From whence with life he never more sprung up.
In few, his death – whose spirit lent a fire
Even to the dullest peasant in his camp –
Being bruited once, took fire and heat away
From the best-temper'd courage in his troops;
For from his metal was his party steeled;
Which once in him abated, all the rest
Turn'd on themselves, like dull and heavy lead.
And as the thing that's heavy in itself
Upon enforcement flies with greatest speed,
So did our men, heavy in Hotspur's loss,
Lend to this weight such lightness with their fear
That arrows fled not swifter toward their aim
Than did our soldiers, aiming at their safety,
Fly from the field. Then was that noble Worcester
Too soon ta'en prisoner; and that furious Scot,
The bloody Douglas, whose well-labouring sword
Had three times slain th' appearance of the King,
Gan vail his stomach and did grace the shame
Of those that turn'd their backs, and in his flight,
Stumbling in fear, was took. The sum of all

Is that the King hath won, and hath sent out
A speedy power to encounter you, my lord,
Under the conduct of young Lancaster
And Westmoreland. This is the news at full.

Henry IV, Part 2 | **Act I, scene 1**

19 APRIL

The city of Derry is burned down by Irish rebels in 1608

Two centuries earlier, Ireland was already hostile to an English presence.

POST
Great lords, from Ireland am I come amain,
To signify that rebels there are up
And put the Englishmen unto the sword:
Send succors, lords, and stop the rage betime,
Before the wound do grow uncurable;
For, being green, there is great hope of help.
[...]

WINCHESTER
My Lord of York, try what your fortune is.
The uncivil kerns of Ireland are in arms
And temper clay with blood of Englishmen:
To Ireland will you lead a band of men,
Collected choicely, from each county some,
And try your hap against the Irishmen?
[...]

RICHARD PLANTAGENET (DUKE OF GLOUCESTER)
My Lord of Suffolk, within fourteen days
At Bristol I expect my soldiers;
For there I'll ship them all for Ireland.

Henry VI, Part 2 | Act III, scene 1

20 APRIL

Birthday in 1924 of English actor Leslie Phillips, often cast as a lothario

Phillips, who played the part of the elderly Falstaff for the Royal Shakespeare Company in 1997, lived to the age of 98.

Crabbed age and youth cannot live together:
Youth is full of pleasance, age is full of care;
Youth like summer morn, age like winter weather;
Youth like summer brave, age like winter bare.
Youth is full of sport, age's breath is short;
Youth is nimble, age is lame;
Youth is hot and bold, age is weak and cold;
Youth is wild, and age is tame.
Age, I do abhor thee; youth, I do adore thee;
O, my love, my love is young!
Age, I do defy thee: O, sweet shepherd, hie thee,
For methinks thou stay'st too long,

From The Passionate Pilgrim

21 APRIL

Date of Mark Antony's defeat at the Battle of Mutina (Modena) in 43 BCE

Mark Antony, a pro-Caesarite, was laying siege to a town governed by Brutus, Caesar's assassin.

OCTAVIUS
Antony,
Leave thy lascivious wassails. When thou once
Wast beaten from Modena, where thou slew'st
Hirtius and Pansa, consuls, at thy heel
Did famine follow; whom thou fought'st against,
Though daintily brought up, with patience more
Than savages could suffer: thou didst drink
The stale of horses, and the gilded puddle
Which beasts would cough at: thy palate then did deign
The roughest berry on the rudest hedge;
Yea, like the stag, when snow the pasture sheets,
The barks of trees thou browsed'st; on the Alps
It is reported thou didst eat strange flesh,
Which some did die to look on: and all this –
It wounds thine honour that I speak it now –
Was borne so like a soldier, that thy cheek
So much as lank'd not.

Antony and Cleopatra | Act I, scene 4

22 APRIL

The death in 1933 of Henry Royce, co-founder of luxury car manufacturer Rolls-Royce

Mercutio describes the chariot of Queen Mab, the fairy who plays tricks on sleeping humans. Both 'queen' and 'mab' were nicknames for a prostitute.

MERCUTIO
O, then, I see Queen Mab hath been with you.
She is the fairies' midwife, and she comes
In shape no bigger than an agate-stone
On the fore-finger of an alderman,
Drawn with a team of little atomies
Athwart men's noses as they lie asleep;
Her wagon-spokes made of long spiders' legs,
The cover of the wings of grasshoppers,
The traces of the smallest spider's web,
The collars of the moonshine's watery beams,
Her whip of cricket's bone, the lash of film,
Her wagoner a small grey-coated gnat,
Not so big as a round little worm
Prick'd from the lazy finger of a maid;
Her chariot is an empty hazel-nut
Made by the joiner squirrel or old grub,
Time out o' mind the fairies' coachmakers.
And in this state she gallops night by night
Through lovers' brains, and then they dream of love;
O'er courtiers' knees, that dream on court'sies straight,
O'er lawyers' fingers, who straight dream on fees,
O'er ladies' lips, who straight on kisses dream,
Which oft the angry Mab with blisters plagues,
Because their breaths with sweetmeats tainted are:
Sometime she gallops o'er a courtier's nose,
And then dreams he of smelling out a suit;

And sometime comes she with a tithe-pig's tail
Tickling a parson's nose as a' lies asleep,
Then dreams, he of another benefice:
Sometime she driveth o'er a soldier's neck,
And then dreams he of cutting foreign throats,
Of breaches, ambuscadoes, Spanish blades,
Of healths five-fathom deep; and then anon
Drums in his ear, at which he starts and wakes,
And being thus frighted swears a prayer or two
And sleeps again. This is that very Mab
That plats the manes of horses in the night,
And bakes the elflocks in foul sluttish hairs,
Which once untangled, much misfortune bodes:
This is the hag, when maids lie on their backs,
That presses them and learns them first to bear,
Making them women of good carriage:
This is she.

Romeo and Juliet | Act I, scene 4

23 APRIL

St George's Day, and the anniversary of William Shakespeare's death in 1616

In one of Shakespeare's most stirring speeches, a king rallies his troops at the Battle of Agincourt.

HENRY V

Once more unto the breach, dear friends, once more;
Or close the wall up with our English dead.
In peace there's nothing so becomes a man
As modest stillness and humility:
But when the blast of war blows in our ears,
Then imitate the action of the tiger;
Stiffen the sinews, summon up the blood,
Disguise fair nature with hard-favour'd rage;
Then lend the eye a terrible aspect;
Let pry through the portage of the head
Like the brass cannon; let the brow o'erwhelm it
As fearfully as doth a galled rock
O'erhang and jutty his confounded base,
Swill'd with the wild and wasteful ocean.
Now set the teeth and stretch the nostril wide,
Hold hard the breath and bend up every spirit
To his full height. On, on, you noblest English.
Whose blood is fet from fathers of war-proof!
Fathers that, like so many Alexanders,
Have in these parts from morn till even fought
And sheathed their swords for lack of argument:
Dishonour not your mothers; now attest
That those whom you call'd fathers did beget you.
Be copy now to men of grosser blood,
And teach them how to war. And you, good yeoman,
Whose limbs were made in England, show us here
The mettle of your pasture; let us swear

That you are worth your breeding; which I doubt not;
For there is none of you so mean and base,
That hath not noble lustre in your eyes.
I see you stand like greyhounds in the slips,
Straining upon the start. The game's afoot:
Follow your spirit, and upon this charge
Cry 'God for Harry, England, and Saint George!'

Henry V | **Act III, scene 1**

24 APRIL

On this day in 1895 Joshua Slocum sets sail from Boston. He will be the first man to sail single-handed around the world

A queen uses an extended nautical metaphor to encourage her supporters not to abandon ship.

QUEEN MARGARET

Great lords, wise men ne'er sit and wail their loss,
But cheerly seek how to redress their harms.
What though the mast be now blown overboard,
The cable broke, the holding-anchor lost,
And half our sailors swallow'd in the flood?
Yet lives our pilot still. Is't meet that he
Should leave the helm and like a fearful lad
With tearful eyes add water to the sea
And give more strength to that which hath too much,
Whiles, in his moan, the ship splits on the rock,
Which industry and courage might have saved?
Ah, what a shame! ah, what a fault were this!
Say Warwick was our anchor; what of that?
And Montague our topmost; what of him?
Our slaughter'd friends the tackles; what of these?
Why, is not Oxford here another anchor?
And Somerset another goodly mast?
The friends of France our shrouds and tacklings?
And, though unskilful, why not Ned and I
For once allow'd the skilful pilot's charge?
We will not from the helm to sit and weep,
But keep our course, though the rough wind say no,
From shelves and rocks that threaten us with wreck.
As good to chide the waves as speak them fair.
And what is Edward but ruthless sea?

Henry VI, Part 3 | Act V, scene 4

25 APRIL

St Mark's Day, also known in Venice as the Festival of the Rosebud

Like the scent within a rosebud, beauty is enhanced by the release of inner beauty.

SONNET 54

O, how much more doth beauty beauteous seem
By that sweet ornament which truth doth give!
The rose looks fair, but fairer we it deem
For that sweet odour which doth in it live.
The canker-blooms have full as deep a dye
As the perfumed tincture of the roses,
Hang on such thorns and play as wantonly
When summer's breath their masked buds discloses:
But, for their virtue only is their show,
They live unwoo'd and unrespected fade,
Die to themselves. Sweet roses do not so;
Of their sweet deaths are sweetest odours made:
And so of you, beauteous and lovely youth,
When that shall fade, my verse distills your truth.

26 APRIL

The day in 1564 when William Shakespeare was baptized

*The great playwright celebrates the world of the
imagination which the theatre can invoke. The 'wooden
O' is the circular, timber-built theatre itself.*

THE CHORUS

O for a Muse of fire, that would ascend
The brightest heaven of invention,
A kingdom for a stage, princes to act
And monarchs to behold the swelling scene!
Then should the warlike Harry, like himself,
Assume the port of Mars; and at his heels,
Leash'd in like hounds, should famine, sword and fire
Crouch for employment. But pardon, and gentles all,
The flat unraised spirits that have dared
On this unworthy scaffold to bring forth
So great an object: can this cockpit hold
The vasty fields of France? or may we cram
Within this wooden O the very casques
That did affright the air at Agincourt?
O, pardon! since a crooked figure may
Attest in little place a million;
And let us, ciphers to this great accompt,
On your imaginary forces work.
Suppose within the girdle of these walls
Are now confined two mighty monarchies,
Whose high upreared and abutting fronts
The perilous narrow ocean parts asunder:
Piece out our imperfections with your thoughts;
Into a thousand parts divide on man,
And make imaginary puissance;
Think when we talk of horses, that you see them
Printing their proud hoofs i' the receiving earth;

For 'tis your thoughts that now must deck our kings,
Carry them here and there; jumping o'er times,
Turning the accomplishment of many years
Into an hour-glass: for the which supply,
Admit me Chorus to this history;
Who prologue-like your humble patience pray,
Gently to hear, kindly to judge, our play.

Henry V | Prologue

27 APRIL

The Feast of St Assicus, who made precious-metal book covers for churches founded by his friend St Patrick

Juliet's mother wants her to marry Paris, whom she describes in terms of a beautifully bound book.

LADY CAPULET
What say you? can you love the gentleman?
This night you shall behold him at our feast;
Read o'er the volume of young Paris' face,
And find delight writ there with beauty's pen;
Examine every married lineament,
And see how one another lends content
And what obscured in this fair volume lies
Find written in the margent of his eyes.
This precious book of love, this unbound lover,
To beautify him, only lacks a cover:
The fish lives in the sea, and 'tis much pride
For fair without the fair within to hide:
That book in many's eyes doth share the glory,
That in gold clasps locks in the golden story;
So shall you share all that he doth possess,
By having him, making yourself no less.

Romeo and Juliet | Act I, scene 3

28 APRIL

In 1503, the Battle of Cerignola is the first to be won by the use of small arms and gunpowder

In the blood and sweat of battle, a soldier encounters an effeminate courtier who dislikes guns.

HOTSPUR

My liege, I did deny no prisoners.
But I remember, when the fight was done,
When I was dry with rage and extreme toil,
Breathless and faint, leaning upon my sword,
Came there a certain lord, neat, and trimly dress'd,
Fresh as a bridegroom; and his chin new reap'd
Show'd like a stubble-land at harvest-home;
He was perfumed like a milliner;
And 'twixt his finger and his thumb he held
A pouncet-box, which ever and anon
He gave his nose and took't away again;
Who therewith angry, when it next came there,
Took it in snuff; and still he smiled and talk'd,
And as the soldiers bore dead bodies by,
He call'd them untaught knaves, unmannerly,
To bring a slovenly unhandsome corse
Betwixt the wind and his nobility.
With many holiday and lady terms
He question'd me; amongst the rest, demanded
My prisoners in your majesty's behalf.
I then, all smarting with my wounds being cold,
To be so pester'd with a popinjay,
Out of my grief and my impatience,
Answer'd neglectingly I know not what,
He should or he should not; for he made me mad
To see him shine so brisk and smell so sweet
And talk so like a waiting-gentlewoman

Of guns and drums and wounds – God save the mark! –
And telling me the sovereign'st thing on earth
Was parmaceti for an inward bruise;
And that it was great pity, so it was,
This villainous salt-petre should be digg'd
Out of the bowels of the harmless earth,
Which many a good tall fellow had destroy'd
So cowardly; and but for these vile guns,
He would himself have been a soldier.

Henry IV, Part 1 | Act I, scene 3

29 APRIL

UNESCO International Dance Day, and the birthday of the father of classical ballet, Jean-Georges Noverre

In a scene to please his London audience, Shakespeare imagines the French in awe of English virility and dancing.

CONSTABLE OF FRANCE
Dieu de batailles! where have they this mettle?
Is not their climate foggy, raw and dull,
On whom, as in despite, the sun looks pale,
Killing their fruit with frowns? Can sodden water,
A drench for sur-rein'd jades, their barley-broth,
Decoct their cold blood to such valiant heat?
And shall our quick blood, spirited with wine,
Seem frosty? O, for honour of our land,
Let us not hang like roping icicles
Upon our houses' thatch, whiles a more frosty people
Sweat drops of gallant youth in our rich fields!
Poor we may call them in their native lords.

THE DAUPHIN
By faith and honour,
Our madams mock at us, and plainly say
Our mettle is bred out and they will give
Their bodies to the lust of English youth
To new-store France with bastard warriors.

DUKE OF BOURBON
They bid us to the English dancing-schools,
And teach lavoltas high and swift corantos;
Saying our grace is only in our heels,
And that we are most lofty runaways.

Henry V | Act III, scene 5

30 APRIL

Walpurgis Night, which celebrates St Walpurga's fight against disease and witchcraft

Bonfires are still lit on the eve of St Walpurga's Day to ward off evil spirits.

[A cavern. In the middle, a boiling cauldron. Thunder. Enter the three Witches]

FIRST WITCH
Thrice the brinded cat hath mew'd.

SECOND WITCH
Thrice and once the hedge-pig whined.

THIRD WITCH
Harpier cries 'Tis time, 'tis time.

FIRST WITCH
Round about the cauldron go;
In the poison'd entrails throw.
Toad, that under cold stone
Days and nights has thirty-one
Swelter'd venom sleeping got,
Boil thou first i' the charmed pot.

ALL
Double, double toil and trouble;
Fire burn, and cauldron bubble.

SECOND WITCH
Fillet of a fenny snake,
In the cauldron boil and bake;
Eye of newt and toe of frog,

Wool of bat and tongue of dog,
Adder's fork and blind-worm's sting,
Lizard's leg and owlet's wing,
For a charm of powerful trouble,
Like a hell-broth boil and bubble.

ALL
Double, double toil and trouble;
Fire burn and cauldron bubble.

THIRD WITCH
Scale of dragon, tooth of wolf,
Witches' mummy, maw and gulf
Of the ravin'd salt-sea shark,
Root of hemlock digg'd i' the dark,
Liver of blaspheming Jew,
Gall of goat, and slips of yew
Silver'd in the moon's eclipse,
Nose of Turk and Tartar's lips,
Finger of birth-strangled babe
Ditch-deliver'd by a drab,
Make the gruel thick and slab:
Add thereto a tiger's chaudron,
For the ingredients of our cauldron.

ALL
Double, double toil and trouble;
Fire burn and cauldron bubble.

SECOND WITCH
Cool it with a baboon's blood,
Then the charm is firm and good.

Macbeth | Act IV, scene 1

MAY

All the world's a stage,
And all the men and women merely players;
They have their exits and their entrances;
And one man in his time plays many parts,
His acts being seven ages.

As You Like It | Act II, scene 7

1 MAY

May Day, traditionally the start of summer in the Northern Hemisphere

Being in love is better than sunshine.

SONNET 18

Shall I compare thee to a summer's day?
Thou art more lovely and more temperate:
Rough winds do shake the darling buds of May,
And summer's lease hath all too short a date:
Sometime too hot the eye of heaven shines,
And often is his gold complexion dimm'd;
And every fair from fair sometime declines,
By chance or nature's changing course untrimm'd;
But thy eternal summer shall not fade
Nor lose possession of that fair thou owest;
Nor shall Death brag thou wander'st in his shade,
When in eternal lines to time thou growest:
So long as men can breathe or eyes can see,
So long lives this and this gives life to thee.

2 MAY

Anniversary of the first passenger-carrying flight by a jet-propelled plane, a De Havilland Comet, in 1952

The Duke of Bedford expects portentous astrological events to mark the death of Henry V.

DUKE OF BEDFORD
Hung be the heavens with black, yield day to night!
Comets, importing change of times and states,
Brandish your crystal tresses in the sky,
And with them scourge the bad revolting stars
That have consented unto Henry's death!
King Henry the Fifth, too famous to live long!
England ne'er lost a king of so much worth.

Henry VI, Part 1 | Act I, scene 1

3 MAY

The day in 1979 when Margaret Thatcher was elected Britain's first female Prime Minister

In Shakespeare's first tragedy, Tamora, Queen of the Goths, becomes Empress of Rome.

AARON
Now climbeth Tamora Olympus' top,
Safe out of fortune's shot; and sits aloft,
Secure of thunder's crack or lightning flash;
Advanced above pale envy's threatening reach.
As when the golden sun salutes the morn,
And, having gilt the ocean with his beams,
Gallops the zodiac in his glistering coach,
And overlooks the highest-peering hills;
So Tamora:
Upon her wit doth earthly honour wait,
And virtue stoops and trembles at her frown.
Then, Aaron, arm thy heart, and fit thy thoughts,
To mount aloft with thy imperial mistress,
And mount her pitch, whom thou in triumph long
Hast prisoner held, fetter'd in amorous chains
And faster bound to Aaron's charming eyes
Than is Prometheus tied to Caucasus.
Away with slavish weeds and servile thoughts!
I will be bright, and shine in pearl and gold,
To wait upon this new-made empress.
To wait, said I? to wanton with this queen,
This goddess, this Semiramis, this nymph,
This siren, that will charm Rome's Saturnine,
And see his shipwreck and his commonweal's.

Titus Andronicus | Act II, scene 1

4 MAY

Remembrance Day in the Netherlands, when the military dead are honoured

A bishop urges Henry V to fight the French by invoking the battles won by his ancestors.

BISHOP OF ELY
Awake remembrance of these valiant dead
And with your puissant arm renew their feats:
You are their heir; you sit upon their throne;
The blood and courage that renowned them
Runs in your veins; and my thrice-puissant liege
Is in the very May-morn of his youth,
Ripe for exploits and mighty enterprises.

Henry V | Act I, scene 2

5 MAY

The Feast Day of St Jutta of Kulmsee and St Aventinus of Tours, who both gave up worldly wealth to become hermits

Richard II agrees to return the lands which he confiscated, but fears that he will be impoverished by the concession.

RICHARD II
What must the king do now? must he submit?
The king shall do it: must he be deposed?
The king shall be contented: must he lose
The name of king? o' God's name, let it go:
I'll give my jewels for a set of beads,
My gorgeous palace for a hermitage,
My gay apparel for an almsman's gown,
My figured goblets for a dish of wood,
My sceptre for a palmer's walking staff,
My subjects for a pair of carved saints
And my large kingdom for a little grave,
A little little grave, an obscure grave;
Or I'll be buried in the king's highway,
Some way of common trade, where subjects' feet
May hourly trample on their sovereign's head;
For on my heart they tread now whilst I live;
And buried once, why not upon my head?

Richard II | Act III, scene 3

6 MAY

The birth in 1904 of English actor Catherine Lacey who made many appearances with the Royal Shakespeare Company, and whose voice can still be heard in an acclaimed audio recording of Romeo and Juliet *opposite Albert Finney, Dame Edith Evans and other greats.*

Juliet, in love with Romeo, desperately seeks a way out of an arranged marriage with Count Paris.

JULIET

O, bid me leap, rather than marry Paris,
From off the battlements of yonder tower;
Or walk in thievish ways; or bid me lurk
Where serpents are; chain me with roaring bears;
Or shut me nightly in a charnel-house,
O'er-cover'd quite with dead men's rattling bones,
With reeky shanks and yellow chapless skulls;
Or bid me go into a new-made grave
And hide me with a dead man in his shroud;
Things that, to hear them told, have made me tremble;
And I will do it without fear or doubt,
To live an unstain'd wife to my sweet love.

Romeo and Juliet | Act IV, scene 1

7 MAY

Radio Day in Russia and Bulgaria, celebrating the work of radio pioneer Alexander Popov

Shipwrecked on a mysterious island, Ferdinand hears music from an invisible source.

[Enter Ariel, invisible, playing and singing]

ARIEL

> *Come unto these yellow sands,*
> *And then take hands:*
> *Courtsied when you have and kiss'd*
> *The wild waves whist,*
> *Foot it featly here and there;*
> *And, sweet sprites, the burthen bear.*
> *Hark, hark! The watch-dogs bark!*
> *Hark, hark! I hear*
> *The strain of strutting chanticleer*
> *Cry, Cock-a-diddle-dow.*

FERDINAND

Where should this music be? i' the air or the earth?
It sounds no more: and sure, it waits upon
Some god o' the island. Sitting on a bank,
Weeping again the king my father's wreck,
This music crept by me upon the waters,
Allaying both their fury and my passion
With its sweet air: thence I have follow'd it,
Or it hath drawn me rather. But 'tis gone.
No, it begins again.

ARIEL

>*Full fathom five thy father lies;*
>*Of his bones are coral made;*
>*Those are pearls that were his eyes:*
>*Nothing of him that doth fade*
>*But doth suffer a sea-change*
>*Into something rich and strange.*
>*Sea-nymphs hourly ring his knell –*
>*Hark! now I hear them – Ding-dong, bell.*

The Tempest | Act I, scene 2

8 MAY

In 1429, Joan of Arc breaks the English siege of Orléans

*An Englishman describes the victory of Joan (known
as la Pucelle) at the head of the French army.*

LORD TALBOT

My thoughts are whirled like a potter's wheel;
I know not where I am, nor what I do;
A witch, by fear, not force, like Hannibal,
Drives back our troops and conquers as she lists:
So bees with smoke and doves with noisome stench
Are from their hives and houses driven away.
They call'd us for our fierceness English dogs;
Now, like to whelps, we crying run away.
[A short alarum]
Hark, countrymen! either renew the fight,
Or tear the lions out of England's coat;
Renounce your soil, give sheep in lions' stead:
Sheep run not half so treacherous from the wolf,
Or horse or oxen from the leopard,
As you fly from your oft-subdued slaves.
[Alarum. Here another skirmish]
It will not be: retire into your trenches:
You all consented unto Salisbury's death,
For none would strike a stroke in his revenge.
Pucelle is enter'd into Orleans,
In spite of us or aught that we could do.
O, would I were to die with Salisbury!
The shame hereof will make me hide my head.

Henry VI, Part 1 | Act I, scene 5

9 MAY

The official opening of Australia's first parliament in Melbourne in 1901, of the first Parliament House in Canberra in 1927, and of New Parliament House there in 1988

Playboy Prince Harry becomes king and demonstrates his new seriousness by summoning his parliament of nobles.

HENRY V
[...] My father is gone wild into his grave,
For in his tomb lie my affections;
And with his spirits sadly I survive,
To mock the expectation of the world,
To frustrate prophecies, and to raze out
Rotten opinion, who hath writ me down
After my seeming. The tide of blood in me
Hath proudly flow'd in vanity till now.
Now doth it turn and ebb back to the sea,
Where it shall mingle with the state of floods,
And flow henceforth in formal majesty.
Now call we our high court of parliament;
And let us choose such limbs of noble counsel,
That the great body of our state may go
In equal rank with the best govern'd nation;
That war, or peace, or both at once, may be
As things acquainted and familiar to us;
In which you, father, shall have foremost hand.
Our coronation done, we will accite,
As I before rememb'red, all our state;
And – God consigning to my good intents –
No prince nor peer shall have just cause to say,
God shorten Harry's happy life one day.

Henry IV, Part 2 | Act V, scene 2

10 MAY

The Astor Place riot breaks out in Manhattan in 1849, between supporters of two Shakespearean greats, over which was the better actor – the American or the Englishman

The riot left at least 22 dead and 120 injured. John of Gaunt, dying, fears for the future of England after King Richard II has made a series of rash decisions, including a commitment to war in Ireland.

JOHN OF GAUNT

Methinks I am a prophet new inspired
And thus expiring do foretell of him:
His rash fierce blaze of riot cannot last,
For violent fires soon burn out themselves;
Small showers last long, but sudden storms are short;
He tires betimes that spurs too fast betimes;
With eager feeding food doth choke the feeder:
Light vanity, insatiate cormorant,
Consuming means, soon preys upon itself.
This royal throne of kings, this scepter'd isle,
This earth of majesty, this seat of Mars,
This other Eden, demi-paradise,
This fortress built by Nature for herself
Against infection and the hand of war,
This happy breed of men, this little world,
This precious stone set in the silver sea,
Which serves it in the office of a wall,
Or as a moat defensive to a house,
Against the envy of less happier lands,
This blessed plot, this earth, this realm, this England,
This nurse, this teeming womb of royal kings,
Fear'd by their breed and famous by their birth,
Renowned for their deeds as far from home,
For Christian service and true chivalry,

As is the sepulchre in stubborn Jewry,
Of the world's ransom, blessed Mary's Son,
This land of such dear souls, this dear dear land,
Dear for her reputation through the world,
Is now leased out, I die pronouncing it,
Like to a tenement or pelting farm:
England, bound in with the triumphant sea
Whose rocky shore beats back the envious siege
Of watery Neptune, is now bound in with shame,
With inky blots and rotten parchment bonds:
That England, that was wont to conquer others,
Hath made a shameful conquest of itself.
Ah, would the scandal vanish with my life,
How happy then were my ensuing death!

Richard II | Act II, scene 1

11 MAY

The death in 1988 of the spy Kim Philby, who betrayed British secrets to the Soviet Union

*Shakespeare plays on the two meanings of the word
'betray' while complaining of his lover's infidelity.*

SONNET 151

Love is too young to know what conscience is;
Yet who knows not conscience is born of love?
Then, gentle cheater, urge not my amiss,
Lest guilty of my faults thy sweet self prove:
For, thou betraying me, I do betray
My nobler part to my gross body's treason;
My soul doth tell my body that he may
Triumph in love; flesh stays no father reason;
But, rising at thy name, doth point out thee
As his triumphant prize. Proud of this pride,
He is contented thy poor drudge to be,
To stand in thy affairs, fall by thy side.
No want of conscience hold it that I call
Her 'love' for whose dear love I rise and fall.

12 MAY

Arrest in 1593 of playwright Thomas Kyd, a contemporary of Shakespeare, for libel; his confession under torture may have led to the death of his roommate, the playwright Christopher Marlowe

Kyd's version of Hamlet *predates Shakespeare's. Here Shakespeare's Hamlet admires the emotional ability of actors and the power of drama to move audiences.*

HAMLET

O what a rogue and peasant slave am I!
Is it not monstrous that this player here,
But in a fiction, in a dream of passion,
Could force his soul so to his own conceit
That, from her working, all his visage wann'd,
Tears in his eyes, distraction in his aspect,
A broken voice, and his whole function suiting
With forms to his conceit? And all for nothing!
For Hecuba!
What's Hecuba to him, or he to Hecuba,
That he should weep for her? What would he do,
Had he the motive and the cue for passion
That I have? He would drown the stage with tears
And cleave the general ear with horrid speech;
Make mad the guilty and appal the free,
Confound the ignorant, and amaze indeed
The very faculties of eyes and ears.
Yet I, a dull and muddy-mettled rascal, peak
Like John-a-dreams, unpregnant of my cause,
And can say nothing! No, not for a king,
Upon whose property and most dear life
A damn'd defeat was made. Am I a coward?
Who calls me villain? breaks my pate across?
Plucks off my beard and blows it in my face?
Tweaks me by th' nose? gives me the lie i' th' throat

As deep as to the lungs? Who does me this, ha?
'Swounds, I should take it! for it cannot be
But I am pigeon-liver'd and lack gall
To make oppression bitter, or ere this
I should have fatted all the region kites
With this slave's offal. Bloody bawdy villain!
Remorseless, treacherous, lecherous, kindless villain!
O, vengeance!
Why, what an ass am I! This is most brave,
That I, the son of a dear father murder'd,
Prompted to my revenge by heaven and hell,
Must (like a whore) unpack my heart with words
And fall a-cursing like a very drab,
A scullion!
Fie upon't! foh! About, my brain! Hum, I have heard
That guilty creatures, sitting at a play,
Have by the very cunning of the scene
Been struck so to the soul that presently
They have proclaim'd their malefactions;
For murder, though it have no tongue, will speak
With most miraculous organ, I'll have these Players
Play something like the murder of my father
Before mine uncle. I'll observe his looks;
I'll tent him to the quick. If he but blench,
I know my course. The spirit that I have seen
May be a devil; and the devil hath power
T' assume a pleasing shape; yea, and perhaps
Out of my weakness and my melancholy,
As he is very potent with such spirits,
Abuses me to damn me. I'll have grounds
More relative than this. The play's the thing
Wherein I'll catch the conscience of the King.

Hamlet | Act II, scene 2

198

13 MAY

Abbotsbury Garland Day, when the children of the Dorset village weave flowers together

Hamlet's mother reports the death of Ophelia, who was hanging garlands on a tree.

GERTRUDE
There is a willow grows aslant a brook,
That shows his hoar leaves in the glassy stream.
There with fantastic garlands did she come
Of crowflowers, nettles, daisies, and long purples,
That liberal shepherds give a grosser name,
But our cold maids do dead men's fingers call them.
There on the pendant boughs her coronet weeds
Clamb'ring to hang, an envious sliver broke,
When down her weedy trophies and herself
Fell in the weeping brook. Her clothes spread wide
And, mermaid-like, awhile they bore her up;
Which time she chaunted snatches of old tunes,
As one incapable of her own distress,
Or like a creature native and indued
Unto that element; but long it could not be
Till that her garments, heavy with their drink,
Pull'd the poor wretch from her melodious lay
To muddy death.

Hamlet | Act IV, scene 7

14 MAY

Birthday in 1553 of Margaret of Valois, queen of France in Shakespeare's time and an enlightened woman of letters

The queen's reputation was sullied after her death by male writers of history. Constable Dogberry has arrested some men accused of similar misrepresentations.

DON PEDRO
Officers, what offence have these men done?

DOGBERRY
Marry, sir, they have committed false report; moreover, they have spoken untruths; secondarily, they are slanders; sixth and lastly, they have belied a lady; thirdly, they have verified unjust things; and, to conclude, they are lying knaves.

DON PEDRO
First, I ask thee what they have done; thirdly, I ask thee what's their offence; sixth and lastly, why they are committed; and, to conclude, what you lay to their charge?
[...]
[he turns to the prisoners]
Who have you offended, masters, that you are thus bound to your answer? This learned constable is too cunning to be understood: what's your offence?

BORACHIO
Sweet prince, let me go no farther to mine answer: do you hear me, and let this count kill me. I have deceived even your very eyes: what your wisdoms could not discover, these shallow fools have brought to light: who

in the night overheard me confessing to this man how
Don John your brother incensed me to slander the
Lady Hero, how you were brought into the orchard and
saw me court Margaret in Hero's garments, how you
disgraced her, when you should marry her: my villany
they have upon record; which I had rather seal with my
death than repeat over to my shame. The lady is dead
upon mine and my master's false accusation; and, briefly,
I desire nothing but the reward of a villain.

Much Ado about Nothing | **Act V, scene 1**

15 MAY

Birthday in 1856 of L. Frank Baum, author of the Wizard of Oz *novels*

A dubious seance is staged for the benefit of Eleanor, Duchess of Gloucester, who wants to know whether her husband will become king – and, more importantly, whether she will become queen.

FATHER JOHN HUME
Come, my masters; the duchess, I tell you, expects performance of your promises.

BOLINGBROKE
Master Hume, we are therefore provided: will her ladyship behold and hear our exorcisms?

FATHER JOHN HUME
Ay, what else? fear you not her courage.

BOLINGBROKE
I have heard her reported to be a woman of an invincible spirit: but it shall be convenient, Master Hume, that you be by her aloft, while we be busy below; and so, I pray you, go, in God's name, and leave us.
[Exit Hume]
Mother Jourdain, be you prostrate and grovel on the earth; John Southwell, read you; and let us to our work.
[Enter Eleanor aloft]

ELEANOR
Well said, my masters; and welcome all. To this gear the sooner the better.

BOLINGBROKE

Patience, good lady; wizards know their times:
Deep night, dark night, the silent of the night,
The time of night when Troy was set on fire;
The time when screech-owls cry and ban-dogs howl,
And spirits walk and ghosts break up their graves,
That time best fits the work we have in hand.
Madam, sit you and fear not: whom we raise,
We will make fast within a hallow'd verge.
[Here they do the ceremonies belonging, and make the circle;
Southwell reads, 'Conjuro te', etc. It thunders and lightens
terribly; then the Spirit riseth]

SPIRIT

Adsum.

MARGARET JOURDAIN

Asmath,
By the eternal God, whose name and power
Thou tremblest at, answer that I shall ask;
For, till thou speak, thou shalt not pass from hence.

SPIRIT

Ask what thou wilt. That I had said and done!

BOLINGBROKE

[Reading out of a paper] 'First of the king: what shall of
him become?'
[As the Spirit speaks, Southwell writes the answer]

SPIRIT

The duke yet lives that Henry shall depose;
But him outlive, and die a violent death.

BOLINGBROKE

'What fates await the Duke of Suffolk?'

SPIRIT

By water shall he die, and take his end.

BOLINGBROKE

'What shall befall the Duke of Somerset?'

SPIRIT

Let him shun castles;

Safer shall he be upon the sandy plains

Than where castles mounted stand.

Have done, for more I hardly can endure.

BOLINGBROKE

Descend to darkness and the burning lake!

False fiend, avoid!

[Thunder and lightning. Exit Spirit]

Henry VI, Part 2 | Act I, scene 4

16 MAY

In 1204 Baldwin of Flanders becomes the first Emperor of the Latin Empire, set up after the Fourth Crusade

The use of Latin declined in England after Henry VIII's decisive break with Roman Catholicism.

CARDINAL WOLSEY
Tanta est erga te mentis integritas, regina Serenissima –

QUEEN KATHARINE
O, good my lord, no Latin;
I am not such a truant since my coming,
As not to know the language I have lived in:
A strange tongue makes my cause more strange, suspicious;
Pray, speak in English: here are some will thank you,
If you speak truth, for their poor mistress' sake;
Believe me, she has had much wrong: lord cardinal,
The willing'st sin I ever yet committed
May be absolved in English.

Henry VIII | Act III, scene 1

17 MAY

A fleet of warships departs from France with a rebel army to overthrow the tyrant English king.

EARL OF NORTHUMBERLAND
Then thus: I have from Port le Blanc, a bay
In Brittany, received intelligence
That Harry Duke of Hereford, Rainold Lord Cobham,
That late broke from the Duke of Exeter,
His brother, Archbishop late of Canterbury,
Sir Thomas Erpingham, Sir John Ramston,
Sir John Norbery, Sir Robert Waterton and Francis Quoint,
All these well furnish'd by the Duke of Bretagne
With eight tall ships, three thousand men of war,
Are making hither with all due expedience
And shortly mean to touch our northern shore:
Perhaps they had ere this, but that they stay
The first departing of the king for Ireland.
If then we shall shake off our slavish yoke,
Imp out our drooping country's broken wing,
Redeem from broking pawn the blemish'd crown,
Wipe off the dust that hides our sceptres gilt
And make high majesty look like itself,
Away with me in post to Ravenspurgh;
But if you faint, as fearing to do so,
Stay and be secret, and myself will go.

Richard II | Act II, scene 1

18 MAY

During in the First Crusade in 1096, 800 Jews are massacred in Worms, in Germany

When the guarantor of a loan mocks the lender, the lender vows to claim his pound of flesh in revenge.

SALARINO
Why, I am sure, if he forfeit, thou wilt not take his flesh: what's that good for?

SHYLOCK
To bait fish withal: if it will feed nothing else, it will feed my revenge. He hath disgraced me, and hindered me half a million; laughed at my losses, mocked at my gains, scorned my nation, thwarted my bargains, cooled my friends, heated mine enemies; and what's his reason? I am a Jew. Hath not a Jew eyes? hath not a Jew hands, organs, dimensions, senses, affections, passions? fed with the same food, hurt with the same weapons, subject to the same diseases, healed by the same means, warmed and cooled by the same winter and summer, as a Christian is? If you prick us, do we not bleed? if you tickle us, do we not laugh? if you poison us, do we not die? and if you wrong us, shall we not revenge? If we are like you in the rest, we will resemble you in that. If a Jew wrong a Christian, what is his humility? Revenge. If a Christian wrong a Jew, what should his sufferance be by Christian example? Why, revenge. The villany you teach me, I will execute, and it shall go hard but I will better the instruction.

The Merchant of Venice | Act III, scene 1

19 MAY

In 1536, the day of the execution of Henry VIII's second wife, Anne Boleyn, for adultery, treason and incest

The Machiavellian Cardinal Wolsey disapproves of Henry's interest in Anne at a masqued ball.

[They choose Ladies for the dance. Henry VIII chooses Anne]

HENRY VIII
The fairest hand I ever touch'd! O beauty,
Till now I never knew thee!
[Music. Dance]
[...]

HENRY VIII
You hold a fair assembly; you do well, lord:
You are a churchman, or, I'll tell you, cardinal,
I should judge now unhappily.

CARDINAL WOLSEY
I am glad Your Grace is grown so pleasant.

HENRY VIII
My lord chamberlain,
Prithee, come hither: what fair lady's that?

LORD CHAMBERLAIN
An't please your grace, Sir Thomas Boleyn's daughter –
The Viscount Rochford – one of her highness' women.

HENRY VIII
By heaven, she is a dainty one. Sweetheart,
I were unmannerly, to take you out,
And not to kiss you. A health, gentlemen!
[...]

CARDINAL WOLSEY
Your grace, I fear, with dancing is a little heated.

HENRY VIII
I fear, too much.

CARDINAL WOLSEY
There's fresher air, my lord, in the next chamber.

Henry VIII | Act I, scene 4

20 MAY

World Bee Day, the birthday in 1734 of pioneering Slovenian apiarist Anton Janša

A well-ordered society is like a bee-hive.

ARCHBISHOP OF CANTERBURY
Therefore doth heaven divide
The state of man in divers functions,
Setting endeavour in continual motion;
To which is fixed, as an aim or butt,
Obedience: for so work the honey-bees,
Creatures that by a rule in nature teach
The act of order to a peopled kingdom.
They have a king and officers of sorts;
Where some, like magistrates, correct at home,
Others, like merchants, venture trade abroad,
Others, like soldiers, armed in their stings,
Make boot upon the summer's velvet buds,
Which pillage they with merry march bring home
To the tent-royal of their emperor;
Who, busied in his majesty, surveys
The singing masons building roofs of gold,
The civil citizens kneading up the honey,
The poor mechanic porters crowding in
Their heavy burdens at his narrow gate,
The sad-eyed justice, with his surly hum,
Delivering o'er to executors pale
The lazy yawning drone.

Henry V | Act I, scene 2

21 MAY

The death in 1607 of English churchman John Rainolds, who instigated the Authorized Version of the Bible

The future Richard III, about to have his brother murdered, admits to cloaking his villainy in biblical piety.

RICHARD OF GLOUCESTER
I do the wrong, and first begin to brawl.
The secret mischiefs that I set abroad
I lay unto the grievous charge of others.
Clarence, whom I, indeed, have laid in darkness,
I do beweep to many simple gulls
Namely, to Hastings, Derby, Buckingham;
And say it is the queen and her allies
That stir the king against the duke my brother.
Now, they believe it; and withal whet me
To be revenged on Rivers, Vaughan, Grey:
But then I sigh; and, with a piece of scripture,
Tell them that God bids us do good for evil:
And thus I clothe my naked villany
With old odd ends stolen out of holy writ;
And seem a saint, when most I play the devil.

Richard III | Act I, scene 3

22 MAY

Birthday in 1907 of the actor Sir Laurence Olivier

Many Shakespearean roles are indelibly associated with Olivier's performances of them.

JAQUES

All the world's a stage,
And all the men and women merely players;
They have their exits and their entrances;
And one man in his time plays many parts,
His acts being seven ages. At first the infant,
Mewling and puking in the nurse's arms;
Then the whining school-boy, with his satchel
And shining morning face, creeping like snail
Unwillingly to school. And then the lover,
Sighing like furnace, with a woeful ballad
Made to his mistress' eyebrow. Then a soldier,
Full of strange oaths, and bearded like the pard,
Jealous in honour, sudden and quick in quarrel,
Seeking the bubble reputation
Even in the cannon's mouth. And then the justice,
In fair round belly with good capon lin'd,
With eyes severe and beard of formal cut,
Full of wise saws and modern instances;
And so he plays his part. The sixth age shifts
Into the lean and slipper'd pantaloon,
With spectacles on nose and pouch on side,
His youthful hose, well sav'd, a world too wide
For his shrunk shank; and his big manly voice,
Turning again toward childish treble, pipes
And whistles in his sound. Last scene of all,
That ends this strange eventful history,

Is second childishness and mere oblivion;
Sans teeth, sans eyes, sans taste, sans every thing.

As You Like It | **Act II, scene 7**

23 MAY

The deaths of the notorious American robbers Bonnie and Clyde in a police ambush in 1934

Hearts may be stolen as easily as banknotes.

SONNET 40

Take all my loves, my love, yea, take them all;
What hast thou then more than thou hadst before?
No love, my love, that thou mayst true love call;
All mine was thine before thou hadst this more.
Then if for my love thou my love receivest,
I cannot blame thee for my love thou usest;
But yet be blamed, if thou thyself deceivest
By wilful taste of what thyself refusest.
I do forgive thy robbery, gentle thief,
Although thou steal thee all my poverty;
And yet, love knows, it is a greater grief
To bear love's wrong than hate's known injury.
Lascivious grace, in whom all ill well shows,
Kill me with spites; yet we must not be foes.

24 MAY

Birthday in 1576 of Elizabeth Carey, Lady Berkeley

Her family were patrons of Shakespeare, and A Midsummer Night's Dream, with these opening lines, may have had its premiere at her wedding.

THESEUS
Now, fair Hippolyta, our nuptial hour
Draws on apace; four happy days bring in
Another moon: but, O, methinks, how slow
This old moon wanes! she lingers my desires,
Like to a step-dame or a dowager
Long withering out a young man revenue.

HIPPOLYTA
Four days will quickly steep themselves in night;
Four nights will quickly dream away the time;
And then the moon, like to a silver bow
New-bent in heaven, shall behold the night
Of our solemnities.

THESEUS
Go, Philostrate,
Stir up the Athenian youth to merriments;
Awake the pert and nimble spirit of mirth;
Turn melancholy forth to funerals;
The pale companion is not for our pomp.
[Exit Philostrate]
Hippolyta, I woo'd thee with my sword,
And won thy love, doing thee injuries;
But I will wed thee in another key,
With pomp, with triumph and with revelling.

A Midsummer Night's Dream | Act I, scene 1

The Diet of Worms concludes with the outlawing of German theologian Martin Luther in 1521

Hamlet, in accidentally killing Polonius, has made him the diet of worms.

CLAUDIUS
Now, Hamlet, where's Polonius?

HAMLET
At supper.

CLAUDIUS
At supper? Where?

HAMLET
Not where he eats, but where he is eaten. A certain convocation of politic worms are e'en at him. Your worm is your only emperor for diet. We fat all creatures else to fat us, and we fat ourselves for maggots. Your fat king and your lean beggar is but variable service – two dishes, but to one table. That's the end.

CLAUDIUS
Alas, alas!

HAMLET
A man may fish with the worm that hath eat of a king, and eat of the fish that hath fed of that worm.

CLAUDIUS
What dost thou mean by this?

HAMLET

Nothing but to show you how a king may go a progress
through the guts of a beggar.

CLAUDIUS

Where is Polonius?

HAMLET

In heaven. Send thither to see. If your messenger find
him not there, seek him i' th' other place yourself. But
indeed, if you find him not within this month, you shall
nose him as you go up the stair, into the lobby.

CLAUDIUS

[To Attendants.] Go seek him there.

HAMLET

He will stay till you come.

Hamlet | Act IV, scene 3

26 MAY

The day in 1938 when the House Un-American Activities Committee began its first session

When Macbeth's paranoia sees traitors in every corner, his countrymen dare not even trust themselves. Macduff has fled, leaving his wife defenceless.

LADY MACDUFF
What had he done, to make him fly the land?

ROSS
You must have patience, madam.

LADY MACDUFF
He had none:
His flight was madness: when our actions do not,
Our fears do make us traitors.

ROSS
You know not
Whether it was his wisdom or his fear.

LADY MACDUFF
Wisdom! to leave his wife, to leave his babes,
His mansion and his titles in a place
From whence himself does fly? He loves us not.
All is the fear and nothing is the love;
As little is the wisdom, where the flight
So runs against all reason.

ROSS
My dearest coz,
I pray you, school yourself: but for your husband,
He is noble, wise, judicious, and best knows

The fits o' the season. I dare not speak much further;
But cruel are the times, when we are traitors
And do not know ourselves, when we hold rumour
From what we fear, yet know not what we fear,
But float upon a wild and violent sea
Each way and move.

Macbeth | Act IV, scene 2

27 MAY

Slavery Abolition Day in Guadeloupe

Like many assassins, Brutus tries to justify the murder of Julius Caesar as an act of liberation.

BRUTUS
Be patient till the last.
Romans, countrymen, and lovers! hear me for my cause, and be silent, that you may hear: believe me for mine honour, and have respect to mine honour, that you may believe: censure me in your wisdom, and awake your senses, that you may the better judge. If there be any in this assembly, any dear friend of Caesar's, to him I say, that Brutus' love to Caesar was no less than his. If then that friend demand why Brutus rose against Caesar, this is my answer: not that I loved Caesar less, but that I loved Rome more. Had you rather Caesar were living and die all slaves, than that Caesar were dead, to live all free men? As Caesar loved me, I weep for him; as he was fortunate, I rejoice at it; as he was valiant, I honour him: but, as he was ambitious, I slew him. There is tears for his love; joy for his fortune; honour for his valour; and death for his ambition. Who is here so base that would be a bondman? If any, speak; for him have I offended. Who is here so rude that would not be a Roman? If any, speak; for him have I offended. Who is here so vile that will not love his country? If any, speak; for him have I offended. I pause for a reply.

Julius Caesar | Act III, scene 2

28 MAY

St Bernard's Day, dedicated to the saint who gave his name to the breed of mountain rescue dogs

The demented King Lear, imagining that his disloyal daughters are on trial, refers to them as dogs.

FOOL
He's mad that trusts in the tameness of a wolf, a horse's health, a boy's love, or a whore's oath.

KING LEAR
It shall be done; I will arraign them straight.
[To Edgar] Come, sit thou here, most learned justicer.
[To the Fool] Thou, sapient sir, sit here.
Now, you she-foxes! [...] The little dogs and all,
Tray, Blanch, and Sweetheart, see, they bark at me.

EDGAR *[DISGUISED AS TOM O'BEDLAM]*
Tom will throw his head at them. Avaunt, you curs!
Be thy mouth or black or white,
Tooth that poisons if it bite;
Mastiff, greyhound, mongrel grim,
Hound or spaniel, brach or lym,
Bobtail tyke or trundle-tail –
Tom will make them weep and wail;
For, with throwing thus my head,
Dogs leap the hatch, and all are fled.
Do de, de, de. Sessa! Come,
March to wakes and fairs and market towns.
Poor Tom, thy horn is dry.

King Lear | Act III, scene 6

29 MAY

After the Interregnum created by the English Civil War, Charles II is restored to the throne in 1660

Newly crowned Edward IV considers the human cost of an earlier civil war.

KING EDWARD IV
Once more we sit in England's royal throne,
Re-purchased with the blood of enemies.
What valiant foemen, like to autumn's corn,
Have we mow'd down, in tops of all their pride!
Three Dukes of Somerset, threefold renown'd
For hardy and undoubted champions;
Two Cliffords, as the father and the son,
And two Northumberlands; two braver men
Ne'er spurr'd their coursers at the trumpet's sound;
With them, the two brave bears, Warwick and Montague,
That in their chains fetter'd the kingly lion
And made the forest tremble when they roar'd.
Thus have we swept suspicion from our seat
And made our footstool of security.
Come hither, Bess, and let me kiss my boy.
Young Ned, for thee, thine uncles and myself
Have in our armours watch'd the winter's night,
Went all afoot in summer's scalding heat,
That thou mightst repossess the crown in peace;
And of our labours thou shalt reap the gain.

Henry VI, Part 3 | Act V, scene 7

30 MAY

*Birth in 1464 of Barbara, Queen of Bohemia: married aged 8,
widowed and remarried aged 12, then divorced aged 36 after her
husband secretly remarried and she secretly became engaged*

*Nobleman Camillo says there is nothing in Leontes'
suspicion of an affair between the King of Bohemia
and Leontes' wife.*

LEONTES
Is whispering nothing?
Is leaning cheek to cheek? is meeting noses?
Kissing with inside lip? stopping the career
Of laughing with a sigh? – a note infallible
Of breaking honesty – horsing foot on foot?
Skulking in corners? wishing clocks more swift?
Hours, minutes? noon, midnight? and all eyes
Blind with the pin and web but theirs, theirs only,
That would unseen be wicked? is this nothing?
Why, then the world and all that's in't is nothing;
The covering sky is nothing; Bohemia nothing;
My wife is nothing; nor nothing have these nothings,
If this be nothing.

CAMILLO
Good my lord, be cured
Of this diseased opinion, and betimes;
For 'tis most dangerous.

LEONTES
Say it be, 'tis true.

CAMILLO
No, no, my lord.

LEONTES
It is; you lie, you lie:
I say thou liest, Camillo, and I hate thee,
Pronounce thee a gross lout, a mindless slave,
Or else a hovering temporizer, that
Canst with thine eyes at once see good and evil,
Inclining to them both: were my wife's liver
Infected as her life, she would not live
The running of one glass.

CAMILLO
Who does infect her?

LEONTES
Why, he that wears her like a medal, hanging
About his neck, Bohemia.

The Winter's Tale | Act I, scene 2

31 MAY

In 1610 a pageant, London's Love to Prince Henry, is performed on the River Thames to mark the investiture of Prince Henry as Prince of Wales – the fireworks alone cost £700

Sir Richard Vernon describes the appearance of an earlier Prince Harry, prepared to do battle.

VERNON
All furnish'd, all in arms;
All plumed like estridges that with the wind
Baited like eagles having lately bathed;
Glittering in golden coats, like images;
As full of spirit as the month of May,
And gorgeous as the sun at midsummer;
Wanton as youthful goats, wild as young bulls.
I saw young Harry, with his beaver on,
His cuisses on his thighs, gallantly arm'd
Rise from the ground like feather'd Mercury,
And vaulted with such ease into his seat,
As if an angel dropp'd down from the clouds,
To turn and wind a fiery Pegasus
And witch the world with noble horsemanship.

Henry IV, Part 1 | Act IV, scene 1

JUNE

I know a bank where the wild thyme blows,
Where oxlips and the nodding violet grows,
Quite over-canopied with luscious woodbine,
With sweet musk-roses and with eglantine...

A Midsummer Night's Dream | Act II, scene 1

1 JUNE

Crop-Over – a celebration since 1687 of the end of the harvest of the West Indian sugar cane crop

Juno, God of Marriage, and Ceres, God of Agriculture, bestow their blessings on a couple.

JUNO
Honour, riches, marriage-blessing,
Long continuance, and increasing,
Hourly joys be still upon you!
Juno sings her blessings upon you.

CERES
Earth's increase, foison plenty,
Barns and garners never empty,
Vines and clustering bunches growing,
Plants with goodly burthen bowing;
Spring come to you at the farthest
In the very end of harvest!
Scarcity and want shall shun you;
Ceres' blessing so is on you.

The Tempest | Act IV, scene 1

2 JUNE

St Elmo's Day: Elmo continued to preach even after a thunderbolt struck the ground beside him

Lear rages against the natural world.

KING LEAR
Blow, winds, and crack your cheeks! rage! blow!
You cataracts and hurricanoes, spout
Till you have drench'd our steeples, drown'd the cocks!
You sulph'rous and thought-executing fires,
Vaunt-couriers to oak-cleaving thunderbolts,
Singe my white head! And thou, all-shaking thunder,
Strike flat the thick rotundity o' th' world,
Crack Nature's moulds, all germains spill at once,
That makes ingrateful man!

King Lear | Act III, scene 2

3 JUNE

On this day in 1980 a bomb is detonated at the Statue of Liberty, suspected to be the work of Croatian nationalists

Shakespeare claims, with some justification, that his poetry will outlast statues.

SONNET 55

Not marble, nor the gilded monuments
Of princes, shall outlive this powerful rhyme;
But you shall shine more bright in these contents
Than unswept stone besmear'd with sluttish time.
When wasteful war shall statues overturn,
And broils root out the work of masonry,
Nor Mars his sword nor war's quick fire shall burn
The living record of your memory.
'Gainst death and all-oblivious enmity
Shall you pace forth; your praise shall still find room
Even in the eyes of all posterity
That wear this world out to the ending doom.
So, till the judgment that yourself arise,
You live in this, and dwell in lover's eyes.

4 JUNE

In Lyon, in 1784, Elizabeth Thible is the first woman to fly in an untethered hot-air balloon

Thible ascends dressed as Minerva the Roman Goddess of Wisdom, singing two operatic arias and stoking the balloon's heat source.

SIR NATHANIEL

[...] If knowledge be the mark, to know thee shall suffice;
Well learned is that tongue that well can thee commend,
All ignorant that soul that sees thee without wonder;
Which is to me some praise that I thy parts admire:
Thy eye Jove's lightning bears, thy voice his dreadful thunder,
Which not to anger bent, is music and sweet fire.
Celestial as thou art, O, pardon, love, this wrong,
That sings heaven's praise with such an earthly tongue.

Love's Labour's Lost | Act IV, scene 2

5 JUNE

In 1610 courtiers perform the masque Tethys' Festival, by Shakespeare's contemporary Samuel Daniel, to celebrate the investiture of the Prince of Wales

Shylock has been invited to a dinner at which masques may be presented. He warns his daughter.

SHYLOCK

What, are there masques? Hear you me, Jessica:
Lock up my doors; and when you hear the drum
And the vile squealing of the wry-neck'd fife,
Clamber not you up to the casements then,
Nor thrust your head into the public street
To gaze on Christian fools with varnish'd faces,
But stop my house's ears, I mean my casements:
Let not the sound of shallow foppery enter
My sober house. By Jacob's staff, I swear,
I have no mind of feasting forth to-night:
But I will go. Go you before me, sirrah;
Say I will come.

The Merchant of Venice | Act II, scene 5

6 JUNE

In 1844 the YMCA – Young Men's Christian Association – is founded in London

The Duke of Buckingham, spin doctor to the scheming Richard of Gloucester, proclaims his Christian virtue.

LORD MAYOR OF LONDON
See, where he stands between two clergymen!

DUKE OF BUCKINGHAM
Two props of virtue for a Christian prince,
To stay him from the fall of vanity:
And, see, a book of prayer in his hand,
True ornaments to know a holy man.
Famous Plantagenet, most gracious prince,
Lend favourable ears to our request;
And pardon us the interruption
Of thy devotion and right Christian zeal.

RICHARD, DUKE OF GLOUCESTER *[THE FUTURE RICHARD III]*
My lord, there needs no such apology:
I rather do beseech you pardon me,
Who, earnest in the service of my God,
Neglect the visitation of my friends.

Richard III | Act III, scene 7

7 JUNE

The death in 1937 of silver screen legend Jean Harlow at the age of only 26

In a film career lasting only nine years, Harlow, known as 'the blonde bombshell', captured many hearts.

Sweet rose, fair flower, untimely pluck'd, soon vaded,
Pluck'd in the bud, and vaded in the spring!
Bright orient pearl, alack, too timely shaded!
Fair creature, kill'd too soon by death's sharp sting!
Like a green plum that hangs upon a tree,
And falls, through wind, before the fall should be.

From Passionate Pilgrim

8 JUNE

In 1918 scientists and a US Navy artist observe a solar eclipse from Baker City in Oregon

Eclipses and other astronomical irregularities were often seen as foreshadows of disaster.

EARL OF GLOUCESTER

These late eclipses in the sun and moon portend no good to us. Though the wisdom of nature can reason it thus and thus, yet nature finds itself scourg'd by the sequent effects. Love cools, friendship falls off, brothers divide. In cities, mutinies; in countries, discord; in palaces, treason; and the bond crack'd 'twixt son and father. This villain of mine comes under the prediction; there's son against father: the King falls from bias of nature; there's father against child. We have seen the best of our time. Machinations, hollowness, treachery, and all ruinous disorders follow us disquietly to our graves.

King Lear | Act I, scene 2

9 JUNE

Death in 68 CE of the Roman emperor Nero, famed for callously playing a lute during the Great Fire of Rome

Lord Talbot threatens to be as cruel and heartless as Nero in avenging the dying Earl of Salisbury during the siege of Orléans.

LORD TALBOT
What chance is this that suddenly hath cross'd us?
Speak, Salisbury; at least, if thou canst speak:
How farest thou, mirror of all martial men?
One of thy eyes and thy cheek's side struck off!
Yet livest thou, Salisbury? though thy speech doth fail,
One eye thou hast, to look to heaven for grace:
The sun with one eye vieweth all the world.
Heaven, be thou gracious to none alive,
If Salisbury wants mercy at thy hands!
Bear hence his body; I will help to bury it.
Salisbury, cheer thy spirit with this comfort;
Thou shalt not die whiles –
He beckons with his hand and smiles on me.
As who should say 'When I am dead and gone,
Remember to avenge me on the French.'
Plantagenet, I will; and like thee, Nero,
Play on the lute, beholding the towns burn:
Wretched shall France be only in my name.

Henry VI, Part 1 | Act I, scene 4

10 JUNE

Birthday in 1804 of the naturalist Hermann Schlegel after whom
Osteochilus schlegelii, the predatory giant sharkminnow, is named

Shipwrecked Pericles overhears three fishermen
wishing they were bigger fish.

THIRD FISHERMAN
[...] Master, I marvel how the fishes live in the sea.

FIRST FISHERMAN
Why, as men do a-land; the great ones eat up the little
ones: I can compare our rich misers to nothing so fitly
as to a whale; he plays and tumbles, driving the poor fry
before him, and at last devours them all at a mouthful:
such whales have I heard on o' the land, who never leave
gaping till they've swallowed the whole parish, church,
steeple, bells, and all.

PERICLES
[Aside] A pretty moral.

THIRD FISHERMAN
But, master, if I had been the sexton, I would have been
that day in the belfry.

SECOND FISHERMAN
Why, man?

THIRD FISHERMAN
Because he should have swallowed me too: and when I
had been in his belly, I would have kept such a jangling
of the bells, that he should never have left, till he cast
bells, steeple, church, and parish up again. [...]

PERICLES

[Aside] How from the finny subject of the sea
These fishers tell the infirmities of men;
And from their watery empire recollect
All that may men approve or men detect!
Peace be at your labour, honest fishermen.
[...]
A man whom both the waters and the wind,
In that vast tennis-court, have made the ball
For them to play upon, entreats you pity him:
He asks of you, that never used to beg.

FIRST FISHERMAN

No, friend, cannot you beg? Here's them in our
country Greece gets more with begging than we can
do with working.

SECOND FISHERMAN

Canst thou catch any fishes, then?

PERICLES

I never practised it.

SECOND FISHERMAN

Nay, then thou wilt starve, sure; for here's nothing to be
got now-a-days, unless thou canst fish for't.

Pericles | Act II, scene 1

238

11 JUNE

In 980, Vladimir the Great unites Kievan Rus', the vast territory from Ukraine to the Baltic Sea

Shakespeare has fun with Fluellen's Welsh accent as he compares Henry V to Alexander the Great.

GOWER
[...] O, 'tis a gallant king!

FLUELLEN
Ay, he was porn at Monmouth, Captain Gower. What call you the town's name where Alexander the Pig was born?

GOWER
Alexander the Great.

FLUELLEN
Why, I pray you, is not pig great? the pig, or the great, or the mighty, or the huge, or the magnanimous, are all one reckonings, save the phrase is a little variations.

GOWER
I think Alexander the Great was born in Macedon; his father was called Philip of Macedon, as I take it.

FLUELLEN
I think it is in Macedon where Alexander is porn. I tell you, captain, if you look in the maps of the 'orld, I warrant you sall find, in the comparisons between Macedon and Monmouth, that the situations, look you, is both alike. There is a river in Macedon; and there is also moreover a river at Monmouth: it is called Wye at Monmouth; but it is out of my prains what is the name of the other river; but 'tis all one, 'tis alike as my fingers

is to my fingers, and there is salmons in both. If you
mark Alexander's life well, Harry of Monmouth's life
is come after it indifferent well; for there is figures in
all things. Alexander, God knows, and you know, in his
rages, and his furies, and his wraths, and his cholers, and
his moods, and his displeasures, and his indignations, and
also being a little intoxicates in his prains, did, in his ales
and his angers, look you, kill his best friend, Cleitus.

GOWER
Our king is not like him in that: he never killed any of
his friends.

FLUELLEN
It is not well done, mark you now take the tales out of
my mouth, ere it is made and finished. I speak but in
the figures and comparisons of it: as Alexander killed
his friend Cleitus, being in his ales and his cups; so
also Harry Monmouth, being in his right wits and his
good judgments, turned away the fat knight with the
great belly-doublet: he was full of jests, and gipes, and
knaveries, and mocks; I have forgot his name.

GOWER
Sir John Falstaff.

FLUELLEN
That is he: I'll tell you there is good men porn at
Monmouth.

Henry V | Act IV, scene 7

12 JUNE

Brazil's Dia dos Namorados – Lovers' Day

Juliet longs for the night, and for love.

JULIET

Gallop apace, you fiery-footed steeds,
Towards Phoebus' lodging: such a wagoner
As Phaethon would whip you to the west,
And bring in cloudy night immediately.
Spread thy close curtain, love-performing night,
That runaway's eyes may wink and Romeo
Leap to these arms, untalk'd of and unseen.
Lovers can see to do their amorous rites
By their own beauties; or, if love be blind,
It best agrees with night. Come, civil night,
Thou sober-suited matron, all in black,
And learn me how to lose a winning match,
Play'd for a pair of stainless maidenhoods:
Hood my unmann'd blood, bating in my cheeks,
With thy black mantle; till strange love, grown bold,
Think true love acted simple modesty.
Come, night; come, Romeo; come, thou day in night;
For thou wilt lie upon the wings of night
Whiter than new snow on a raven's back.
Come, gentle night, come, loving, black-brow'd night,
Give me my Romeo; and, when he shall die,
Take him and cut him out in little stars,
And he will make the face of heaven so fine
That all the world will be in love with night
And pay no worship to the garish sun.
O, I have bought the mansion of a love,
But not possess'd it, and, though I am sold,

Not yet enjoy'd: so tedious is this day
As is the night before some festival
To an impatient child that hath new robes
And may not wear them.

Romeo and Juliet | **Act III, scene 2**

13 JUNE

Birthday in 1892 of actor Basil Rathbone, known for his screen performances as Sherlock Holmes

Rathbone made his stage debut as Hortensio, who has been teaching shrewish Katherine to play the lute.

[Re-enter Hortensio, with his head broke]

BAPTISTA MINOLA
How now, my friend! Why dost thou look so pale?

HORTENSIO
For fear, I promise you, if I look pale.

BAPTISTA MINOLA
What, will my daughter prove a good musician?

HORTENSIO
I think she'll sooner prove a soldier:
Iron may hold with her, but never lutes.

BAPTISTA MINOLA
Why, then thou canst not break her to the lute?

HORTENSIO
Why, no; for she hath broke the lute to me.
I did but tell her she mistook her frets,
And bow'd her hand to teach her fingering,
When, with a most impatient devilish spirit,
'Frets, call you these?' quoth she 'I'll fume with them.'
And with that word she struck me on the head,
And through the instrument my pate made way;
And there I stood amazed for a while,
As on a pillory, looking through the lute,

While she did call me rascal fiddler
And twangling Jack, with twenty such vile terms,
As she had studied to misuse me so.

The Taming of the Shrew | Act II, scene 1

14 JUNE

The Marijuana Tax Act is passed in the United States. It is signed into law seven weeks later, levying a tax on the sale of Cannabis sativa

A priest sees similarities between the characteristics of herbs and the character of human beings.

FRIAR LAURENCE

The grey-eyed morn smiles on the frowning night,
Chequering the eastern clouds with streaks of light,
And flecked darkness like a drunkard reels
From forth day's path and Titan's fiery wheels:
Now, ere the sun advance his burning eye,
The day to cheer and night's dank dew to dry,
I must up-fill this osier cage of ours
With baleful weeds and precious-juiced flowers.
The earth that's nature's mother is her tomb;
What is her burying grave that is her womb,
And from her womb children of divers kind
We sucking on her natural bosom find,
Many for many virtues excellent,
None but for some and yet all different.
O, mickle is the powerful grace that lies
In herbs, plants, stones, and their true qualities:
For nought so vile that on the earth doth live
But to the earth some special good doth give,
Nor aught so good but strain'd from that fair use
Revolts from true birth, stumbling on abuse:
Virtue itself turns vice, being misapplied;
And vice sometimes by action dignified.
Within the infant rind of this small flower
Poison hath residence and medicine power:
For this, being smelt, with that part cheers each part;
Being tasted, slays all senses with the heart.
Two such opposed kings encamp them still

In man as well as herbs, grace and rude will;
And where the worser is predominant,
Full soon the canker death eats up that plant.

Romeo and Juliet | **Act II, scene 3**

15 JUNE

King John sets his seal to the Magna Carta in 1215, guaranteeing the rights and privileges of his nobles

A noble objects to the king's seizure of property from John of Gaunt and the Duke of Hereford, who are father and son.

EDMUND OF LANGLEY
O my liege,
Pardon me, if you please; if not, I, pleased
Not to be pardon'd, am content withal.
Seek you to seize and gripe into your hands
The royalties and rights of banish'd Hereford?
Is not Gaunt dead, and doth not Hereford live?
Was not Gaunt just, and is not Harry true?
Did not the one deserve to have an heir?
Is not his heir a well-deserving son?
Take Hereford's rights away, and take from Time
His charters and his customary rights;
Let not to-morrow then ensue to-day;
Be not thyself; for how art thou a king
But by fair sequence and succession?
Now, afore God – God forbid I say true! –
If you do wrongfully seize Hereford's rights,
Call in the letters patent that he hath
By his attorneys-general to sue
His livery, and deny his offer'd homage,
You pluck a thousand dangers on your head,
You lose a thousand well-disposed hearts
And prick my tender patience, to those thoughts
Which honour and allegiance cannot think.

KING RICHARD II
Think what you will, we seize into our hands
His plate, his goods, his money and his lands.

EDMUND OF LANGLEY
I'll not be by the while: my liege, farewell:
What will ensue hereof, there's none can tell;
But by bad courses may be understood
That their events can never fall out good.

Richard II | Act II, scene 1

16 JUNE

The death in 1858 of epidemiologist John Snow, who ended an outbreak of cholera by removing the handle of an infected water pump

A Roman general wishes illness and disease on his troops, who have fled from an attacking army.

CORIOLANUS
All the contagion of the south light on you,
You shames of Rome! you herd of – Boils and plagues
Plaster you o'er, that you may be abhorr'd
Further than seen and one infect another
Against the wind a mile! You souls of geese,
That bear the shapes of men, how have you run
From slaves that apes would beat! Pluto and hell!
All hurt behind; backs red, and faces pale
With flight and agued fear! Mend and charge home,
Or, by the fires of heaven, I'll leave the foe
And make my wars on you: look to't: come on;
If you'll stand fast, we'll beat them to their wives,
As they us to our trenches followed.

Coriolanus | Act I, scene 4

17 JUNE

Mumtaz Mahal, empress consort of the Mughal Empire, dies in childbirth in 1631: her memorial will be the Taj Mahal

Pericles, who thought his wife had died in childbirth, has been told by Dionyza that his daughter Marina is also dead.

JOHN GOWER
[...] And Pericles, in sorrow all devour'd,
With sighs shot through, and biggest tears o'ershower'd,
Leaves Tarsus and again embarks. He swears
Never to wash his face, nor cut his hairs:
He puts on sackcloth, and to sea. He bears
A tempest, which his mortal vessel tears,
And yet he rides it out. Now please you wit.
The epitaph is for Marina writ
By wicked Dionyza.
[Reads the inscription on Marina's monument]
'The fairest, sweet'st, and best lies here,
Who wither'd in her spring of year.
She was of Tyrus the king's daughter,
On whom foul death hath made this slaughter;
Marina was she call'd; and at her birth,
Thetis, being proud, swallow'd some part o' the earth:
Therefore the earth, fearing to be o'erflow'd,
Hath Thetis' birth-child on the heavens bestow'd:
Wherefore she does, and swears she'll never stint,
Make raging battery upon shores of flint.'
No visor does become black villany
So well as soft and tender flattery.

Pericles | Act IV, scene 4

18 JUNE

Britain and Prussia defeat Napoleon Bonaparte at the Battle of Waterloo in 1815

Henry V fears leaving England defenceless against the marauding Scots if he attacks France.

ARCHBISHOP OF CANTERBURY
[...] I this infer,
That many things, having full reference
To one consent, may work contrariously:
As many arrows, loosed several ways,
Come to one mark; as many ways meet in one town;
As many fresh streams meet in one salt sea;
As many lines close in the dial's centre;
So may a thousand actions, once afoot.
End in one purpose, and be all well borne
Without defeat. Therefore to France, my liege.
Divide your happy England into four;
Whereof take you one quarter into France,
And you withal shall make all Gallia shake.
If we, with thrice such powers left at home,
Cannot defend our own doors from the dog,
Let us be worried and our nation lose
The name of hardiness and policy.

Henry V | Act I, scene 2

19 JUNE

The Feast of the Forests in the Philippines province of Palawan

Trees show the passing of the seasons, ageing only imperceptibly. Perhaps their greatest beauty is already passed.

SONNET 104

To me, fair friend, you never can be old,
For as you were when first your eye I eyed,
Such seems your beauty still. Three winters cold
Have from the forests shook three summers' pride,
Three beauteous springs to yellow autumn turn'd
In process of the seasons have I seen,
Three April perfumes in three hot Junes burn'd,
Since first I saw you fresh, which yet are green.
Ah! yet doth beauty, like a dial-hand,
Steal from his figure and no pace perceived;
So your sweet hue, which methinks still doth stand,
Hath motion and mine eye may be deceived:
For fear of which, hear this, thou age unbred;
Ere you were born was beauty's summer dead.

20 JUNE

In 1791 Louis XVI attempts to escape revolutionary Paris disguised as a valet

Viola, disguised as a man called Cesario, loves the Duke Orsino. Orsino loves the Countess Olivia. Olivia loves Cesario and uses one of her rings to lure 'him' to her.

VIOLA
I left no ring with her: what means this lady?
Fortune forbid my outside have not charm'd her!
She made good view of me; indeed, so much,
That sure methought her eyes had lost her tongue,
For she did speak in starts distractedly.
She loves me, sure; the cunning of her passion
Invites me in this churlish messenger.
None of my lord's ring! why, he sent her none.
I am the man: if it be so, as 'tis,
Poor lady, she were better love a dream.
Disguise, I see, thou art a wickedness,
Wherein the pregnant enemy does much.
How easy is it for the proper-false
In women's waxen hearts to set their forms!
Alas, our frailty is the cause, not we!
For such as we are made of, such we be.
How will this fadge? my master loves her dearly;
And I, poor monster, fond as much on him;
And she, mistaken, seems to dote on me.
What will become of this? As I am man,
My state is desperate for my master's love;
As I am woman – now alas the day! –
What thriftless sighs shall poor Olivia breathe!
O time! thou must untangle this, not I;
It is too hard a knot for me to untie!

Twelfth Night | Act II, scene 2

253

21 JUNE

The Summer Solstice, in the northern hemisphere, the Winter Solstice in the southern

Oberon, king of the fairies, commands a spell on Midsummer Night which will make his queen fall in love with the first creature she sees. Unfortunately, that will prove to be a donkey.

OBERON

I know a bank where the wild thyme blows,
Where oxlips and the nodding violet grows,
Quite over-canopied with luscious woodbine,
With sweet musk-roses and with eglantine:
There sleeps Titania sometime of the night,
Lull'd in these flowers with dances and delight;
And there the snake throws her enamell'd skin,
Weed wide enough to wrap a fairy in:
And with the juice of this I'll streak her eyes,
And make her full of hateful fantasies.
Take thou some of it, and seek through this grove:
A sweet Athenian lady is in love
With a disdainful youth: anoint his eyes;
But do it when the next thing he espies
May be the lady: thou shalt know the man
By the Athenian garments he hath on.
Effect it with some care, that he may prove
More fond on her than she upon her love:
And look thou meet me ere the first cock crow.

A Midsummer Night's Dream | Act II, scene 1

22 JUNE

In 1633 Galileo Galilei is forced to recant his claim that the Earth revolves around the Sun, not the other way round

Cleopatra is distracted and her universe turned upside down.

CLEOPATRA
I dream'd there was an Emperor Antony:
O, such another sleep, that I might see
But such another man!

DOLABELLA
If it might please ye,—

CLEOPATRA
His face was as the heavens; and therein stuck
A sun and moon, which kept their course, and lighted
The little O, the earth.

DOLABELLA
Most sovereign creature,—

CLEOPATRA
His legs bestrid the ocean: his rear'd arm
Crested the world: his voice was propertied
As all the tuned spheres, and that to friends;
But when he meant to quail and shake the orb,
He was as rattling thunder. For his bounty,
There was no winter in't; an autumn 'twas
That grew the more by reaping: his delights
Were dolphin-like; they show'd his back above
The element they lived in: in his livery
Walk'd crowns and crownets; realms and islands were
As plates dropp'd from his pocket.

DOLABELLA
Cleopatra!

CLEOPATRA
Think you there was, or might be, such a man
As this I dream'd of?

DOLABELLA
Gentle madam, no.

Antony and Cleopatra | **Act V, scene 2**

23 JUNE

International Widows Day, which draws attention to the poverty and injustice often met by widows

Two widows compare their losses. George, Duke of Clarence, and King Edward IV are both sons of the Duchess of York.

QUEEN ELIZABETH
[...] Edward – my lord, your son, our king – is dead.
Why grow the branches now the root is wither'd?
Why wither not the leaves the sap being gone?
If you will live, lament; if die, be brief,
That our swift-winged souls may catch the king's;
Or, like obedient subjects, follow him
To his new kingdom of perpetual rest.

DUCHESS OF YORK
Ah, so much interest have I in thy sorrow
As I had title in thy noble husband!
I have bewept a worthy husband's death,
And lived by looking on his images:
But now two mirrors of his princely semblance
Are crack'd in pieces by malignant death,
And I for comfort have but one false glass,
Which grieves me when I see my shame in him.
Thou art a widow; yet thou art a mother,
And hast the comfort of thy children left thee:
But death hath snatch'd my husband from mine arms,
And pluck'd two crutches from my feeble limbs,
Edward and Clarence. O, what cause have I,
Thine being but a moiety of my grief,
To overgo thy plaints and drown thy cries!

Richard III | Act II, scene 2

24 JUNE

Fors Fortuna, the ancient Roman festival of the goddess of fortune, usually depicted blindfold and with a wheel

Pistol pleads for mercy on behalf of Bardolph, who is to be hung for looting a religious artefact.

PISTOL
Bardolph, a soldier, firm and sound of heart,
And of buxom valour, hath, by cruel fate,
And giddy Fortune's furious fickle wheel,
That goddess blind,
That stands upon the rolling restless stone—

FLUELLEN
By your patience, Aunchient Pistol. Fortune is painted blind, with a muffler afore her eyes, to signify to you that Fortune is blind; and she is painted also with a wheel, to signify to you, which is the moral of it, that she is turning, and inconstant, and mutability, and variation: and her foot, look you, is fixed upon a spherical stone, which rolls, and rolls, and rolls: in good truth, the poet makes a most excellent description of it: Fortune is an excellent moral.

Henry V | Act III, scene 6

25 JUNE

Death in 1634 of the satirical poet John Marston, noted for his obscure and idiosyncratic language

Marston is said to have influenced the speech of several of Shakespeare's characters, including Lear's at his maddest.

KING LEAR
Thou think'st 'tis much that this contentious storm
Invades us to the skin. So 'tis to thee;
But where the greater malady is fix'd,
The lesser is scarce felt. Thou'dst shun a bear;
But if thy flight lay toward the raging sea,
Thou'dst meet the bear i' th' mouth. When the mind's free,
The body's delicate. The tempest in my mind
Doth from my senses take all feeling else
Save what beats there. Filial ingratitude!
Is it not as this mouth should tear this hand
For lifting food to't? But I will punish home!
No, I will weep no more. In such a night
To shut me out! Pour on; I will endure.
In such a night as this! O Regan, Goneril!
Your old kind father, whose frank heart gave all!
O, that way madness lies; let me shun that!
No more of that.

King Lear | Act III, scene 4

26 JUNE

Ratcatchers' Day, marking the day in 1284 when, in the fairy tale, the Pied Piper led the children out of Hamelin

Edgar pretends to be Tom O'Bedlam, down on his luck, catching rats and drinking ditchwater.

EARL OF GLOUCESTER
What are you there? Your names?

EDGAR
Poor Tom, that eats the swimming frog, the toad, the todpole, the wall-newt and the water; that in the fury of his heart, when the foul fiend rages, eats cow-dung for sallets, swallows the old rat and the ditch-dog, drinks the green mantle of the standing pool; who is whipp'd from tithing to tithing, and stock-punish'd and imprison'd; who hath had three suits to his back, six shirts to his body, horse to ride, and weapons to wear;
But mice and rats, and such small deer,
Have been Tom's food for seven long year.
Beware my follower. Peace, Smulkin! peace, thou fiend!

King Lear | Act III, scene 4

27 JUNE

Seven Sleepers Day in southern Germany, when meteorological conditions may predict the weather of the following seven weeks of summer

Twisted Richard appears to celebrate his brother Edward IV's return to the throne, while plotting his downfall.

RICHARD III

Now is the winter of our discontent
Made glorious summer by this sun of York;
And all the clouds that lour'd upon our house
In the deep bosom of the ocean buried.
Now are our brows bound with victorious wreaths;
Our bruised arms hung up for monuments;
Our stern alarums changed to merry meetings,
Our dreadful marches to delightful measures.
Grim-visaged war hath smooth'd his wrinkled front;
And now, instead of mounting barded steeds
To fright the souls of fearful adversaries,
He capers nimbly in a lady's chamber
To the lascivious pleasing of a lute.
But I, that am not shaped for sportive tricks,
Nor made to court an amorous looking-glass;
I, that am rudely stamp'd, and want love's majesty
To strut before a wanton ambling nymph;
I, that am curtail'd of this fair proportion,
Cheated of feature by dissembling nature,
Deformed, unfinish'd, sent before my time
Into this breathing world, scarce half made up,
And that so lamely and unfashionable
That dogs bark at me as I halt by them;
Why, I, in this weak piping time of peace,
Have no delight to pass away the time,

Unless to spy my shadow in the sun
And descant on mine own deformity:
And therefore, since I cannot prove a lover,
To entertain these fair well-spoken days,
I am determined to prove a villain
And hate the idle pleasures of these days.
Plots have I laid, inductions dangerous,
By drunken prophecies, libels and dreams,
To set my brother Clarence and the king
In deadly hate the one against the other:
And if King Edward be as true and just
As I am subtle, false and treacherous,
This day should Clarence closely be mew'd up,
About a prophecy, which says that 'G'
Of Edward's heirs the murderer shall be.
Dive, thoughts, down to my soul: here
Clarence comes.

Richard III | Act I, scene 1

28 JUNE

The day in 1919 of the signing of the Treaty of Versailles, settling the peace exactly five years after the assassination which sparked World War One

At the baptism of the future Queen Elizabeth, Cranmer predicts peaceful reigns for her and her son and successor (James, who just happens to be king when this play is first performed).

ARCHBISHOP CRANMER
Let me speak, sir,
For heaven now bids me; and the words I utter
Let none think flattery, for they'll find 'em truth.
This royal infant – heaven still move about her! –
Though in her cradle, yet now promises
Upon this land a thousand thousand blessings,
Which time shall bring to ripeness: she shall be –
But few now living can behold that goodness –
A pattern to all princes living with her,
And all that shall succeed: Saba was never
More covetous of wisdom and fair virtue
Than this pure soul shall be: all princely graces,
That mould up such a mighty piece as this is,
With all the virtues that attend the good,
Shall still be doubled on her: truth shall nurse her,
Holy and heavenly thoughts still counsel her:
She shall be loved and fear'd: her own shall bless her;
Her foes shake like a field of beaten corn,
And hang their heads with sorrow: good grows with her:
In her days every man shall eat in safety,
Under his own vine, what he plants; and sing
The merry songs of peace to all his neighbours:
God shall be truly known; and those about her
From her shall read the perfect ways of honour,

And by those claim their greatness, not by blood.
Nor shall this peace sleep with her: but as when
The bird of wonder dies, the maiden phoenix,
Her ashes new create another heir,
As great in admiration as herself;
So shall she leave her blessedness to one,
When heaven shall call her from this cloud of darkness,
Who from the sacred ashes of her honour
Shall star-like rise, as great in fame as she was,
And so stand fix'd: peace, plenty, love, truth, terror,
That were the servants to this chosen infant,
Shall then be his, and like a vine grow to him:
Wherever the bright sun of heaven shall shine,
His honour and the greatness of his name
Shall be, and make new nations: he shall flourish,
And, like a mountain cedar, reach his branches
To all the plains about him: our children's children
Shall see this, and bless heaven.

Henry VIII | Act V, scene 5

29 JUNE

The day in 1613 when Shakespeare's theatre, the Globe, was burned down by a special effects cannon

Hamlet was among the plays which received their premieres on the stage of the Globe Theatre. Here, the prince has just learned from the ghost of his father that he was murdered.

THE GHOST OF HAMLET'S FATHER
[...] Adieu, adieu, adieu! Remember me. *[Exit.]*

HAMLET
O all you host of heaven! O earth! What else?
And shall I couple hell? Hold, hold, my heart!
And you, my sinews, grow not instant old,
But bear me stiffly up. Remember thee?
Ay, thou poor ghost, while memory holds a seat
In this distracted globe. Remember thee?
Yea, from the table of my memory
I'll wipe away all trivial fond records,
All saws of books, all forms, all pressures past
That youth and observation copied there,
And thy commandment all alone shall live
Within the book and volume of my brain,
Unmix'd with baser matter. Yes, by heaven!
O most pernicious woman!
O villain, villain, smiling, damned villain!
My tables! Meet it is I set it down
That one may smile, and smile, and be a villain;
At least I am sure it may be so in Denmark.

Hamlet | Act I, scene 5

30 JUNE

The death of Henrietta, youngest daughter of England's Charles I, in 1670, aged only 26

The death of his youngest daughter, Cordelia, breaks King Lear's heart, his spirit and his body.

[Enter Lear, with Cordelia dead in his arms]

KING LEAR
Howl, howl, howl, howl! O, you are men of stone.
Had I your tongues and eyes, I'd use them so
That heaven's vault should crack. She's gone for ever!
I know when one is dead, and when one lives.
She's dead as earth. Lend me a looking glass.
If that her breath will mist or stain the stone,
Why, then she lives.

EARL OF KENT
Is this the promis'd end?
[...]

LEAR
This feather stirs; she lives! If it be so,
It is a chance which does redeem all sorrows
That ever I have felt.

EARL OF KENT
O my good master!

KING LEAR
I might have sav'd her; now she's gone for ever!
Cordelia, Cordelia! stay a little. Ha!
What is't thou say'st? Her voice was ever soft,
Gentle, and low – an excellent thing in woman.

[...]
Why should a dog, a horse, a rat, have life,
And thou no breath at all? Thou'lt come no more,
Never, never, never, never, never!
Pray you undo this button. Thank you, sir.
Do you see this? Look on her! look! her lips!
Look there, look there! *[He dies.]*

King Lear | Act V, scene 3

JULY

To be, or not to be – that is the question:
Whether 'tis nobler in the mind to suffer
The slings and arrows of outrageous fortune
Or to take arms against a sea of troubles,
And by opposing end them.

Hamlet | Act III, scene 1

1 JULY

Birthday in 1553 of carpenter Peter Street, who built five London theatres including the Globe

In warfare, as in building, it is sometimes okay to go back to the drawing board.

LORD BARDOLPH
[...] When we mean to build,
We first survey the plot, then draw the model;
And when we see the figure of the house,
Then we must rate the cost of the erection;
Which if we find outweighs ability,
What do we then but draw anew the model
In fewer offices, or at least desist
To build at all? Much more, in this great work –
Which is almost to pluck a kingdom down
And set another up – should we survey
The plot of situation and the model,
Consent upon a sure foundation,
Question surveyors, know our own estate
How able such a work to undergo –
To weigh against his opposite; or else
We fortify in paper and in figures,
Using the names of men instead of men;
Like one that draws the model of a house
Beyond his power to build it; who, half through,
Gives o'er and leaves his part-created cost
A naked subject to the weeping clouds
And waste for churlish winter's tyranny.

Henry IV, Part 2 | Act I, scene 3

2 JULY

The birthday in 1900 of Sophie Harris, renowned costume designer for British theatre, opera and film

Benedick's friends mock him for his dress sense, and for being in love. Civet is a perfume.

DON PEDRO
There is no appearance of fancy in him, unless it be a fancy that he hath to strange disguises; as, to be a Dutchman today, a Frenchman to-morrow, or in the shape of two countries at once, as, a German from the waist downward, all slops, and a Spaniard from the hip upward, no doublet. Unless he have a fancy to this foolery, as it appears he hath, he is no fool for fancy, as you would have it appear he is.

CLAUDIO
If he be not in love with some woman, there is no believing old signs: he brushes his hat o' mornings; what should that bode?

DON PEDRO
Nay, he rubs himself with civet: can you smell him out by that?

CLAUDIO
And when was he wont to wash his face?

DON PEDRO
Indeed, that tells a heavy tale for him: conclude, conclude he is in love.

Much Ado about Nothing | Act III, scene 2

3 JULY

The final night of David Bowie's Ziggy Stardust tour in 1973, when he announced that he was killing off the Ziggy persona

The reported death of Falstaff must have shocked his audience just as Bowie distressed his.

PISTOL
[...] Boy, bristle thy courage up; for Falstaff he is dead, and we must yearn therefore.

BARDOLPH
Would I were with him, wheresome'er he is, either in heaven or in hell!

HOSTESS QUICKLY
Nay, sure, he's not in hell: he's in Arthur's bosom, if ever man went to Arthur's bosom. He made a finer end and went away an it had been any christom child; he parted even just between twelve and one, even at the turning o' the tide: for after I saw him fumble with the sheets and play with flowers and smile upon his fingers' ends, I knew there was but one way; for his nose was as sharp as a pen, and he babbled of green fields. 'How now, Sir John!' quoth I. 'what, man! be o' good cheer.' So he cried out 'God, God, God!' three or four times. Now I, to comfort him, bid him he should not think of God; I hoped there was no need to trouble himself with any such thoughts yet. So he bade me lay more clothes on his feet: I put my hand into the bed and felt them, and they were as cold as any stone; then I felt to his knees, and they were as cold as any stone, and so upward and upward, and all was as cold as any stone.

Henry V | Act II, scene 3

4 JULY

Independence Day in the United States of America

By assassinating Julius Caesar, the conspirators hope to usher in a new age of Roman politics.

CINNA
Liberty! Freedom! Tyranny is dead!
Run hence, proclaim, cry it about the streets.

CASSIUS
Some to the common pulpits, and cry out
'Liberty, freedom, and enfranchisement!'
[...]

BRUTUS
Fates, we will know your pleasures:
That we shall die, we know; 'tis but the time
And drawing days out, that men stand upon.

CASSIUS
Why, he that cuts off twenty years of life
Cuts off so many years of fearing death.

BRUTUS
Grant that, and then is death a benefit:
So are we Caesar's friends, that have abridged
His time of fearing death. Stoop, Romans, stoop,
And let us bathe our hands in Caesar's blood
Up to the elbows, and besmear our swords:
Then walk we forth, even, to the market-place,
And, waving our red weapons o'er our heads,
Let's all cry 'Peace, freedom and liberty!'

Julius Caesar | **Act III, scene 1**

5 JULY

English travel agent Thomas Cook runs his first ever holiday excursion, from Leicester to Loughborough, in 1841

Prince Hal claims that his dissolute behaviour is an act which will only make his eventual reformation seem more remarkable.

HENRY
[...] If all the year were playing holidays,
To sport would be as tedious as to work;
But when they seldom come, they wish'd for come,
And nothing pleaseth but rare accidents.
So, when this loose behavior I throw off
And pay the debt I never promised,
By how much better than my word I am,
By so much shall I falsify men's hopes;
And like bright metal on a sullen ground,
My reformation, glittering o'er my fault,
Shall show more goodly and attract more eyes
Than that which hath no foil to set it off.
I'll so offend, to make offence a skill;
Redeeming time when men think least I will.

Henry IV, Part 1 | Act I, scene 2

6 JULY

Death in 1960 of Aneurin Bevan, who created Britain's National Health Service

Like an emetic which induces sickness to prevent disease, the poet's efforts to fix a relationship which wasn't broken have poisoned it.

SONNET 118

Like as, to make our appetites more keen,
With eager compounds we our palate urge,
As, to prevent our maladies unseen,
We sicken to shun sickness when we purge,
Even so, being tuff of your ne'er-cloying sweetness,
To bitter sauces did I frame my feeding
And, sick of welfare, found a kind of meetness
To be diseased ere that there was true needing.
Thus policy in love, to anticipate
The ills that were not, grew to faults assured
And brought to medicine a healthful state
Which, rank of goodness, would by ill be cured:
But thence I learn, and find the lesson true,
Drugs poison him that so fell sick of you.

7 JULY

The day in 1928 when sliced bread went on sale for the first time, thanks to a machine invented by water repairer Otto Rohwedder of Davenport, Iowa

Once-wealthy Tarsus has fallen on hard times.

CLEON
[...] These mouths, who but of late, earth, sea, and air,
Were all too little to content and please,
Although they gave their creatures in abundance,
As houses are defiled for want of use,
They are now starved for want of exercise:
Those palates who, not yet two summers younger,
Must have inventions to delight the taste,
Would now be glad of bread, and beg for it:
Those mothers who, to nousle up their babes,
Thought nought too curious, are ready now
To eat those little darlings whom they loved.
So sharp are hunger's teeth, that man and wife
Draw lots who first shall die to lengthen life:
Here stands a lord, and there a lady weeping;
Here many sink, yet those which see them fall
Have scarce strength left to give them burial.

Pericles | Act I, scene 4

8 JULY

The death in 1898 of con artist and crime boss Soapy Smith in a shoot-out in Skagway, Alaska

The king finds the Earl of Gloucester innocent of all charges; but the queen is suspicious.

QUEEN MARGARET
Ah, what's more dangerous than this fond affiance!
Seems he a dove? his feathers are but borrowed,
For he's disposed as the hateful raven:
Is he a lamb? his skin is surely lent him,
For he's inclined as is the ravenous wolf.
Who cannot steal a shape that means deceit?
Take heed, my lord; the welfare of us all
Hangs on the cutting short that fraudful man.

Henry VI, Part 2 | Act III, scene 1

9 JULY

In 1877, the first day of the first Wimbledon Tennis Championship

The French Dauphin, in response to England's claims of sovereignty, mocks Henry V's youth with a gift.

FIRST AMBASSADOR
Your highness, lately sending into France,
Did claim some certain dukedoms, in the right
Of your great predecessor, King Edward the Third.
In answer of which claim, the prince our master
Says that you savour too much of your youth,
And bids you be advised there's nought in France
That can be with a nimble galliard won;
You cannot revel into dukedoms there.
He therefore sends you, meeter for your spirit,
This tun of treasure; and, in lieu of this,
Desires you let the dukedoms that you claim
Hear no more of you. This the Dauphin speaks.

HENRY V
What treasure, uncle?

DUKE OF EXETER
[opening the barrel] Tennis-balls, my liege.

Henry V | Act I, scene 2

10 JULY

*In 1925 in Dayton, Tennessee, the trial begins of science teacher
John T. Scopes, accused of teaching evolution*

*Guests take advantage of Timon's unguarded generosity.
Cynical Apemantus is unimpressed.*

MESSENGER
'Tis Alcibiades, and some twenty horse,
All of companionship.

TIMON
Pray, entertain them; give them guide to us.
[Exeunt some Attendants]
You must needs dine with me: go not you hence
Till I have thank'd you: when dinner's done,
Show me this piece. I am joyful of your sights.
[Enter Alcibiades, with the rest]
Most welcome, sir!

APEMANTUS
So, so, there!
Aches contract and starve your supple joints!
That there should be small love 'mongst these sweet knaves,
And all this courtesy! The strain of man's bred out
Into baboon and monkey.

Timon of Athens | Act I, scene 1

11 JULY

Kōkichi Mikimoto produces the world's first cultured pearl on this day in 1893

Proteus has fallen in love at first sight of Valentine's bride-to-be, Sylvia.

VALENTINE
Pardon me, Proteus: all I can is nothing
To her whose worth makes other worthies nothing;
She is alone.

PROTEUS
Then let her alone.

VALENTINE
Not for the world: why, man, she is mine own,
And I as rich in having such a jewel
As twenty seas, if all their sand were pearl,
The water nectar and the rocks pure gold.
Forgive me that I do not dream on thee,
Because thou see'st me dote upon my love.
My foolish rival, that her father likes
Only for his possessions are so huge,
Is gone with her along, and I must after,
For love, thou know'st, is full of jealousy.

The Two Gentlemen of Verona | **Act II, scene 4**

12 JULY

Death in 2012 of children's author Else Holmelund Minarik, who wrote the Little Bear *series of books*

Minarik also wrote No Fighting, No Biting!, *about two children who are always quarrelling.*

MARGARELON
Turn, slave, and fight.

THERSITES
What art thou?

MARGARELON
A bastard son of Priam's.

THERSITES
I am a bastard too; I love bastards: I am a bastard
begot, bastard instructed, bastard in mind, bastard
in valour, in every thing illegitimate. One bear will
not bite another, and wherefore should one bastard?
Take heed, the quarrel's most ominous to us: if the
son of a whore fight for a whore, he tempts judgment:
farewell, bastard. *[He runs away]*

MARGARELON
The devil take thee, coward!

Troilus and Cressida | **Act V, scene 7**

13 JULY

The day in 1985 when Live Aid rock concerts took place around the world to raise funds for famine relief in Africa

Wealthy Timon has not yet realized that most of his visitors are only there to take advantage of his unguarded generosity.

TIMON
I take all and your several visitations
So kind to heart, 'tis not enough to give;
Methinks, I could deal kingdoms to my friends,
And ne'er be weary. Alcibiades,
Thou art a soldier, therefore seldom rich;
It comes in charity to thee: for all thy living
Is 'mongst the dead, and all the lands thou hast
Lie in a pitch'd field.

Timon of Athens | Act I, scene 2

14 JULY

The birth in 1901 of English composer Gerald Finzi

Finzi wrote incidental music for Love's Labour's Lost *and a cycle of Shakespearean songs called* Let Us Garlands Bring, *which includes this ditty.*

TOUCHSTONE
By my troth, well met. Come sit, sit, and a song.

SECOND PAGE
We are for you; sit i' th' middle.

FIRST PAGE
Shall we clap into't roundly, without hawking, or spitting, or saying we are hoarse, which are the only prologues to a bad voice?

SECOND PAGE
I'faith, i'faith; and both in a tune, like two gipsies on a horse.
[they sing]

    It was a lover and his lass,
    With a hey, and a ho, and a hey nonino,
    That o'er the green corn-field did pass
    In the spring time, the only pretty ring time,
    When birds do sing, hey ding a ding, ding.
    Sweet lovers love the spring.
    Between the acres of the rye,
    With a hey, and a ho, and a hey nonino,
    These pretty country folks would lie,
    In the spring time, the only pretty ring time,
    When birds do sing, hey ding a ding, ding.
    Sweet lovers love the spring.
    This carol they began that hour,
    With a hey, and a ho, and a hey nonino,

How that a life was but a flower,
In the spring time, the only pretty ring time,
When birds do sing, hey ding a ding, ding.
Sweet lovers love the spring.
And therefore take the present time,
With a hey, and a ho, and a hey nonino,
For love is crowned with the prime,
In the spring time, the only pretty ring time,
When birds do sing, hey ding a ding, ding.
Sweet lovers love the spring.

As You Like It | **Act V, scene 3**

15 JULY

The annual Obon Festival in eastern Japan, in which families gather to honour their ancestors. Other parts of the country celebrate in August

An archbishop urges a king to remember the deeds of his ancestors and the spirit of England.

ARCHBISHOP OF CANTERBURY
[...] Gracious lord,
Stand for your own; unwind your bloody flag;
Look back into your mighty ancestors:
Go, my dread lord, to your great-grandsire's tomb,
From whom you claim; invoke his warlike spirit,
And your great-uncle's, Edward the Black Prince,
Who on the French ground play'd a tragedy,
Making defeat on the full power of France,
Whiles his most mighty father on a hill
Stood smiling to behold his lion's whelp
Forage in blood of French nobility.
O noble English. that could entertain
With half their forces the full Pride of France
And let another half stand laughing by,
All out of work and cold for action!

Henry V | Act I, scene 2

16 JULY

*In 1956, the last performance in a marquee by the Ringling Bros, and
Barnum & Bailey Circus*

*All future performances would take place in permanent
arenas, not the circus tents of tradition.*

TOUCHSTONE
It is meat and drink to me to see a clown. By my troth,
we that have good wits have much to answer for: we
shall be flouting; we cannot hold.

As You Like It | Act V, scene 1

17 JULY

Charles VII is crowned King of France in 1429, thanks to the efforts of Joan of Arc

Two years later Joan is captured and, defiant to the end, burned at the stake.

DUKE OF GLOUCESTER
Take her away; for she hath lived too long,
To fill the world with vicious qualities.

JOAN LA PUCELLE
First, let me tell you whom you have condemn'd:
Not me begotten of a shepherd swain,
But issued from the progeny of kings;
Virtuous and holy; chosen from above,
By inspiration of celestial grace,
To work exceeding miracles on earth.
I never had to do with wicked spirits:
But you, that are polluted with your lusts,
Stain'd with the guiltless blood of innocents,
Corrupt and tainted with a thousand vices,
Because you want the grace that others have,
You judge it straight a thing impossible
To compass wonders but by help of devils.
No, misconceived! Joan of Arc hath been
A virgin from her tender infancy,
Chaste and immaculate in very thought;
Whose maiden blood, thus rigorously effused,
Will cry for vengeance at the gates of heaven.

DUKE OF GLOUCESTER
Ay, ay: away with her to execution!

Henry VI, Part 1 | Act V, scene 4

18 JULY

The birthday in 1908 of Mildred Lisette Norman, self-styled Peace Pilgrim, who walked about 50,000 miles to promote spiritual and temporal peace

Medieval pilgrim routes were dotted with lodging houses where weary 'palmers' could spend the night on their way. St Francis, best known for his patronage of animals, also looks after travellers.

[Enter Helena, disguised like a Pilgrim]

WIDOW
Look, here comes a pilgrim: I know she will lie at
my house; thither they send one another: I'll
question her. God save you, pilgrim! whither are you bound?

HELENA
To Saint Jaques le Grand.
Where do the palmers lodge, I do beseech you?

WIDOW
At the Saint Francis here beside the port.

HELENA
Is this the way?

WIDOW
Ay, marry, is't.
[A march afar]
Hark you! they come this way.
If you will tarry, holy pilgrim,
But till the troops come by,
I will conduct you where you shall be lodged;
The rather, for I think I know your hostess
As ample as myself.

HELENA
Is it yourself?

WIDOW
If you shall please so, pilgrim.

HELENA
I thank you, and will stay upon your leisure.

All's Well That Ends Well | Act III, scene 5

19 JULY

The foundation of the British Medical Association in 1832

The earliest understanding of human anatomy was the insight of surgeons tending wounds in battle.

DUNCAN
What bloody man is that? He can report,
As seemeth by his plight, of the revolt
The newest state.

MALCOLM
This is the sergeant
Who like a good and hardy soldier fought
'Gainst my captivity. Hail, brave friend!
Say to the king the knowledge of the broil
As thou didst leave it.

SERGEANT
Doubtful it stood;
As two spent swimmers, that do cling together
And choke their art. The merciless Macdonald
Worthy to be a rebel, for to that
The multiplying villanies of nature
Do swarm upon him – from the western isles
Of kerns and gallowglasses is supplied;
And fortune, on his damned quarrel smiling,
Show'd like a rebel's whore: but all's too weak:
For brave Macbeth – well he deserves that name –
Disdaining fortune, with his brandish'd steel,
Which smoked with bloody execution,
Like valour's minion carved out his passage
Till he faced the slave;

Which ne'er shook hands, nor bade farewell to him,
Till he unseam'd him from the nave to the chaps,
And fix'd his head upon our battlements.
[...]
But I am faint, my gashes cry for help.

DUNCAN
So well thy words become thee as thy wounds;
They smack of honour both. Go get him surgeons.

Macbeth | Act I, scene 2

20 JULY

The birthday in 1583 of the colourful, temperamental Saint Alban Roe

The saint conducted his ministry in London pubs,
gambling with cards not for money but for prayers.

ISABELLA
Hark how I'll bribe you: good my lord, turn back.

ANGELO
How! bribe me?

ISABELLA
Ay, with such gifts that heaven shall share with you.
[...]
Not with fond shekels of the tested gold,
Or stones whose rates are either rich or poor
As fancy values them; but with true prayers
That shall be up at heaven and enter there
Ere sun-rise, prayers from preserved souls,
From fasting maids whose minds are dedicate
To nothing temporal.

Measure for Measure | Act II, scene 2

21 JULY

In 1969, at 2:56 GMT, Neil Armstrong becomes the first man to walk on the Moon

Some workmen are performing Pyramus and Thisbe, *a play for Theseus, Hippolyta and their guests, who are not taking it seriously.*

STARVELING
[as Moonshine] This lanthorn doth the horned moon present;—

DEMETRIUS
He should have worn the horns on his head.

THESEUS
He is no crescent, and his horns are
invisible within the circumference.

STARVELING
[as Moonshine] This lanthorn doth the horned moon present;
Myself the man i' the moon do seem to be.

THESEUS
This is the greatest error of all the rest: the man
should be put into the lanthorn. How is it else the
man i' the moon?

DEMETRIUS
He dares not come there for the candle; for, you
see, it is already in snuff.

HIPPOLYTA
I am aweary of this moon: would he would change!

THESEUS
It appears, by his small light of discretion, that
he is in the wane; but yet, in courtesy, in all
reason, we must stay the time.

LYSANDER
Proceed, Moon.

STARVELING
[as Moonshine] All that I have to say, is, to tell you that the
lanthorn is the moon; I, the man in the moon; this
thorn-bush, my thorn-bush; and this dog, my dog.

DEMETRIUS
Why, all these should be in the lanthorn; for all
these are in the moon. But, silence! here comes Thisbe.
[Enter Thisbe]

FLUTE
[as Thisbe] This is old Ninny's tomb. Where is my love?

SNUG
[as Lion] [Roars] Oh—
[Thisbe runs off]

DEMETRIUS
Well roared, Lion.

THESEUS
Well run, Thisbe.

HIPPOLYTA
Well shone, Moon. Truly, the moon shines with a
good grace.

22 JULY

The birthday in 1908 of Amy Vanderbilt, the doyenne of etiquette in New York society

Different manners may apply in different situations.

TOUCHSTONE
Why, if thou never wast at court thou never saw'st good manners; if thou never saw'st good manners, then thy manners must be wicked; and wickedness is sin, and sin is damnation. Thou art in a parlous state, shepherd.

CORIN
Not a whit, Touchstone. Those that are good manners at the court are as ridiculous in the country as the behaviour of the country is most mockable at the court. You told me you salute not at the court, but you kiss your hands; that courtesy would be uncleanly if courtiers were shepherds.

As You Like It | Act III, scene 2

23 JULY

In 1829 William Austin Burt is granted a patent for his typographer machine, the forerunner of the typewriter

Some things are still best written by hand.

SONNET 17

Who will believe my verse in time to come,
If it were fill'd with your most high deserts?
Though yet, heaven knows, it is but as a tomb
Which hides your life and shows not half your parts.
If I could write the beauty of your eyes
And in fresh numbers number all your graces,
The age to come would say 'This poet lies:
Such heavenly touches ne'er touch'd earthly faces.'
So should my papers yellow'd with their age
Be scorn'd like old men of less truth than tongue,
And your true rights be term'd a poet's rage
And stretched metre of an antique song:
But were some child of yours alive that time,
You should live twice; in it and in my rhyme.

The death in 1612 of John Salusbury, patron of allegorical poetry who sponsored Robert Chester's book Love's Martyr

Love's Martyr *includes Shakespeare's metaphysical masterpiece* The Phoenix and the Turtle, *about the funeral of a turtle dove and his queen.*

Here the anthem doth commence:
Love and constancy is dead;
Phoenix and the turtle fled
In a mutual flame from hence.

So they loved, as love in twain
Had the essence but in one;
Two distincts, division none:
Number there in love was slain.

Hearts remote, yet not asunder;
Distance, and no space was seen
'Twixt the turtle and his queen:
But in them it were a wonder.

So between them love did shine,
That the turtle saw his right
Flaming in the phoenix' sight;
Either was the other's mine.

From The Phoenix and the Turtle

25 JULY

The Union of the Crowns in 1603, with the coronation at Westminster Abbey of James I of England and Ireland. He has been James VI of Scotland since 1567

James, son of Mary Queen of Scots, was patron of Shakespeare's acting company when the playwright wrote Macbeth.

MACBETH

[...] Is this a dagger which I see before me,
The handle toward my hand? Come, let me clutch thee.
I have thee not, and yet I see thee still.
Art thou not, fatal vision, sensible
To feeling as to sight? or art thou but
A dagger of the mind, a false creation,
Proceeding from the heat-oppressed brain?
I see thee yet, in form as palpable
As this which now I draw.
Thou marshall'st me the way that I was going;
And such an instrument I was to use.
Mine eyes are made the fools o' the other senses,
Or else worth all the rest; I see thee still,
And on thy blade and dudgeon gouts of blood,
Which was not so before. There's no such thing:
It is the bloody business which informs
Thus to mine eyes. Now o'er the one halfworld
Nature seems dead, and wicked dreams abuse
The curtain'd sleep; witchcraft celebrates
Pale Hecate's offerings, and wither'd murder,
Alarum'd by his sentinel, the wolf,
Whose howl's his watch, thus with his stealthy pace.
With Tarquin's ravishing strides, towards his design
Moves like a ghost. Thou sure and firm-set earth,
Hear not my steps, which way they walk, for fear

Thy very stones prate of my whereabout,
And take the present horror from the time,
Which now suits with it. Whiles I threat, he lives:
Words to the heat of deeds too cold breath gives.
[A bell rings]
I go, and it is done; the bell invites me.
Hear it not, Duncan; for it is a knell
That summons thee to heaven or to hell.

Macbeth | Act II, scene 1

26 JULY

The birthday in 1875 of the psychoanalyst Carl Jung

Hamlet ponders his very existence.

HAMLET
To be, or not to be – that is the question:
Whether 'tis nobler in the mind to suffer
The slings and arrows of outrageous fortune
Or to take arms against a sea of troubles,
And by opposing end them. To die – to sleep –
No more; and by a sleep to say we end
The heartache, and the thousand natural shocks
That flesh is heir to. 'Tis a consummation
Devoutly to be wish'd. To die – to sleep.
To sleep, perchance to dream: ay, there's the rub!
For in that sleep of death what dreams may come
When we have shuffled off this mortal coil,
Must give us pause. There's the respect
That makes calamity of so long life.
For who would bear the whips and scorns of time,
Th' oppressor's wrong, the proud man's contumely,
The pangs of despis'd love, the law's delay,
The insolence of office, and the spurns
That patient merit of th' unworthy takes,
When he himself might his quietus make
With a bare bodkin? Who would these fardels bear,
To grunt and sweat under a weary life,
But that the dread of something after death –
The undiscover'd country, from whose bourn
No traveller returns – puzzles the will,
And makes us rather bear those ills we have
Than fly to others that we know not of?
Thus conscience does make cowards of us all,
And thus the native hue of resolution

Is sicklied o'er with the pale cast of thought,
And enterprises of great pith and moment
With this regard their currents turn awry
And lose the name of action.

Hamlet | **Act III, scene 1**

27 JULY

In 1054 Siward, Earl of Northumbria defeats King Macbeth of Scotland, somewhere north of the River Forth

As Scotland suffers under Macbeth's rule, the Thane of Ross hopes for good news from Malcolm, son of the assassinated King Duncan.

MACDUFF
Stands Scotland where it did?

ROSS
Alas, poor country!
Almost afraid to know itself. It cannot
Be call'd our mother, but our grave; where nothing,
But who knows nothing, is once seen to smile;
Where sighs and groans and shrieks that rend the air
Are made, not mark'd; where violent sorrow seems
A modern ecstasy; the dead man's knell
Is there scarce ask'd for who; and good men's lives
Expire before the flowers in their caps,
Dying or ere they sicken.
[...]

MALCOLM
Be't their comfort
We are coming thither: gracious England hath
Lent us good Siward and ten thousand men;
An older and a better soldier none
That Christendom gives out.

Macbeth | Act IV, scene 3

28 JULY

The 9000-year-old skeleton of Kennewick Man is found on the bank of the Columbia River in 1996

Hamlet, in a graveyard, muses on death and bones.

[The gravedigger throws up a skull]

HAMLET
That skull had a tongue in it, and could sing once. How the knave jowls it to the ground, as if 'twere Cain's jawbone, that did the first murder! This might be the pate of a Politician, which this ass now o'erreaches; one that would circumvent God, might it not?

HORATIO
It might, my lord.

HAMLET
Or of a courtier, which could say 'Good morrow, sweet lord! How dost thou, good lord?' This might be my Lord Such-a-one, that prais'd my Lord Such-a-one's horse when he meant to beg it – might it not?

HORATIO
Ay, my lord.

HAMLET
Why, e'en so! and now my Lady Worm's, chapless, and knock'd about the mazzard with a sexton's spade. Here's fine revolution, and we had the trick to see't. Did these bones cost no more the breeding but to play at loggets with 'em? Mine ache to think on't.

GRAVEDIGGER

[Sings]

> *A pickaxe and a spade, a spade,*
> *For and a shrouding sheet;*
> *O, a Pit of clay for to be made*
> *For such a guest is meet.*

[Throws up another skull]

HAMLET

There's another. Why may not that be the skull of a lawyer? Where be his quiddits now, his quillets, his cases, his tenures, and his tricks? Why does he suffer this rude knave now to knock him about the sconce with a dirty shovel, and will not tell him of his action of battery? Hum! This fellow might be in's time a great buyer of land, with his statutes, his recognizances, his fines, his double vouchers, his recoveries. Is this the fine of his fines, and the recovery of his recoveries, to have his fine pate full of fine dirt? Will his vouchers vouch him no more of his purchases, and double ones too, than the length and breadth of a pair of indentures? The very conveyances of his lands will scarcely lie in this box; and must th' inheritor himself have no more, ha?

Hamlet | Act V, scene 1

29 JULY

The end in 1148 of the Siege of Damascus, when Christian crusaders were repelled by Muslim forces

Damascus has lent its name to damask, a woven fabric with a reversible pattern which was traded in the city in the Middle Ages. Shakespeare often uses it as a metaphor for the softness of a lady's skin.

SONNET 130

My mistress' eyes are nothing like the sun;
Coral is far more red than her lips' red;
If snow be white, why then her breasts are dun;
If hairs be wires, black wires grow on her head.
I have seen roses damask'd, red and white,
But no such roses see I in her cheeks;
And in some perfumes is there more delight
Than in the breath that from my mistress reeks.
I love to hear her speak, yet well I know
That music hath a far more pleasing sound;
I grant I never saw a goddess go;
My mistress, when she walks, treads on the ground:
And yet, by heaven, I think my love as rare
As any she belied with false compare.

30 JULY

The death in 1996 of Claudette Colbert, Hollywood star, beloved for her charm and comedic timing

Colbert starred as Cleopatra in the 1934 Cecil B. DeMille epic. Here the Queen of the Nile is playful and in love.

CLEOPATRA
Give me some music; music, moody food
Of us that trade in love.

ATTENDANTS
The music, ho!
[...]

CLEOPATRA
My music playing far off, I will betray
Tawny-finn'd fishes; my bended hook shall pierce
Their slimy jaws; and, as I draw them up,
I'll think them every one an Antony,
And say 'Ah, ha! you're caught.'

CHARMIAN
'Twas merry when
You wager'd on your angling; when your diver
Did hang a salt-fish on his hook, which he
With fervency drew up.

CLEOPATRA

That time – O times! –

I laugh'd him out of patience; and that night

I laugh'd him into patience; and next morn,

Ere the ninth hour, I drunk him to his bed;

Then put my tires and mantles on him, whilst

I wore his sword Philippan.

Antony and Cleopatra | Act II, scene 5

31 JULY

After victory at the Battle of Alexandria in 30 BCE, Mark Antony's army deserts him and he commits suicide

Mark Antony, dying of self-inflicted wounds, is brought to Cleopatra.

CLEOPATRA
Noblest of men, woo't die?
Hast thou no care of me? Shall I abide
In this dull world, which in thy absence is
No better than a sty? O see, my women,
The crown o' th' Earth doth melt. My lord!
[Antony dies]
O, withered is the garland of the war;
The soldier's pole is fall'n; young boys and girls
Are level now with men. The odds is gone,
And there is nothing left remarkable
Beneath the visiting moon.

CHARMIAN
O, quietness, lady!
[...]

CLEOPATRA
No more but e'en a woman, and commanded
By such poor passion as the maid that milks
And does the meanest chares. It were for me
To throw my scepter at the injurious gods,
To tell them that this world did equal theirs
Till they had stolen our jewel. All's but naught.
Patience is sottish, and impatience does
Become a dog that's mad. Then is it sin
To rush into the secret house of death
Ere death dare come to us? How do you, women?

308

What, what, good cheer! Why, how now, Charmian?
My noble girls! Ah, women, women! Look,
Our lamp is spent; it's out. Good sirs, take heart.
We'll bury him; and then, what's brave, what's noble,
Let's do 't after the high Roman fashion
And make death proud to take us. Come, away.
This case of that huge spirit now is cold.
Ah women, women! Come, we have no friend
But resolution and the briefest end.

Antony and Cleopatra | Act IV, scene 15

AUGUST

But, soft! what light through yonder window breaks?
It is the east, and Juliet is the sun.
Arise, fair sun, and kill the envious moon...

Romeo and Juliet | Act II, scene 2

1 AUGUST

Lammas Day, celebrating the first grain harvests; the word lammas means loaf mass in Old English

Juliet's birthday was late on Lammas Eve, and her nurse remembers weaning her.

NURSE
Even or odd, of all days in the year,
Come Lammas-eve at night shall she be fourteen.
Susan and she – God rest all Christian souls! –
Were of an age: well, Susan is with God;
She was too good for me: but, as I said,
On Lammas-eve at night shall she be fourteen;
That shall she, marry; I remember it well.
'Tis since the earthquake now eleven years;
And she was wean'd – I never shall forget it –
Of all the days of the year, upon that day:
For I had then laid wormwood to my dug,
Sitting in the sun under the dove-house wall;
My lord and you were then at Mantua: as –
Nay, I do bear a brain: – but, as I said,
When it did taste the wormwood on the nipple
Of my dug and felt it bitter, pretty fool,
To see it tetchy and fall out with the dug!

Romeo and Juliet | Act I, scene 3

2 AUGUST

In the United States, the signing of the Declaration of Independence in 1776

Jack Cade was a commoner who led a rebellious army of working men against the corrupt English nobility in 1450.

JACK CADE
And you that love the commons, follow me.
Now show yourselves men; 'tis for liberty.
We will not leave one lord, one gentleman:
Spare none but such as go in clouted shoon;
For they are thrifty honest men, and such
As would, but that they dare not, take our parts.

Henry VI, Part 2 | Act IV, scene 2

3 AUGUST

The birthday in 1803 of Joseph Paxton, architect of glasshouses and London's Crystal Palace

The god Jupiter reassures imprisoned Posthumus that the future is bright, and banishes ghosts who have been tormenting him.

JUPITER
No more, you petty spirits of region low,
Offend our hearing; hush! How dare you ghosts
Accuse the thunderer, whose bolt, you know,
Sky-planted batters all rebelling coasts?
Poor shadows of Elysium, hence, and rest
Upon your never-withering banks of flowers:
Be not with mortal accidents opprest;
No care of yours it is; you know 'tis ours.
Whom best I love I cross; to make my gift,
The more delay'd, delighted. Be content;
Your low-laid son our godhead will uplift:
His comforts thrive, his trials well are spent.
Our Jovial star reign'd at his birth, and in
Our temple was he married. Rise, and fade.
He shall be lord of lady Imogen,
And happier much by his affliction made.
This tablet lay upon his breast, wherein
Our pleasure his full fortune doth confine:
and so, away: no further with your din
Express impatience, lest you stir up mine.
Mount, eagle, to my palace crystalline.

Cymbeline | Act V, scene 4

4 AUGUST

The death in 1875 of Danish storyteller Hans Christian Andersen

King Richard II learns that his enemy Bolingbroke is gaining support, and meditates on mortality.

RICHARD II

[...] Let's talk of graves, of worms, and epitaphs;
Make dust our paper and with rainy eyes
Write sorrow on the bosom of the earth,
Let's choose executors and talk of wills:
And yet not so, for what can we bequeath
Save our deposed bodies to the ground?
Our lands, our lives and all are Bolingbroke's,
And nothing can we call our own but death
And that small model of the barren earth
Which serves as paste and cover to our bones.
For God's sake, let us sit upon the ground
And tell sad stories of the death of kings;
How some have been deposed; some slain in war,
Some haunted by the ghosts they have deposed;
Some poison'd by their wives: some sleeping kill'd;
All murder'd: for within the hollow crown
That rounds the mortal temples of a king
Keeps Death his court and there the antic sits,
Scoffing his state and grinning at his pomp,
Allowing him a breath, a little scene,
To monarchize, be fear'd and kill with looks,
Infusing him with self and vain conceit,
As if this flesh which walls about our life,
Were brass impregnable, and humour'd thus
Comes at the last and with a little pin
Bores through his castle wall, and farewell king!

Richard II | Act III, scene 2

5 AUGUST

The death in 2000 of the Star Wars actor Alec Guinness, whose many Shakespearean roles included an acclaimed Romeo in 1939

Romeo is in love.

ROMEO

But, soft! what light through yonder window breaks?

It is the east, and Juliet is the sun.

Arise, fair sun, and kill the envious moon,

Who is already sick and pale with grief,

That thou her maid art far more fair than she:

Be not her maid, since she is envious;

Her vestal livery is but sick and green

And none but fools do wear it; cast it off.

It is my lady, O, it is my love!

O, that she knew she were!

She speaks yet she says nothing: what of that?

Her eye discourses; I will answer it.

I am too bold, 'tis not to me she speaks:

Two of the fairest stars in all the heaven,

Having some business, do entreat her eyes

To twinkle in their spheres till they return.

What if her eyes were there, they in her head?

The brightness of her cheek would shame those stars,

As daylight doth a lamp; her eyes in heaven

Would through the airy region stream so bright

That birds would sing and think it were not night.

See, how she leans her cheek upon her hand!

O, that I were a glove upon that hand,

That I might touch that cheek!

Romeo and Juliet. | **Act II, scene 2**

6 AUGUST

In 1926 American athlete Gertrude Ederle becomes the first woman to swim across the English Channel

Ederle was popularly known as the Queen of the Waves.

SONNET 60

Like as the waves make towards the pebbled shore,
So do our minutes hasten to their end;
Each changing place with that which goes before,
In sequent toil all forwards do contend.
Nativity, once in the main of light,
Crawls to maturity, wherewith being crown'd,
Crooked elipses 'gainst his glory fight,
And Time that gave doth now his gift confound.
Time doth transfix the flourish set on youth
And delves the parallels in beauty's brow,
Feeds on the rarities of nature's truth,
And nothing stands but for his scythe to mow:
And yet to times in hope my verse shall stand,
Praising thy worth, despite his cruel hand.

7 AUGUST

In 1909 Alice Huyler Ramsey becomes the first woman to cross the US by car, from NYC to SF

Imogen is in a hurry to get to Milford Haven, where her beloved Posthumus is waiting.

IMOGEN
[...] O, for a horse with wings! Hear'st thou, Pisanio?
He is at Milford-Haven: read, and tell me
How far 'tis thither. If one of mean affairs
May plod it in a week, why may not I
Glide thither in a day? Then, true Pisanio, –
Who long'st, like me, to see thy lord; who long'st, –
let me bate, – but not like me – yet long'st,
But in a fainter kind: – O, not like me;
For mine's beyond beyond – say, and speak thick;
Love's counsellor should fill the bores of hearing,
To the smothering of the sense – how far it is
To this same blessed Milford: and by the way
Tell me how Wales was made so happy as
To inherit such a haven: but first of all,
How we may steal from hence, and for the gap
That we shall make in time, from our hence-going
And our return, to excuse: but first, how get hence:
Why should excuse be born or e'er begot?
We'll talk of that hereafter. Prithee, speak,
How many score of miles may we well ride
'Twixt hour and hour?

Cymbeline | Act III, scene 2

8 AUGUST

In 1576 the cornerstone of astronomer Tycho Brahe's new observatory, Uraniborg, is laid on the Swedish island of Hven

The illegitimate son of the Earl of Gloucester has no time for horoscopes.

EDMUND
This is the excellent foppery of the world, that, when we are sick in fortune, often the surfeit of our own behaviour, we make guilty of our disasters the sun, the moon, and the stars; as if we were villains on necessity; fools by heavenly compulsion; knaves, thieves, and treachers by spherical pre-dominance; drunkards, liars, and adulterers by an enforc'd obedience of planetary influence; and all that we are evil in, by a divine thrusting on. An admirable evasion of whore-master man, to lay his goatish disposition to the charge of a star! My father compounded with my mother under the Dragon's Tail, and my nativity was under Ursa Major, so that it follows I am rough and lecherous. Fut! I should have been that I am, had the maidenliest star in the firmament twinkled on my bastardizing.

King Lear | Act I, scene 2

9 AUGUST

President Nixon resigns from office in 1974

With his rival Bolingbroke in the ascendency, the king surrenders his crown.

RICHARD II
Ay, no; no, ay; for I must nothing be;
Therefore no no, for I resign to thee.
Now mark me, how I will undo myself;
I give this heavy weight from off my head
And this unwieldy sceptre from my hand,
The pride of kingly sway from out my heart;
With mine own tears I wash away my balm,
With mine own hands I give away my crown,
With mine own tongue deny my sacred state,
With mine own breath release all duty's rites:
All pomp and majesty I do forswear;
My manors, rents, revenues I forego;
My acts, decrees, and statutes I deny:
God pardon all oaths that are broke to me!
God keep all vows unbroke that swear to thee!
Make me, that nothing have, with nothing grieved,
And thou with all pleased, that hast all achieved!
Long mayst thou live in Richard's seat to sit,
And soon lie Richard in an earthly pit!
God save King Harry, unking'd Richard says,
And send him many years of sunshine days!
What more remains?

Richard II | Act IV, scene 1

10 AUGUST

Shakespeare's date for the 1429 Battle of Patay, at which Lord Talbot was captured by the French

The battle actually took place on 18 June but the playwright was often flexible with historical detail. It's true about Sir John Fastolfe though.

MESSENGER
O, no; wherein Lord Talbot was o'erthrown:
The circumstance I'll tell you more at large.
The tenth of August last this dreadful lord,
Retiring from the siege of Orleans,
Having full scarce six thousand in his troop.
By three and twenty thousand of the French
Was round encompassed and set upon.
No leisure had he to enrank his men;
He wanted pikes to set before his archers;
Instead whereof sharp stakes pluck'd out of hedges
They pitched in the ground confusedly,
To keep the horsemen off from breaking in.
More than three hours the fight continued;
Where valiant Talbot above human thought
Enacted wonders with his sword and lance:
Hundreds he sent to hell, and none durst stand him;
Here, there, and every where, enraged he flew:
The French exclaim'd, the devil was in arms;
All the whole army stood agazed on him:
His soldiers spying his undaunted spirit
'A Talbot! a Talbot!' cried out amain
And rush'd into the bowels of the battle.
Here had the conquest fully been seal'd up,
If Sir John Fastolfe had not play'd the coward:
He, being in the vaward, placed behind
With purpose to relieve and follow them,

Cowardly fled, not having struck one stroke.
Hence grew the general wreck and massacre;
Enclosed were they with their enemies:
A base Walloon, to win the Dauphin's grace,
Thrust Talbot with a spear into the back,
Whom all France with their chief assembled strength
Durst not presume to look once in the face.

Henry VI, Part 1 | Act I, scene 1

11 AUGUST

Movie star Hedy Lamarr and composer George Antheil patent a secure guidance system for radio-controlled torpedoes in 1942

Lamarr is best known for playing opposite Victor Mature in Cecil B. DeMille's epic Samson and Delilah. *Samson was brought down by love, as fantastical Spaniard Don Adriano explains.*

DON ADRIANO DE ARMADO
I do affect the very ground, which is base, where
her shoe, which is baser, guided by her foot, which
is basest, doth tread. I shall be forsworn, which
is a great argument of falsehood, if I love. And
how can that be true love which is falsely
attempted? Love is a familiar; Love is a devil:
there is no evil angel but Love. Yet was Samson so
tempted, and he had an excellent strength; yet was
Solomon so seduced, and he had a very good wit.
Cupid's butt-shaft is too hard for Hercules' club;
and therefore too much odds for a Spaniard's rapier.
The first and second cause will not serve my turn;
the passado he respects not, the duello he regards
not: his disgrace is to be called boy; but his
glory is to subdue men. Adieu, valour! rust rapier!
be still, drum! for your manager is in love; yea,
he loveth. Assist me, some extemporal god of rhyme,
for I am sure I shall turn sonnet. Devise, wit;
write, pen; for I am for whole volumes in folio.

Love's Labour's Lost | Act I, scene 2

12 AUGUST

World Elephant Day

Shakespeare characterizes the Greek warrior Ajax as a lumbering elephant, a man of too many ill-fitting parts.

ALEXANDER
They say he is a very man per se,
And stands alone.

CRESSIDA
So do all men, unless they are drunk, sick, or have no legs.

ALEXANDER
This man, lady, hath robbed many beasts of their
particular additions; he is as valiant as the lion,
churlish as the bear, slow as the elephant: a man
into whom nature hath so crowded humours that his
valour is crushed into folly, his folly sauced with
discretion: there is no man hath a virtue that he
hath not a glimpse of, nor any man an attaint but he
carries some stain of it: he is melancholy without
cause, and merry against the hair: he hath the
joints of every thing, but everything so out of joint
that he is a gouty Briareus, many hands and no use,
or purblind Argus, all eyes and no sight.

CRESSIDA
But how should this man, that makes
me smile, make Hector angry?

ALEXANDER

They say he yesterday coped Hector in the battle and struck him down, the disdain and shame whereof hath ever since kept Hector fasting and waking.

Troilus and Cressida | **Act I, scene 2**

13 AUGUST

The death in 1910 of Florence Nightingale, who nursed the injured during the Crimean War

The king, rallying his troops, urges them to wear their wounds with pride.

HENRY V

[...] He that shall live this day, and see old age,
Will yearly on the vigil feast his neighbours,
And say 'To-morrow is Saint Crispian:'
Then will he strip his sleeve and show his scars.
And say 'These wounds I had on Crispin's day.'
Old men forget: yet all shall be forgot,
But he'll remember with advantages
What feats he did that day: then shall our names.
Familiar in his mouth as household words
Harry the king, Bedford and Exeter,
Warwick and Talbot, Salisbury and Gloucester,
Be in their flowing cups freshly remember'd.
This story shall the good man teach his son;
And Crispin Crispian shall ne'er go by,
From this day to the ending of the world,
But we in it shall be remember'd;
We few, we happy few, we band of brothers;
For he to-day that sheds his blood with me
Shall be my brother; be he ne'er so vile,
This day shall gentle his condition:
And gentlemen in England now a-bed
Shall think themselves accursed they were not here,
And hold their manhoods cheap whiles any speaks
That fought with us upon Saint Crispin's day.

Henry V | Act IV, scene 3

14 AUGUST

In 1040, King Duncan of Scotland is killed during a battle with the forces of his cousin Macbeth

Shakespeare has Macbeth murder Duncan in Macbeth's castle, using the daggers of the king's drugged guards.

LADY MACBETH
Alack, I am afraid they have awaked,
And 'tis not done. The attempt and not the deed
Confounds us. Hark! I laid their daggers ready;
He could not miss 'em. Had he not resembled
My father as he slept, I had done't.   *[Enter Macbeth]*
My husband!

MACBETH
I have done the deed. Didst thou not hear a noise?

LADY MACBETH
I heard the owl scream and the crickets cry.
Did not you speak?

MACBETH
When?

LADY MACBETH
Now.

MACBETH
As I descended?

LADY MACBETH
Ay.

Macbeth | Act II, scene 2

15 AUGUST

The birthday in 1912 of Julia Child, who brought French cooking to the American palate

Capulet is throwing a party.

CAPULET
So many guests invite as here are writ.
[Exit First Servant]
Sirrah, go hire me twenty cunning cooks.

Romeo and Juliet | **Act IV, scene 2**

16 AUGUST

The death in 1977 of Elvis Presley, whose first number one hit was 'Heartbreak Hotel'

Hamlet is heartbroken; his mother is to marry his uncle, only a month after the death of his father.

HAMLET
O that this too too solid flesh would melt,
Thaw, and resolve itself into a dew!
Or that the Everlasting had not fix'd
His canon 'gainst self-slaughter! O God! God!
How weary, stale, flat, and unprofitable
Seem to me all the uses of this world!
Fie on't! ah, fie! 'Tis an unweeded garden
That grows to seed; things rank and gross in nature
Possess it merely. That it should come to this!
But two months dead! Nay, not so much, not two.
So excellent a king, that was to this
Hyperion to a satyr; so loving to my mother
That he might not beteem the winds of heaven
Visit her face too roughly. Heaven and earth!
Must I remember? Why, she would hang on him
As if increase of appetite had grown
By what it fed on; and yet, within a month –
Let me not think on't! Frailty, thy name is woman! –
A little month, or ere those shoes were old
With which she followed my poor father's body
Like Niobe, all tears – why she, even she
(O God! a beast that wants discourse of reason
Would have mourn'd longer) married with my uncle;
My father's brother, but no more like my father
Than I to Hercules. Within a month,
Ere yet the salt of most unrighteous tears
Had left the flushing in her galled eyes,

She married. O, most wicked speed, to post
With such dexterity to incestuous sheets!
It is not, nor it cannot come to good.
But break my heart, for I must hold my tongue!

Hamlet | Act I, scene 2

17 AUGUST

The birthday in 1865 in northwest England of the actress Julia Marlowe, famed for her Shakespearean roles

One of Marlowe's final roles was Portia, here trying to persuade Shylock to be merciful and abandon his legal claim.

PORTIA
The quality of mercy is not strain'd,
It droppeth as the gentle rain from heaven
Upon the place beneath: it is twice blest;
It blesseth him that gives and him that takes:
'Tis mightiest in the mightiest: it becomes
The throned monarch better than his crown;
His sceptre shows the force of temporal power,
The attribute to awe and majesty,
Wherein doth sit the dread and fear of kings;
But mercy is above this sceptred sway;
It is enthroned in the hearts of kings,
It is an attribute to God himself;
And earthly power doth then show likest God's
When mercy seasons justice. Therefore, Jew,
Though justice be thy plea, consider this,
That, in the course of justice, none of us
Should see salvation: we do pray for mercy;
And that same prayer doth teach us all to render
The deeds of mercy. I have spoke thus much
To mitigate the justice of thy plea;
Which if thou follow, this strict court of Venice
Must needs give sentence 'gainst the merchant there.

The Merchant of Venice | Act IV, scene 1

18 AUGUST

The birthday in 1587 of Virginia Dare, the first English child to be born on American soil, in the new colony of Roanoke; and the day in 1590 when a supply ship from England found the colony deserted

The fate of Virginia and the other colonists remains a mystery, although they were probably killed by native Americans. In Macbeth, *MacDuff receives terrible news of the fate of his wife and children.*

ROSS
Your castle is surprised; your wife and babes
Savagely slaughter'd: to relate the manner,
Were, on the quarry of these murder'd deer,
To add the death of you.

MALCOLM
Merciful heaven!
What, man! ne'er pull your hat upon your brows;
Give sorrow words: the grief that does not speak
Whispers the o'er-fraught heart and bids it break.

MACDUFF
My children too?

ROSS
Wife, children, servants, all
That could be found.

MACDUFF
And I must be from thence!
My wife kill'd too?

ROSS
I have said.

MALCOLM

Be comforted:

Let's make us medicines of our great revenge,

To cure this deadly grief.

MACDUFF

He has no children. All my pretty ones?

Did you say all? O hell-kite! All?

What, all my pretty chickens and their dam

At one fell swoop?

MALCOLM

Dispute it like a man.

MACDUFF

I shall do so;

But I must also feel it as a man:

I cannot but remember such things were,

That were most precious to me. Did heaven look on,

And would not take their part? Sinful Macduff,

They were all struck for thee! naught that I am,

Not for their own demerits, but for mine,

Fell slaughter on their souls. Heaven rest them now!

Macbeth | Act IV, scene 3

19 AUGUST

The start in 1612 of the trial of the three Samlesbury Witches, falsely accused of child murder and cannibalism by an anti-Catholic priest; all were acquitted

Antipholus, newly arrived in Ephesus, thinks that the place has cast a spell on his servant, making him steal Antipholus's money.

ANTIPHOLUS OF SYRACUSE
Upon my life, by some device or other
The villain is o'er-raught of all my money.
They say this town is full of cozenage,
As, nimble jugglers that deceive the eye,
Dark-working sorcerers that change the mind,
Soul-killing witches that deform the body,
Disguised cheaters, prating mountebanks,
And many such-like liberties of sin:
If it prove so, I will be gone the sooner.
I'll to the Centaur, to go seek this slave:
I greatly fear my money is not safe.

The Comedy of Errors | Act I, scene 2

20 AUGUST

The birthday in 1659 of Henry Every, English pirate, known to his crew as Long Ben

A messenger brings news of a persistent danger to Italian shipping.

MESSENGER
Caesar, I bring thee word,
Menecrates and Menas, famous pirates,
Make the sea serve them, which they ear and wound
With keels of every kind: many hot inroads
They make in Italy; the borders maritime
Lack blood to think on't, and flush youth revolt:
No vessel can peep forth, but 'tis as soon
Taken as seen; for Pompey's name strikes more
Than could his war resisted.

Antony and Cleopatra | Act I, scene 4

21 AUGUST

In 1614, the death of Elizabeth Báthory, Countess of Ecsed in Hungary, accused of torturing and murdering hundreds of young women, and even suspected of vampirism

The accusations may have been politically motivated; too often men resent powerful women. Richard, captured by the French-born Queen Margaret, doesn't hold back in expressing his anger.

RICHARD PLANTAGENET
She-wolf of France, but worse than wolves of France,
Whose tongue more poisons than the adder's tooth!
How ill-beseeming is it in thy sex
To triumph, like an Amazonian trull,
Upon their woes whom fortune captivates!
But that thy face is, vizard-like, unchanging,
Made impudent with use of evil deeds,
I would assay, proud queen, to make thee blush.
To tell thee whence thou camest, of whom derived,
Were shame enough to shame thee, wert thou not shameless.
Thy father bears the type of King of Naples,
Of both the Sicils and Jerusalem,
Yet not so wealthy as an English yeoman.
Hath that poor monarch taught thee to insult?
It needs not, nor it boots thee not, proud queen,
Unless the adage must be verified,
That beggars mounted run their horse to death.
'Tis beauty that doth oft make women proud;
But, God he knows, thy share thereof is small:
'Tis virtue that doth make them most admired;
The contrary doth make thee wonder'd at:
'Tis government that makes them seem divine;
The want thereof makes thee abominable:
Thou art as opposite to every good

As the Antipodes are unto us,
Or as the south to the septentrion.
O tiger's heart wrapt in a woman's hide!
How couldst thou drain the life-blood of the child,
To bid the father wipe his eyes withal,
And yet be seen to bear a woman's face?
Women are soft, mild, pitiful and flexible;
Thou stern, obdurate, flinty, rough, remorseless.
Bids't thou me rage? why, now thou hast thy wish:
Wouldst have me weep? why, now thou hast thy will:
For raging wind blows up incessant showers,
And when the rage allays, the rain begins.
These tears are my sweet Rutland's obsequies:
And every drop cries vengeance for his death,
'Gainst thee, fell Clifford, and thee, false
Frenchwoman.

Henry VI, Part 3 | Act I, scene 4

22 AUGUST

St Guinefort's Day – St Guinefort was a thirteenth-century French greyhound who protected its master's child from a viper

All greyhounds are dogs; but not all dogs are greyhounds; and all murderers are men, but not all men are murderers. Macbeth is interviewing potential assassins.

FIRST MURDERER
We are men, my liege.

MACBETH
Ay, in the catalogue ye go for men;
As hounds and greyhounds, mongrels, spaniels, curs,
Shoughs, water-rugs and demi-wolves, are clept
All by the name of dogs: the valued file
Distinguishes the swift, the slow, the subtle,
The housekeeper, the hunter, every one
According to the gift which bounteous nature
Hath in him closed; whereby he does receive
Particular addition from the bill
That writes them all alike: and so of men.
Now, if you have a station in the file,
Not i' the worst rank of manhood, say 't;
And I will put that business in your bosoms,
Whose execution takes your enemy off,
Grapples you to the heart and love of us,
Who wear our health but sickly in his life,
Which in his death were perfect.

Macbeth | Act III, scene 1

23 AUGUST

In 1991, Tim Berners-Lee, inventor of the World Wide Web, launches the world's first public website – a page of instructions on how to use the internet

Online life is a mixed blessing.

FIRST LORD
The web of our life is of a mingled yarn, good and ill together: our virtues would be proud, if our faults whipped them not; and our crimes would despair, if they were not cherished by our virtues.

All's Well That Ends Well | Act IV, scene 3

24 AUGUST

The birthday in 1578 of John Taylor, Elizabethan ferryman and poet, who used to convey actors, playwrights and audiences across the Thames to the theatres on the south bank

One of Taylor's poems contains the earliest printed reference to Shakespeare's death.

SONNET 71

No longer mourn for me when I am dead
Then you shall hear the surly sullen bell
Give warning to the world that I am fled
From this vile world, with vilest worms to dwell:
Nay, if you read this line, remember not
The hand that writ it; for I love you so
That I in your sweet thoughts would be forgot
If thinking on me then should make you woe.
O, if, I say, you look upon this verse
When I perhaps compounded am with clay,
Do not so much as my poor name rehearse.
But let your love even with my life decay,
Lest the wise world should look into your moan
And mock you with me after I am gone.

25 AUGUST

The day in 1823 when fur trapper Hugh Glass was mauled by a bear and left for dead; he survived

Shakespeare's stage directions can be as entertaining as his dialogue. A sailor urges Antigonus, who is tasked with abandoning an unwanted baby, to board his ship ahead of bad weather.

MARINER
Make your best haste, and go not
Too far i' the land: 'tis like to be loud weather;
Besides, this place is famous for the creatures
Of prey that keep upon't.

ANTIGONUS
Go thou away:
I'll follow instantly. [...] Come, poor babe:
I have heard, but not believed, the spirits o' the dead
May walk again: if such thing be, thy mother
Appear'd to me last night, for ne'er was dream
So like a waking.
[...]
[the storm rises]
The day frowns more and more: thou'rt like to have
A lullaby too rough: I never saw
The heavens so dim by day. A savage clamour!
Well may I get aboard! This is the chase:
I am gone for ever.
[Exit, pursued by a bear]

The Winter's Tale | Act III, scene 3

26 AUGUST

In 1346 the Battle of Crecy in northern France pits the English longbow against the French crossbow

Edward III watched his son the Black Prince lead the English army to a resounding victory, something from which the French still smarted as they prepared for battle at Agincourt in 1415.

KING OF FRANCE
Think we King Harry strong;
And, princes, look you strongly arm to meet him.
The kindred of him hath been flesh'd upon us;
And he is bred out of that bloody strain
That haunted us in our familiar paths:
Witness our too much memorable shame
When Cressy battle fatally was struck,
And all our princes captiv'd by the hand
Of that black name, Edward, Black Prince of Wales;
Whiles that his mountain sire, on mountain standing,
Up in the air, crown'd with the golden sun,
Saw his heroical seed, and smiled to see him,
Mangle the work of nature and deface
The patterns that by God and by French fathers
Had twenty years been made. This is a stem
Of that victorious stock; and let us fear
The native mightiness and fate of him.

Henry V | Act II, scene 4

27 AUGUST

The 'Famous Five' women petition the Canadian government in 1927 to rule on the question, 'Does the word "Persons" in the British North America Act, 1867, include female persons?'

The ruling that women were 'qualified persons' was a breakthrough for gender equality in Canada. Shakespeare's women were acted by men, but here he plays on the ambiguity of a man dressed as a woman appealing to the men and women in the audience.

ROSALIND

It is not the fashion to see the lady the epilogue; but it is no more unhandsome than to see the lord the prologue. If it be true that good wine needs no bush, 'tis true that a good play needs no epilogue. Yet to good wine they do use good bushes; and good plays prove the better by the help of good epilogues. What a case am I in then, that am neither a good epilogue, nor cannot insinuate with you in the behalf of a good play! I am not furnish'd like a beggar; therefore to beg will not become me. My way is to conjure you; and I'll begin with the women. I charge you, O women, for the love you bear to men, to like as much of this play as please you; and I charge you, O men, for the love you bear to women – as I perceive by your simp'ring none of you hates them – that between you and the women the play may please. If I were a woman, I would kiss as many of you as had beards that pleas'd me, complexions that lik'd me, and breaths that I defied not; and, I am sure, as many as have good beards, or good faces, or sweet breaths, will, for my kind offer, when I make curtsy, bid me farewell.

As You Like It | Epilogue

28 AUGUST

In 1963, Martin Luther King Jr delivers his speech, 'I have a dream'

Nick Bottom the weaver wakes up. Did he only dream that he was turned into a donkey and made love with the Queen of the Fairies?

BOTTOM
[Awaking] [...] I have had a most rare vision.
I have had a dream, past the wit of man to
say what dream it was: man is but an ass, if he go
about to expound this dream. Methought I was – there
is no man can tell what. Methought I was – and
methought I had – but man is but a patched fool, if
he will offer to say what methought I had. The eye
of man hath not heard, the ear of man hath not
seen, man's hand is not able to taste, his tongue
to conceive, nor his heart to report, what my dream
was. I will get Peter Quince to write a ballad of
this dream: it shall be called Bottom's Dream,
because it hath no bottom; and I will sing it in the
latter end of a play, before the duke:
peradventure, to make it the more gracious, I shall
sing it at her death.

A Midsummer Night's Dream | Act IV, scene 1

29 AUGUST

The birthday in 1915 of the cinema legend Ingrid Bergman

At Bergman's memorial service in 1982, Sir John Gielgud read this speech from The Tempest.

PROSPERO
You do look, my son, in a moved sort,
As if you were dismay'd: be cheerful, sir.
Our revels now are ended. These our actors,
As I foretold you, were all spirits and
Are melted into air, into thin air:
And, like the baseless fabric of this vision,
The cloud-capp'd towers, the gorgeous palaces,
The solemn temples, the great globe itself,
Ye all which it inherit, shall dissolve
And, like this insubstantial pageant faded,
Leave not a rack behind. We are such stuff
As dreams are made on, and our little life
Is rounded with a sleep. Sir, I am vex'd;
Bear with my weakness; my, brain is troubled:
Be not disturb'd with my infirmity:
If you be pleased, retire into my cell
And there repose: a turn or two I'll walk,
To still my beating mind.

The Tempest | Act IV, scene 1

30 AUGUST

The birthday in 1797 of Mary Shelley, author of Frankenstein; or,
The Modern Prometheus

*The god Prometheus was chained to a rock in the
Caucasus Mountains as punishment for giving
humans the secret of fire. Aaron the Moor professes his
admiration for Tamora, Queen of the Goths.*

AARON
[...] As when the golden sun salutes the morn,
And, having gilt the ocean with his beams,
Gallops the zodiac in his glistering coach,
And overlooks the highest-peering hills;
So Tamora:
Upon her wit doth earthly honour wait,
And virtue stoops and trembles at her frown.
Then, Aaron, arm thy heart, and fit thy thoughts,
To mount aloft with thy imperial mistress,
And mount her pitch, whom thou in triumph long
Hast prisoner held, fetter'd in amorous chains
And faster bound to Aaron's charming eyes
Than is Prometheus tied to Caucasus.
Away with slavish weeds and servile thoughts!
I will be bright, and shine in pearl and gold,
To wait upon this new-made empress.
To wait, said I? to wanton with this queen,
This goddess, this Semiramis, this nymph,
This siren, that will charm Rome's Saturnine,
And see his shipwreck and his commonweal's.

Titus Andronicus | Act II, scene 1

31 AUGUST

The death in Paris of Diana, Princess of Wales, in 1997

Mariana gives the widow's daughter, chaste Diana, some worldly advice.

MARIANA
[...] Well, Diana, take heed of this French earl:
the honour of a maid is her name; and
no legacy is so rich as honesty.

WIDOW
I have told my neighbour how you have been solicited
by a gentleman his companion.

MARIANA
I know that knave; hang him! one Parolles: a
filthy officer he is in those suggestions for the
young earl. Beware of them, Diana; their promises,
enticements, oaths, tokens, and all these engines of
lust, are not the things they go under: many a maid
hath been seduced by them; and the misery is,
example, that so terrible shows in the wreck of
maidenhood, cannot for all that dissuade succession,
but that they are limed with the twigs that threaten
them. I hope I need not to advise you further; but
I hope your own grace will keep you where you are,
though there were no further danger known but the
modesty which is so lost.

All's Well That Ends Well | Act III, scene 5

SEPTEMBER

O' the dreadful thunder-claps, more momentary
And sight-outrunning were not; the fire and cracks
Of sulphurous roaring the most mighty Neptune
Seem to besiege and make his bold waves tremble,
Yea, his dread trident shake.

The Tempest | Act I, scene 2

1 SEPTEMBER

The beginning of meteorological autumn in the Northern Hemisphere

September is a time of harvest and, for the Ancient Romans, games and sporting events before the weather prevents them.

IRIS
You nymphs, call'd Naiads, of the windring brooks,
With your sedged crowns and ever-harmless looks,
Leave your crisp channels and on this green land
Answer your summons; Juno does command:
Come, temperate nymphs, and help to celebrate
A contract of true love; be not too late.
[Enter certain Nymphs]
You sunburnt sicklemen, of August weary,
Come hither from the furrow and be merry:
Make holiday; your rye-straw hats put on
And these fresh nymphs encounter every one
In country footing.
[Enter certain Reapers, properly habited: they join with the Nymphs in a graceful dance; towards the end whereof Prospero starts suddenly, and speaks; after which, to a strange, hollow, and confused noise, they heavily vanish]

The Tempest | Act IV, scene 1

2 SEPTEMBER

A fire in a bakery in Pudding Lane spreads and destroys the medieval centre of London in 1666

Sinon was a Greek spy. He pretended to defect to King Priam's Troy, and persuaded the king to bring the Trojan Horse statue inside the city walls. Greek soldiers hidden inside it then sacked Troy.

Look, look, how listening Priam wets his eyes,
To see those borrow'd tears that Sinon sheds!
Priam, why art thou old and yet not wise?
For every tear he falls a Trojan bleeds:
His eye drops fire, no water thence proceeds;
Those round clear pearls of his, that move thy pity,
Are balls of quenchless fire to burn thy city.

From The Rape of Lucrece

351

3 SEPTEMBER

The death in 1592 of the playwright Robert Greene

*Greene attacked a young Shakespeare for being
an actor who dared to write plays, describing him
as an 'upstart crow beautified with our feathers'.
Shakespeare responded.*

POLONIUS
[...] I have a daughter (have while she is mine),
Who in her duty and obedience, mark,
Hath given me this. Now gather, and surmise.
[Reads a letter from Hamlet]
    To the celestial, and my soul's idol, the most beautified Ophelia—
That's an ill phrase, a vile phrase; 'beautified' is a vile phrase.

Hamlet | Act II, scene 2

4 SEPTEMBER

In 1998 the search engine Google is founded by students at Stanford University

There's no point, Berowne argues, in gaining knowledge just for the sake of having it.

BEROWNE
Why, all delights are vain; but that most vain,
Which with pain purchased doth inherit pain:
As, painfully to pore upon a book
To seek the light of truth; while truth the while
Doth falsely blind the eyesight of his look:
Light seeking light doth light of light beguile:
So, ere you find where light in darkness lies,
Your light grows dark by losing of your eyes.
Study me how to please the eye indeed
By fixing it upon a fairer eye,
Who dazzling so, that eye shall be his heed
And give him light that it was blinded by.
Study is like the heaven's glorious sun
That will not be deep-search'd with saucy looks:
Small have continual plodders ever won
Save base authority from others' books
These earthly godfathers of heaven's lights
That give a name to every fixed star
Have no more profit of their shining nights
Than those that walk and wot not what they are.
Too much to know is to know nought but fame;
And every godfather can give a name.

Love's Labour's Lost | Act I, scene 1

5 SEPTEMBER

*The birthday in 1787 of French geologist François Sulpice Beudant,
after whom the lead- and iron-bearing mineral beudantite is named*

*Hamlet is beside himself with grief, having
accidentally killed his intended father-in-law.*

CLAUDIUS
What, Gertrude? How does Hamlet?

GERTRUDE
Mad as the sea and wind when both contend
Which is the mightier. In his lawless fit
Behind the arras hearing something stir,
Whips out his rapier, cries 'A rat, a rat!'
And in this brainish apprehension kills
The unseen good old man.

CLAUDIUS
O heavy deed!
It had been so with us, had we been there.
His liberty is full of threats to all –
To you yourself, to us, to every one.
Alas, how shall this bloody deed be answer'd?
It will be laid to us, whose providence
Should have kept short, restrain'd, and out of haunt
This mad young man. But so much was our love
We would not understand what was most fit,
But, like the owner of a foul disease,
To keep it from divulging, let it feed
Even on the pith of life. Where is he gone?

GERTRUDE

To draw apart the body he hath kill'd;

O'er whom his very madness, like some ore

Among a mineral of metals base,

Shows itself pure. He weeps for what is done.

Hamlet | Act IV, scene 1

6 SEPTEMBER

The earliest date on which the Abbots Bromley Horn Dance can be performed

Dancers wear reindeer antlers in a ritual which may have its origins in prehistoric fertility rites. On that subject, a clown sees the positive side of his wife's infidelity.

CLOWN
I have been, madam, a wicked creature, as you and all flesh and blood are; and, indeed, I do marry that I may repent.

COUNTESS
Thy marriage, sooner than thy wickedness.

CLOWN
I am out o' friends, madam; and I hope to have friends for my wife's sake.

COUNTESS
Such friends are thine enemies, knave.

CLOWN
You're shallow, madam, in great friends; for the knaves come to do that for me which I am aweary of. He that ears my land spares my team and gives me leave to in the crop; if I be his cuckold, he's my drudge: he that comforts my wife is the cherisher of my flesh and blood; he that cherishes my flesh and blood loves my flesh and blood; he that loves my flesh and blood is my friend: ergo, he that kisses my wife is my friend. If men could be contented to be what they are, there were no fear in marriage; for young Charbon the Puritan and old

Poysam the Papist, howsome'er their hearts are severed in religion, their heads are both one; they may jowl horns together, like any deer i' the herd.

All's Well That Ends Well | Act I, scene 3

7 SEPTEMBER

The birthday in 1533 of the future Queen Elizabeth I, for whom many of Shakespeare's plays were performed

Love's Labour's Lost *was presented at Elizabeth's court over Christmas 1597. At its end, Berowne has been told that he must spend a year in charitable works to win the hand of Rosaline.*

ROSALINE
[...] You shall this twelvemonth term from day to day
Visit the speechless sick and still converse
With groaning wretches; and your task shall be,
With all the fierce endeavor of your wit
To enforce the pained impotent to smile.

BEROWNE
To move wild laughter in the throat of death?
It cannot be; it is impossible:
Mirth cannot move a soul in agony. [...]
A twelvemonth! well; befall what will befall,
I'll jest a twelvemonth in an hospital. [...]
Our wooing doth not end like an old play;
Jack hath not Jill: these ladies' courtesy
Might well have made our sport a comedy.

FERDINAND
Come, sir, it wants a twelvemonth and a day,
And then 'twill end.

BEROWNE
That's too long for a play.

Love's Labour's Lost | Act V, scene 2

8 SEPTEMBER

In 1923, seven US Navy warships run aground on rocks in thick fog at Honda Point, California

Aegeon describes the shipwrecks – his and his wife's – which resulted in two sets of twins being split up, creating the circumstances for the comedy of errors which follows.

AEGEON
[...] For, ere the ships could meet by twice five leagues,
We were encountered by a mighty rock;
Which being violently borne upon,
Our helpful ship was splitted in the midst;
So that, in this unjust divorce of us,
Fortune had left to both of us alike
What to delight in, what to sorrow for.
Her part, poor soul! seeming as burdened
With lesser weight but not with lesser woe,
Was carried with more speed before the wind;
And in our sight they three were taken up
By fishermen of Corinth, as we thought.
At length, another ship had seized on us;
And, knowing whom it was their hap to save,
Gave healthful welcome to their shipwreck'd guests;
And would have reft the fishers of their prey,
Had not their bark been very slow of sail;
And therefore homeward did they bend their course.
Thus have you heard me sever'd from my bliss;
That by misfortunes was my life prolong'd,
To tell sad stories of my own mishaps.

The Comedy of Errors | Act I, scene 1

9 SEPTEMBER

The birthday in 1754 of Captain William Bligh, against whose command the crew of the ship HMS Bounty mutinied

After the murder of Julius Caesar by 'honourable' men, Antony wants Romans to rise up – but insists that he doesn't.

ANTONY
Good friends, sweet friends, let me not stir you up
To such a sudden flood of mutiny.
They that have done this deed are honourable:
What private griefs they have, alas, I know not,
That made them do it: they are wise and honourable,
And will, no doubt, with reasons answer you.
I come not, friends, to steal away your hearts:
I am no orator, as Brutus is;
But, as you know me all, a plain blunt man,
That love my friend; and that they know full well
That gave me public leave to speak of him:
For I have neither wit, nor words, nor worth,
Action, nor utterance, nor the power of speech,
To stir men's blood: I only speak right on;
I tell you that which you yourselves do know;
Show you sweet Caesar's wounds, poor poor dumb mouths,
And bid them speak for me: but were I Brutus,
And Brutus Antony, there were an Antony
Would ruffle up your spirits and put a tongue
In every wound of Caesar that should move
The stones of Rome to rise and mutiny.

ALL
We'll mutiny!

Julius Caesar | Act III, scene 2

10 SEPTEMBER

A patent for a mechanical sewing machine is granted to inventor Elias Howe in 1846

A row breaks out over whether the tailor has fulfilled the order for a dress for Petruchio's wife. Grumio is Petruchio's servant.

PETRUCHIO
Thy gown? Why, ay. Come, tailor, let us see't.
O mercy, God! what masquing stuff is here?
What's this? A sleeve? 'Tis like a demi-cannon.
What, up and down, carv'd like an appletart?
Here's snip and nip and cut and slish and slash,
Like to a censer in a barber's shop.
Why, what a devil's name, tailor, call'st thou this?

TAILOR
You bid me make it orderly and well,
According to the fashion and the time.
[...]

PETRUCHIO
O monstrous arrogance! Thou liest, thou thread, thou thimble,
Thou yard, three-quarters, half-yard, quarter, nail,
Thou flea, thou nit, thou winter-cricket thou –
Brav'd in mine own house with a skein of thread!
Away, thou rag, thou quantity, thou remnant;
Or I shall so bemete thee with thy yard
As thou shalt think on prating whilst thou liv'st!
I tell thee, I, that thou hast marr'd her gown.

TAILOR
Your worship is deceiv'd; the gown is made
Just as my master had direction.

Grumio gave order how it should be done.

[...]

Why, here is the note of the fashion to testify.

[Reads]

    Imprimis, a loose-bodied gown—

GRUMIO

Master, if ever I said loose-bodied gown, sew me in the
skirts of it and beat me to death with a bottom of brown bread; I
said a gown.

TAILOR

[Reads]

    With a small compass'd cape—

GRUMIO

I confess the cape.

TAILOR

[Reads]

    With a trunk sleeve—

GRUMIO

I confess two sleeves.

TAILOR

[Reads]

    The sleeves curiously cut.

GRUMIO

Error i' th' bill, sir; error i' th' bill! I commanded the
sleeves should be cut out, and sew'd up again; and that I'll
prove upon thee, though thy little finger be armed in a thimble.

The Taming of the Shrew | Act IV, scene 3

11 SEPTEMBER

Several sieges end – Drogheda's by Oliver Cromwell in 1649; Vienna's by the Ottoman Empire in 1683; and Barcelona's by the Bourbon army in 1714

The audience is invited to use its imagination in picturing the Siege of Harfleur.

THE CHORUS

[...] Work, work your thoughts, and therein see a siege;
Behold the ordnance on their carriages,
With fatal mouths gaping on girded Harfleur.
Suppose the ambassador from the French comes back;
Tells Harry that the king doth offer him
Katharine his daughter, and with her, to dowry,
Some petty and unprofitable dukedoms.
The offer likes not: and the nimble gunner
With linstock now the devilish cannon touches,
[Alarum, and chambers go off]
And down goes all before them. Still be kind,
And eke out our performance with your mind.

Henry V | Act III, prologue

12 SEPTEMBER

Defenders Day in Baltimore, Maryland, celebrating the 1814 victory of the town over an attacking British army, thanks to defences planned and built long in advance

Local poet Francis Scott Key was there and wrote the words of The Star-Spangled Banner *after the event. In France, the Dauphin advices readiness even in peacetime.*

THE DAUPHIN
My most redoubted father,
It is most meet we arm us 'gainst the foe;
For peace itself should not so dull a kingdom,
Though war nor no known quarrel were in question,
But that defences, musters, preparations,
Should be maintain'd, assembled and collected,
As were a war in expectation.
Therefore, I say 'tis meet we all go forth
To view the sick and feeble parts of France:
And let us do it with no show of fear;
No, with no more than if we heard that England
Were busied with a Whitsun morris-dance:
For, my good liege, she is so idly king'd,
Her sceptre so fantastically borne
By a vain, giddy, shallow, humorous youth,
That fear attends her not.

Henry V | Act II, scene 4

13 SEPTEMBER

The death in 1598 of Philip II, who ruled Spain during its Golden Age and sent fleets of ships to attack England on three unsuccessful occasions

Like many Englishmen before and since, Shakespeare pokes fun at the other countries of Europe.

ANTIPHOLUS OF SYRACUSE
What's her name?

DROMIO OF SYRACUSE
Nell, sir; no longer from head to foot than from hip to hip:
she is spherical, like a globe; I could find out countries in her.

ANTIPHOLUS OF SYRACUSE
In what part of her body stands Ireland?

DROMIO OF SYRACUSE
Marry, in her buttocks: I found it out by the bogs.

ANTIPHOLUS OF SYRACUSE
Where Scotland?

DROMIO OF SYRACUSE
I found it by the barrenness; hard in the palm of the hand.

ANTIPHOLUS OF SYRACUSE
Where France?

DROMIO OF SYRACUSE
In her forehead; armed and reverted, making war
against her heir.

ANTIPHOLUS OF SYRACUSE
Where England?

DROMIO OF SYRACUSE
I looked for the chalky cliffs, but I could find no
whiteness in them; but I guess it stood in her chin,
by the salt rheum that ran between France and it.

ANTIPHOLUS OF SYRACUSE
Where Spain?

DROMIO OF SYRACUSE
Faith, I saw it not; but I felt it hot in her breath.

ANTIPHOLUS OF SYRACUSE
Where America, the Indies?

DROMIO OF SYRACUSE
Oh, sir, upon her nose all o'er embellished with
rubies, carbuncles, sapphires, declining their rich
aspect to the hot breath of Spain; who sent whole
armadoes of caracks to be ballast at her nose.

ANTIPHOLUS OF SYRACUSE
Where stood Belgia, the Netherlands?

DROMIO OF SYRACUSE
Oh, sir, I did not look so low.

The Comedy of Errors | Act III, scene 2

14 SEPTEMBER

In Britain Wednesday, 2 September 1752 was followed by Thursday, 14 September 1752, as the country finally adopted the Gregorian calendar, bringing it into line with most other European nations.

Hamlet, visited by the spirit of his late father, is convinced that the natural order has been disrupted, and that he must right a wrong which is preventing his father's ghost from resting in peace.

HAMLET
Rest, rest, perturbed spirit! So, gentlemen,
With all my love I do commend me to you;
And what so poor a man as Hamlet is
May do t' express his love and friending to you,
God willing, shall not lack. Let us go in together;
And still your fingers on your lips, I pray.
The time is out of joint. O cursed spite
That ever I was born to set it right!

Hamlet | Act I, scene 5

15 SEPTEMBER

In 1835 Charles Darwin, aboard HMS Beagle, *arrives at the Galapagos Islands*

Spanish explorers first visited the islands in the sixteenth century, and named them after their most famous inhabitants – 'galápagos' is Spanish for tortoises. Romeo has seen one.

ROMEO
[...] I do remember an apothecary –
And hereabouts he dwells – which late I noted
In tatter'd weeds, with overwhelming brows,
Culling of simples; meagre were his looks,
Sharp misery had worn him to the bones:
And in his needy shop a tortoise hung,
An alligator stuff'd, and other skins
Of ill-shaped fishes; and about his shelves
A beggarly account of empty boxes,
Green earthen pots, bladders and musty seeds,
Remnants of packthread and old cakes of roses,
Were thinly scatter'd, to make up a show.
Noting this penury, to myself I said
'An if a man did need a poison now,
Whose sale is present death in Mantua,
Here lives a caitiff wretch would sell it him.'
O, this same thought did but forerun my need;
And this same needy man must sell it me.

Romeo and Juliet | **Act V, scene 1**

16 SEPTEMBER

Thirty-five Pilgrims set sail on the Mayflower *from Plymouth in 1620, bound for Virginia*

Misanthropic Timon turns his back on the trappings of the establishment and leaves Athens.

TIMON
[...] Piety, and fear,
Religion to the gods, peace, justice, truth,
Domestic awe, night-rest, and neighbourhood,
Instruction, manners, mysteries, and trades,
Degrees, observances, customs, and laws,
Decline to your confounding contraries,
And let confusion live! Plagues, incident to men,
Your potent and infectious fevers heap
On Athens, ripe for stroke! Thou cold sciatica,
Cripple our senators, that their limbs may halt
As lamely as their manners. Lust and liberty
Creep in the minds and marrows of our youth,
That 'gainst the stream of virtue they may strive,
And drown themselves in riot! Itches, blains,
Sow all the Athenian bosoms; and their crop
Be general leprosy! Breath infect breath,
at their society, as their friendship, may
merely poison! Nothing I'll bear from thee,
But nakedness, thou detestable town!

Timon of Athens | Act IV, scene 1

369

17 SEPTEMBER

Birthday in 1783 of Nadezhda Durova, a woman who fought in the Napoleonic Wars disguised as a man

Cross-dressing abounds in Shakespeare, for plot purposes. Rosalind thinks she will be safer travelling as a young man.

ROSALIND
Were it not better,
Because that I am more than common tall,
That I did suit me all points like a man?
A gallant curtle-axe upon my thigh,
A boar spear in my hand; and – in my heart
Lie there what hidden woman's fear there will –
We'll have a swashing and a martial outside,
As many other mannish cowards have
That do outface it with their semblances.

As You Like It | Act I, scene 3

18 SEPTEMBER

Henry D. Washburn of Indiana names Old Faithful, a geyser in Yellowstone Park, in 1870

Venus invites Adonis to explore the features of her landscape.

'Fondling,' she saith, 'since I have hemm'd thee here
Within the circuit of this ivory pale,
I'll be a park, and thou shalt be my deer;
Feed where thou wilt, on mountain or in dale:
Graze on my lips; and if those hills be dry,
Stray lower, where the pleasant fountains lie.'

From Venus and Adonis

19 SEPTEMBER

In 1846 two French children see a vision of the Virgin Mary while watching their sheep near La Salette

Apparitions often appear in Shakespeare to prick the consciences of murderers.

BRUTUS
[...] Look, Lucius, here's the book I sought for so;
I put it in the pocket of my gown.
[...]
Let me see, let me see; is not the leaf turn'd down
Where I left reading? Here it is, I think.
How ill this taper burns!
[Enter the Ghost of Caesar]
Ha! Who comes here?
I think it is the weakness of mine eyes
That shapes this monstrous apparition.
It comes upon me. Art thou any thing?
Art thou some god, some angel, or some devil,
That makest my blood cold and my hair to stare?
Speak to me what thou art.

CAESAR
Thy evil spirit, Brutus.

Julius Caesar | Act IV, scene 3

20 SEPTEMBER

Birthday in 1924 of American singer Gogi Grant, who recorded an album of songs from the musical Kiss Me Kate *with Howard Keel*

Kiss Me Kate *is based on* The Taming of the Shrew. *Grant sang the songs of Bianca, who is being woo'd by two suitors pretending to be her music and Latin tutors. Neither knows his subject.*

BIANCA
Why, gentlemen, you do me double wrong
To strive for that which resteth in my choice.
I am no breeching scholar in the schools,
I'll not be tied to hours nor 'pointed times,
But learn my lessons as I please myself.
And to cut off all strife: here sit we down;
Take you your instrument, play you the whiles!
His lecture will be done ere you have tun'd.

HORTENSIO [AS MUSIC TUTOR]
You'll leave his lecture when I am in tune?

LUCENTIO [AS LATIN TUTOR]
That will be never – tune your instrument.

BIANCA
Where left we last?

LUCENTIO
Here, madam:
'Hic ibat Simois, hic est Sigeia tellus,
Hic steterat Priami regia celsa senis.'

BIANCA
Construe them.

LUCENTIO

'Hic ibat' – as I told you before

'Simois' – I am Lucentio

'hic est' – son unto Vincentio of Pisa

'Sigeia tellus' – disguised thus to get your love

'celsa senis' – that we might beguile the old pantaloon.

HORTENSIO

Madam, my instrument's in tune.

BIANCA

Let's hear. O fie! the treble jars.

LUCENTIO

Spit in the hole, man, and tune again.

The Taming of the Shrew | Act III, scene 1

21 SEPTEMBER

The death in 1974 of Jacqueline Susann, author of Valley of the Dolls, *a novel of sex, drugs and show business*

Romeo visits a pharmacist whom he knows will be prepared to break the law.

ROMEO
[...] What, ho! apothecary!

APOTHECARY
Who calls so loud?

ROMEO
Come hither, man. I see that thou art poor:
Hold, there is forty ducats: let me have
A dram of poison, such soon-speeding gear
As will disperse itself through all the veins
That the life-weary taker may fall dead
And that the trunk may be discharged of breath
As violently as hasty powder fired
Doth hurry from the fatal cannon's womb.

APOTHECARY
Such mortal drugs I have; but Mantua's law
Is death to any he that utters them.

ROMEO
Art thou so bare and full of wretchedness,
And fear'st to die? famine is in thy cheeks,
Need and oppression starveth in thine eyes,
Contempt and beggary hangs upon thy back;
The world is not thy friend nor the world's law;
The world affords no law to make thee rich;
Then be not poor, but break it, and take this.

APOTHECARY

My poverty, but not my will, consents.

ROMEO

I pay thy poverty, and not thy will.

APOTHECARY

Put this in any liquid thing you will,

And drink it off; and, if you had the strength

Of twenty men, it would dispatch you straight.

Romeo and Juliet | **Act V, scene 1**

22 SEPTEMBER

The Autumn Equinox

Titania and Oberon's quarrel has upset the seasons.

TITANIA
These are the forgeries of jealousy:
And never, since the middle summer's spring,
Met we on hill, in dale, forest or mead,
By paved fountain or by rushy brook,
Or in the beached margent of the sea,
To dance our ringlets to the whistling wind,
But with thy brawls thou hast disturb'd our sport.
Therefore the winds, piping to us in vain,
As in revenge, have suck'd up from the sea
Contagious fogs; which falling in the land
Have every pelting river made so proud
That they have overborne their continents:
The ox hath therefore stretch'd his yoke in vain,
The ploughman lost his sweat, and the green corn
Hath rotted ere his youth attain'd a beard;
The fold stands empty in the drowned field,
And crows are fatted with the murrion flock;
The nine men's morris is fill'd up with mud,
And the quaint mazes in the wanton green
For lack of tread are undistinguishable:
The human mortals want their winter here;
No night is now with hymn or carol blest:
Therefore the moon, the governess of floods,
Pale in her anger, washes all the air,
That rheumatic diseases do abound:
And thorough this distemperature we see
The seasons alter: hoary-headed frosts
Far in the fresh lap of the crimson rose,
And on old Hiems' thin and icy crown

An odorous chaplet of sweet summer buds
Is, as in mockery, set: the spring, the summer,
The childing autumn, angry winter, change
Their wonted liveries, and the mazed world,
By their increase, now knows not which is which:
And this same progeny of evils comes
From our debate, from our dissension;
We are their parents and original.

A Midsummer Night's Dream | Act II, scene 1

23 SEPTEMBER

In 1884, the steamship Arctique *runs aground; a rescue expedition stumbles across rich gold deposits in a local stream, sparking the Tierra del Fuego goldrush*

Romeo has just bought poison in exchange for gold.

ROMEO

There is thy gold, worse poison to men's souls,
Doing more murders in this loathsome world,
Than these poor compounds that thou mayst not sell.
I sell thee poison; thou hast sold me none.
Farewell: buy food, and get thyself in flesh.
Come, cordial and not poison, go with me
To Juliet's grave; for there must I use thee.

Romeo and Juliet | Act V, scene 1

24 SEPTEMBER

Birthday in 1870 of Georges Claude, French inventor of neon lighting

A king in love with a princess reads the sonnet he has written for her, which labours the metaphor of light. A rival in love overhears him.

BEROWNE

[...] Here comes one with a paper: God give him grace to groan!

[Hides – enter King Ferdinand, with a paper]

FERDINAND

Ay me!

BEROWNE

[Aside] Shot, by heaven! Proceed, sweet Cupid: thou hast thumped him with thy bird-bolt under the left pap. In faith, secrets!

FERDINAND

[Reads]

> So sweet a kiss the golden sun gives not
> To those fresh morning drops upon the rose,
> As thy eye-beams, when their fresh rays have smote
> The night of dew that on my cheeks down flows:
> Nor shines the silver moon one half so bright
> Through the transparent bosom of the deep,
> As doth thy face through tears of mine give light;
> Thou shinest in every tear that I do weep:
> No drop but as a coach doth carry thee;
> So ridest thou triumphing in my woe.
> Do but behold the tears that swell in me,
> And they thy glory through my grief will show:
> But do not love thyself; then thou wilt keep

My tears for glasses, and still make me weep.
O queen of queens! how far dost thou excel,
No thought can think, nor tongue of mortal tell.

Love's Labour's Lost | Act IV, scene 3

25 SEPTEMBER

The birthday in 1929 of British comedian Ronnie Barker, who once skipped school to see Laurence Olivier in Henry V, *and later appeared as* Quince *in* A Midsummer Night's Dream

Quince is putting on a play for the Duke. One of his actors is enthusiastically willing to try his hand at anything.

QUINCE
You, Nick Bottom, are set down for Pyramus.

BOTTOM
What is Pyramus? a lover, or a tyrant?

QUINCE
A lover, that kills himself most gallant for love.

BOTTOM
That will ask some tears in the true performing of it: if I do it, let the audience look to their eyes; I will move storms, I will condole in some measure. To the rest: yet my chief humour is for a tyrant: I could play Ercles rarely, or a part to tear a cat in, to make all split:
The raging rocks
And shivering shocks
Shall break the locks
Of prison gates;
And Phibbus' car
Shall shine from far
And make and mar
The foolish Fates.
This was lofty! Now name the rest of the players. This is Ercles' vein, a tyrant's vein; a lover is more condoling.
[...]

QUINCE
Flute, you must take Thisby on you.
[...]

FLUTE
Nay, faith, let me not play a woman; I have a beard coming.
[...]

BOTTOM
An I may hide my face, let me play Thisby too, I'll speak
in a monstrous little voice. 'Thisne, Thisne; Ah, Pyramus,
lover dear! thy Thisby dear, and lady dear!'

QUINCE
No, no; you must play Pyramus: and, Flute, you Thisby.
[...]

SNUG
Have you the lion's part written? pray you, if it be, give it
me, for I am slow of study.

QUINCE
You may do it extempore, for it is nothing but roaring.

BOTTOM
Let me play the lion too: I will roar, that I will do any
man's heart good to hear me; I will roar, that I will make
the duke say 'Let him roar again, let him roar again.'

A Midsummer Night's Dream | Act I, scene 2

26 SEPTEMBER

In 1580 sea captain Sir Francis Drake returns to Plymouth after three years, having circumnavigated the globe

The King of the Fairies hatches a plan to distract his Queen from her lover.

OBERON
That very time I saw, but thou couldst not,
Flying between the cold moon and the earth,
Cupid all arm'd: a certain aim he took.
[...]
Yet mark'd I where the bolt of Cupid fell:
It fell upon a little western flower,
Before milk-white, now purple with love's wound,
And maidens call it love-in-idleness.
Fetch me that flower; the herb I shew'd thee once:
The juice of it on sleeping eye-lids laid
Will make or man or woman madly dote
Upon the next live creature that it sees.
Fetch me this herb; and be thou here again
Ere the leviathan can swim a league.

PUCK
I'll put a girdle round about the earth
In forty minutes. *[Exit]*

OBERON
Having once this juice,
I'll watch Titania when she is asleep,
And drop the liquor of it in her eyes.
The next thing then she waking looks upon,
Be it on lion, bear, or wolf, or bull,
On meddling monkey, or on busy ape,
She shall pursue it with the soul of love:

And ere I take this charm from off her sight,
As I can take it with another herb,
I'll make her render up her page to me.

A Midsummer Night's Dream | Act II, scene 1

27 SEPTEMBER

United Nations World Tourism Day since 1980

A Spanish tourist is causing a stir in King Ferdinand's court.

FERDINAND
Our court, you know, is haunted
With a refined traveller of Spain;
A man in all the world's new fashion planted,
That hath a mint of phrases in his brain;
One whom the music of his own vain tongue
Doth ravish like enchanting harmony;
A man of complements, whom right and wrong
Have chose as umpire of their mutiny:
This child of fancy, that Armado hight,
For interim to our studies shall relate
In high-born words the worth of many a knight
From tawny Spain lost in the world's debate.
How you delight, my lords, I know not, I;
But, I protest, I love to hear him lie
And I will use him for my minstrelsy.

Love's Labour's Lost | **Act I, scene 1**

28 SEPTEMBER

St Leoba's Day – she died on this day in 782, and miracles observed at her grave include the freeing of a man whose arms were bound by iron rings

Although Adonis shows no interest in Venus, his horse's lust is greatly aroused by a pretty jennet – a breeding mare of Spanish blood.

And forth she rushes, snorts and neighs aloud:
The strong-neck'd steed, being tied unto a tree,
Breaketh his rein, and to her straight goes he.

Imperiously he leaps, he neighs, he bounds,
And now his woven girths he breaks asunder;
The bearing earth with his hard hoof he wounds,
Whose hollow womb resounds like heaven's thunder;
The iron bit he crusheth 'tween his teeth,
Controlling what he was controlled with.

His ears up-prick'd; his braided hanging mane
Upon his compass'd crest now stand on end;
His nostrils drink the air, and forth again,
As from a furnace, vapours doth he send:
His eye, which scornfully glisters like fire,
Shows his hot courage and his high desire.

Sometime he trots, as if he told the steps,
With gentle majesty and modest pride;
Anon he rears upright, curvets and leaps,
As who should say 'Lo, thus my strength is tried,
And this I do to captivate the eye
Of the fair breeder that is standing by.'

From Venus and Adonis

387

29 SEPTEMBER

The death in 1902 of Scottish weaver, actor and bad poet William McGonagall, who entertained his fellow weavers with recitations of Shakespeare and once refused to die on stage in the role of Macbeth

As King Malcolm's army gains the upper hand, Macbeth is confronted by the man whose wife and children he murdered.

MACDUFF
Turn, hell-hound, turn!

MACBETH
Of all men else I have avoided thee:
But get thee back; my soul is too much charged
With blood of thine already.

MACDUFF
I have no words:
My voice is in my sword: thou bloodier villain
Than terms can give thee out!
[They fight]

MACBETH
[...] Let fall thy blade on vulnerable crests;
I bear a charmed life, which must not yield,
To one of woman born.

MACDUFF
Despair thy charm;
And let the angel whom thou still hast served
Tell thee, Macduff was from his mother's womb
Untimely ripp'd.

MACBETH

Accursed be that tongue that tells me so,
For it hath cow'd my better part of man!
And be these juggling fiends no more believed,
That palter with us in a double sense;
That keep the word of promise to our ear,
And break it to our hope. I'll not fight with thee.

MACDUFF

Then yield thee, coward,
And live to be the show and gaze o' the time:
We'll have thee, as our rarer monsters are,
Painted on a pole, and underwrit,
'Here may you see the tyrant.'

MACBETH

I will not yield,
To kiss the ground before young Malcolm's feet,
And to be baited with the rabble's curse.
Though Birnam wood be come to Dunsinane,
And thou opposed, being of no woman born,
Yet I will try the last. Before my body
I throw my warlike shield. Lay on, Macduff,
And damn'd be him that first cries, 'Hold, enough!'

Macbeth | Act V, scene 8

30 SEPTEMBER

Henry IV becomes King of England in 1399; his reign will be plagued by rebellion and border warfare

Hal, heir to Henry IV's throne, prefers the company of lowlife criminals and drunkards. Henry urges his son to behave with more dignity, as Henry did when his predecessor Richard II was king.

HENRY IV

God pardon thee! yet let me wonder, Harry,
At thy affections, which do hold a wing
Quite from the flight of all thy ancestors.
Thy place in council thou hast rudely lost,
Which by thy younger brother is supplied,
And art almost an alien to the hearts
Of all the court and princes of my blood:
The hope and expectation of thy time
Is ruin'd, and the soul of every man
Prophetically doth forethink thy fall.
Had I so lavish of my presence been,
So common-hackney'd in the eyes of men,
So stale and cheap to vulgar company,
Opinion, that did help me to the crown,
Had still kept loyal to possession
And left me in reputeless banishment,
A fellow of no mark nor likelihood.
By being seldom seen, I could not stir
But like a comet I was wonder'd at;
That men would tell their children 'This is he;'
Others would say 'Where, which is Bolingbroke?'
And then I stole all courtesy from heaven,
And dress'd myself in such humility
That I did pluck allegiance from men's hearts,
Loud shouts and salutations from their mouths,

Even in the presence of the crowned king.
Thus did I keep my person fresh and new;
My presence, like a robe pontifical,
Ne'er seen but wonder'd at: and so my state,
Seldom but sumptuous, showed like a feast
And won by rareness such solemnity.
The skipping king, he ambled up and down
With shallow jesters and rash bavin wits,
[...]
Grew a companion to the common streets;
That, being daily swallow'd by men's eyes,
They surfeited with honey and began
To loathe the taste of sweetness, whereof a little
More than a little is by much too much.
So when he had occasion to be seen,
He was but as the cuckoo is in June,
Heard, not regarded; seen, but with such eyes
[...]
But rather drowzed and hung their eyelids down,
Slept in his face and render'd such aspect
As cloudy men use to their adversaries,
Being with his presence glutted, gorged and full.
And in that very line, Harry, standest thou;
For thou has lost thy princely privilege
With vile participation: not an eye
But is a-weary of thy common sight,
Save mine, which hath desired to see thee more;
Which now doth that I would not have it do,
Make blind itself with foolish tenderness.

Henry IV, Part 1 | Act III, scene 2

OCTOBER

Double, double toil and trouble;
Fire burn, and cauldron bubble.

Macbeth | Act IV, scene 1

1 OCTOBER

Publication day in 1861 of Mrs Beeton's Book of Household Management, *the housewife's bible*

In an unlikely love match, Petruchio has married the reluctant Kate.

PETRUCHIO
They shall go forward, Kate, at thy command.
Obey the bride, you that attend on her;
Go to the feast, revel and domineer,
Carouse full measure to her maidenhead;
Be mad and merry, or go hang yourselves.
But for my bonny Kate, she must with me.
Nay, look not big, nor stamp, nor stare, nor fret;
I will be master of what is mine own –
She is my goods, my chattels, she is my house,
My household stuff, my field, my barn,
My horse, my ox, my ass, my any thing,
And here she stands; touch her whoever dare;
I'll bring mine action on the proudest he
That stops my way in Padua. Grumio,
Draw forth thy weapon; we are beset with thieves;
Rescue thy mistress, if thou be a man.
Fear not, sweet wench; they shall not touch thee, Kate;
I'll buckler thee against a million.

The Taming of the Shrew | Act III, scene 2

2 OCTOBER

When Vikings try to reassert their dominance of the west coast of Scotland in 1263, they are defeated at the Battle of Largs

King Duncan of Scotland hears reports from another engagement with the Vikings.

SERGEANT
[...] No sooner justice had with valour arm'd
Compell'd these skipping kerns to trust their heels,
But the Norweyan lord surveying vantage,
With furbish'd arms and new supplies of men
Began a fresh assault.

DUNCAN
Dismay'd not this
Our captains, Macbeth and Banquo?

SERGEANT
Yes;
As sparrows eagles, or the hare the lion.
If I say sooth, I must report they were
As cannons overcharged with double cracks, so they
Doubly redoubled strokes upon the foe:
Except they meant to bathe in reeking wounds,
Or memorise another Golgotha,
I cannot tell. [...] *[Enter Ross]*

DUNCAN
Whence camest thou, worthy thane?

ROSS
From Fife, great king;
Where the Norweyan banners flout the sky
And fan our people cold. Norway himself,

With terrible numbers,
Assisted by that most disloyal traitor
The thane of Cawdor, began a dismal conflict;
Till that Bellona's bridegroom, lapp'd in proof,
Confronted him with self-comparisons,
Point against point rebellious, arm 'gainst arm.
Curbing his lavish spirit: and, to conclude,
The victory fell on us.

DUNCAN
Great happiness!

Macbeth | Act I, scene 2

3 OCTOBER

German Unity Day, celebrating the reunification in 1990 of East and West Germany, divided since 1945

The kings of England and France are newly united by the wedding of their niece and son. But the Pope wants war between their two countries. Philip of France protests.

KING PHILIP

[...] This royal hand and mine are newly knit,
And the conjunction of our inward souls
Married in league, coupled and linked together
With all religious strength of sacred vows;
The latest breath that gave the sound of words
Was deep-sworn faith, peace, amity, true love
Between our kingdoms and our royal selves,
And even before this truce, but new before,
No longer than we well could wash our hands
To clap this royal bargain up of peace,
Heaven knows, they were besmear'd and over-stain'd
With slaughter's pencil, where revenge did paint
The fearful difference of incensed kings:
And shall these hands, so lately purged of blood,
So newly join'd in love, so strong in both,
Unyoke this seizure and this kind regreet?
Play fast and loose with faith? so jest with heaven,
Make such unconstant children of ourselves,
As now again to snatch our palm from palm,
Unswear faith sworn, and on the marriage-bed
Of smiling peace to march a bloody host,
And make a riot on the gentle brow
Of true sincerity? O, holy sir,

My reverend father, let it not be so!
Out of your grace, devise, ordain, impose
Some gentle order; and then we shall be blest
To do your pleasure and continue friends.

King John | Act III, scene 1

4 OCTOBER

The death in 1951 of Henrietta Lacks, whose immortalized cancer cells live on as a vital tool for medical research

Shakespeare wrote several so-called procreation sonnets, in which he recommended having children as a way of living on after one's own death.

SONNET 13

O, that you were yourself! but, love, you are
No longer yours than you yourself here live:
Against this coming end you should prepare,
And your sweet semblance to some other give.
So should that beauty which you hold in lease
Find no determination: then you were
Yourself again after yourself's decease,
When your sweet issue your sweet form should bear.
Who lets so fair a house fall to decay,
Which husbandry in honour might uphold
Against the stormy gusts of winter's day
And barren rage of death's eternal cold?
O, none but unthrifts! Dear my love, you know
You had a father: let your son say so.

5 OCTOBER

The death in 1606 of Philippe Desportes, a French sonneteer whose style was a great influence on English poets of the time

Louis, Dauphin of France, unadvisedly admits to having written a sonnet for his horse – a palfrey is a gentle horse, especially one ridden by women.

CONSTABLE OF FRANCE
Indeed, my lord, it is a most absolute and excellent horse.

LOUIS THE DAUPHIN
It is the prince of palfreys; his neigh is like the bidding of a monarch and his countenance enforces homage.

DUKE OF ORLEANS
No more, cousin.

LOUIS THE DAUPHIN
Nay, the man hath no wit that cannot, from the rising of the lark to the lodging of the lamb, vary deserved praise on my palfrey: it is a theme as fluent as the sea: turn the sands into eloquent tongues, and my horse is argument for them all: 'tis a subject for a sovereign to reason on, and for a sovereign's sovereign to ride on; and for the world, familiar to us and unknown to lay apart their particular functions and wonder at him. I once writ a sonnet in his praise and began thus: 'Wonder of nature—

DUKE OF ORLEANS
I have heard a sonnet begin so to one's mistress.

LOUIS THE DAUPHIN

Then did they imitate that which I composed to my courser, for my horse is my mistress.

Henry V | Act III, scene 7

6 OCTOBER

The birthday in 1573 of Henry Wriothesley, 3rd Earl of Southampton, to whom Shakespeare dedicated his narrative poems The Rape of Lucrece *and* Venus and Adonis

Wriothesley may also have been the Fair Youth, the addressee of many of Shakespeare's sonnets.

The love I dedicate to your lordship is without end; whereof this pamphlet, without beginning, is but a superfluous moiety. The warrant I have of your honourable disposition, not the worth of my untutored lines, makes it assured of acceptance. What I have done is yours; what I have to do is yours; being part in all I have, devoted yours. Were my worth greater, my duty would show greater; meantime, as it is, it is bound to your lordship, to whom I wish long life, still lengthened with all happiness.

Shakespeare's dedication to Wriothesley in The Rape of Lucrece

7 OCTOBER

In 1988 three whales trapped under ice are the focus of international efforts to release them

Pericles' wife Thaisa is to be buried at sea, having apparently died on board their ship during childbirth in a storm.

FIRST SAILOR
Sir, your queen must overboard: the sea works high, the wind is loud, and will not lie till the ship be cleared of the dead.

PERICLES
That's your superstition.

FIRST SAILOR
Pardon us, sir; with us at sea it hath been still observed: and we are strong in custom. Therefore briefly yield her; for she must overboard straight.
[...]

PERICLES
A terrible childbed hast thou had, my dear;
No light, no fire: the unfriendly elements
Forgot thee utterly: nor have I time
To give thee hallow'd to thy grave, but straight
Must cast thee, scarcely coffin'd, in the ooze;
Where, for a monument upon thy bones,
And e'er-remaining lamps, the belching whale
And humming water must o'erwhelm thy corpse,
Lying with simple shells. O Lychorida,
Bid Nestor bring me spices, ink and paper,
My casket and my jewels; and bid Nicander

Bring me the satin coffer: lay the babe
Upon the pillow: hie thee, whiles I say
A priestly farewell to her: suddenly, woman.

SECOND SAILOR
Sir, we have a chest beneath the hatches, caulked and
bitumed ready.

Pericles | Act III, scene 1

8 OCTOBER

The birthday in 1872 of US bacteriologist Mary Engle Pennington who set new sanitary standards for the handling of milk and developed systems for refrigeration in transport and the home

The hoot of the owl traditionally presaged change, bringing hope in cold winters.

[SONG]
When icicles hang by the wall
And Dick the shepherd blows his nail
And Tom bears logs into the hall
And milk comes frozen home in pail,
When blood is nipp'd and ways be foul,
Then nightly sings the staring owl; Tu-whit,
Tu-who, a merry note,
While greasy Joan doth keel the pot.
When all aloud the wind doth blow
And coughing drowns the parson's saw
And birds sit brooding in the snow
And Marian's nose looks red and raw,
When roasted crabs hiss in the bowl,
Then nightly sings the staring owl; Tu-whit,
Tu-who, a merry note,
While greasy Joan doth keel the pot.

Love's Labour's Lost | Act V, scene 2

9 OCTOBER

The birthday in 1593 of Nicolaes Tulp, mayor and chief anatomist of Amsterdam, whose anatomy lesson was the subject of a painting by Rembrandt

Lucrece is moved by a painting which shows Hecuba witnessing the death of her husband King Priam at the hands of Pyrrhus.

To this well-painted piece is Lucrece come,
To find a face where all distress is stell'd.
Many she sees where cares have carved some,
But none where all distress and dolour dwell'd,
Till she despairing Hecuba beheld,
Staring on Priam's wounds with her old eyes,
Which bleeding under Pyrrhus' proud foot lies.

In her the painter had anatomized
Time's ruin, beauty's wreck, and grim care's reign:
Her cheeks with chaps and wrinkles were disguised;
Of what she was no semblance did remain:
Her blue blood changed to black in every vein,
Wanting the spring that those shrunk pipes had fed,
Show'd life imprison'd in a body dead.

On this sad shadow Lucrece spends her eyes,
And shapes her sorrow to the beldam's woes,
Who nothing wants to answer her but cries,
And bitter words to ban her cruel foes:
The painter was no god to lend her those;
And therefore Lucrece swears he did her wrong,
To give her so much grief and not a tongue.

From The Rape of Lucrece

10 OCTOBER

The death in 1963 of French chanteuse Édith Piaf, whose nickname was 'the Little Sparrow'

Troilus paces nervously, awaiting the arrival of his beloved Cressida.

TROILUS
I am giddy; expectation whirls me round.
The imaginary relish is so sweet
That it enchants my sense: what will it be,
When that the watery palate tastes indeed
Love's thrice repured nectar? death, I fear me,
Swooning destruction, or some joy too fine,
Too subtle-potent, tuned too sharp in sweetness,
For the capacity of my ruder powers:
I fear it much; and I do fear besides,
That I shall lose distinction in my joys;
As doth a battle, when they charge on heaps
The enemy flying.

PANDARUS
She's making her ready, she'll come straight: you must
be witty now. She does so blush, and fetches her wind so
short, as if she were frayed with a sprite: I'll fetch her. It
is the prettiest villain: she fetches her breath as short as a
new-ta'en sparrow.

Troilus and Cressida | Act III, scene 2

11 OCTOBER

Feast Day of first-century saints Zenaida and Philonella, sisters who devoted their lives to not-for-profit medicine

Helena, daughter of a physician, determines to treat the ailing king. As ever, her ability as a mere woman is brought into question.

HELENA
I will tell truth; by grace itself I swear.
You know my father left me some prescriptions
Of rare and proved effects, such as his reading
And manifest experience had collected
For general sovereignty; and that he will'd me
In heedfull'st reservation to bestow them,
As notes whose faculties inclusive were
More than they were in note: amongst the rest,
There is a remedy, approved, set down,
To cure the desperate languishings whereof
The king is render'd lost.

COUNTESS
But think you, Helen,
If you should tender your supposed aid,
He would receive it? he and his physicians
Are of a mind; he, that they cannot help him,
They, that they cannot help: how shall they credit
A poor unlearned virgin, when the schools,
Embowell'd of their doctrine, have left off
The danger to itself?

HELENA
There's something in't,
More than my father's skill, which was the greatest
Of his profession, that his good receipt

Shall for my legacy be sanctified
By the luckiest stars in heaven: and, would your honour
But give me leave to try success, I'd venture
The well-lost life of mine on his grace's cure
By such a day and hour.

All's Well That Ends Well | Act I, scene 3

12 OCTOBER

The death in 1991 of Australian actress Sheila Florance, best known for her role as Lizzie Birdsworth in the TV series Prisoner: Cell Block H

Florance appeared as Lady Macbeth in Melbourne's Union Theatre in 1962. Hearing that her husband has been made Thane of Cawdor as the witches foretold, and that they also predicted he would be king, Lady Macbeth decides to help matters along by killing the present monarch, Duncan.

LADY MACBETH
The raven himself is hoarse
That croaks the fatal entrance of Duncan
Under my battlements. Come, you spirits
That tend on mortal thoughts, unsex me here,
And fill me from the crown to the toe top-full
Of direst cruelty! make thick my blood;
Stop up the access and passage to remorse,
That no compunctious visitings of nature
Shake my fell purpose, nor keep peace between
The effect and it! Come to my woman's breasts,
And take my milk for gall, you murdering ministers,
Wherever in your sightless substances
You wait on nature's mischief! Come, thick night,
And pall thee in the dunnest smoke of hell,
That my keen knife see not the wound it makes,
Nor heaven peep through the blanket of the dark,
To cry 'Hold, hold!'

Macbeth | Act I, scene 5

13 OCTOBER

The Miracle of the Sun, prophesied by three shepherd children, is witnessed by a large crowd at Fátima in Portugal in 1917

Simpcox claims that his sight has been restored by a miracle. He also claims to be lame. The Duke of Gloucester is sceptical.

[Enter a Townsman of Saint Alban's, crying 'A miracle!']

DUKE OF GLOUCESTER
What means this noise? Fellow, what miracle dost
thou proclaim?
[...]

TOWNSMAN
Forsooth, a blind man at Saint Alban's shrine,
Within this half-hour, hath received his sight;
A man that ne'er saw in his life before.
[...]

KING HENRY
Good fellow, tell us here the circumstance,
That we for thee may glorify the Lord.
What, hast thou been long blind and now restored?

SIMPCOX
Born blind, an 't please your Grace.
[...]

WINCHESTER
What, art thou lame?

SIMPCOX
Ay, God Almighty help me!

EARL OF SUFFOLK
How camest thou so?

SIMPCOX
A fall off of a tree.

DUKE OF GLOUCESTER
How long hast thou been blind?

SIMPCOX
Born so, master.

DUKE OF GLOUCESTER
What, and wouldst climb a tree?
[...]
My lords, Saint Alban here hath done a miracle; and
would ye not think his cunning to be great, that could
restore this cripple to his legs again?

SIMPCOX
O master, that you could!

DUKE OF GLOUCESTER
My masters of Saint Alban's, have you not beadles in
your town, and things called whips?

MAYOR OF SAINT ALBAN'S
Yes, my lord, if it please your grace.
[...]

DUKE OF GLOUCESTER
Now fetch me a stool hither by and by. Now, sirrah, if
you mean to save yourself from whipping, leap me over
this stool and run away.

SIMPCOX

Alas, master, I am not able to stand alone: you go about
to torture me in vain.

[Enter a Beadle with whips]

DUKE OF GLOUCESTER

Well, sir, we must have you find your legs. Sirrah beadle,
whip him till he leap over that same stool.

BEADLE

I will, my lord. Come on, sirrah; off with your
doublet quickly.

SIMPCOX

Alas, master, what shall I do? I am not able to stand.

*[After the Beadle hath hit him once, he leaps over the stool
and runs away; and they follow and cry, 'A miracle!']*

Henry VI, Part 2 | Act II, scene 1

14 OCTOBER

The Battle of Hastings in 1066, which marked the start of the Norman conquest of England

Although those Normans were French, English Normans who attack France three hundred years later are not welcomed as brothers.

DUKE OF BOURBON
Normans, but bastard Normans, Norman bastards!
Mort de ma vie! if they march along
Unfought withal, but I will sell my dukedom,
To buy a slobbery and a dirty farm
In that nook-shotten isle of Albion.

Henry V | Act III, scene 5

15 OCTOBER

*The execution by firing squad in 1917 of the glamorous Dutch dancer
Mata Hari, who spied for Germany*

*To prove his disloyalty, friends of Parolles blindfold
him, pretend to be enemy soldiers, and encourage him
to betray Damian and Bertram, Count Rousillon.*

FIRST SOLDIER

I perceive, sir, by the general's looks, we shall be fain to
hang you.

[...]

We'll see what may be done, so you confess freely;
therefore, once more to this Captain Dumain: you have
answered to his reputation with the duke and to his
valour: what is his honesty?

PAROLLES

He will steal, sir, an egg out of a cloister: for rapes and
ravishments he parallels Nessus: he professes not keeping
of oaths; in breaking 'em he is stronger than Hercules:
he will lie, sir, with such volubility, that you would think
truth were a fool: drunkenness is his best virtue, for he
will be swine-drunk; and in his sleep he does little harm,
save to his bed-clothes about him; but they know his
conditions and lay him in straw. I have but little more to
say, sir, of his honesty: he has every thing that an honest
man should not have; what an honest man should have,
he has nothing.

[...]

FIRST SOLDIER

If your life be saved, will you undertake to betray
the Florentine?

PAROLLES

Ay, and the captain of his horse, Count Rousillon.

FIRST SOLDIER

I'll whisper with the general, and know his pleasure.

[He pretends to whisper]

There is no remedy, sir, but you must die: the general says,
you that have so traitorously discovered the secrets of your
army and made such pestiferous reports of men very nobly
held, can serve the world for no honest use; therefore you
must die. Come, headsman, off with his head.

PAROLLES

O Lord, sir, let me live, or let me see my death!

FIRST LORD

That shall you, and take your leave of all your friends.

[Unblinding him so that he can see his friends around him]

So, look about you: know you any here?

BERTRAM

Good morrow, noble captain.

All's Well That Ends Well | Act IV, scene 3

16 OCTOBER

The birthday in 1854 of the Irish playwright Oscar Wilde, who during his trial for gross indecency invoked Shakespeare's sonnets in his description of 'the love that dare not speak its name'

Wilde wrote a short story which speculated on the identity of the Fair Youth to whom so many of the sonnets were dedicated. Here Shakespeare advises passing on one's beauty to one's children.

SONNET 2

When forty winters shall besiege thy brow,
And dig deep trenches in thy beauty's field,
Thy youth's proud livery, so gazed on now,
Will be a tatter'd weed, of small worth held:
Then being ask'd where all thy beauty lies,
Where all the treasure of thy lusty days,
To say, within thine own deep-sunken eyes,
Were an all-eating shame and thriftless praise.
How much more praise deserved thy beauty's use,
If thou couldst answer 'This fair child of mine
Shall sum my count and make my old excuse,'
Proving his beauty by succession thine!
This were to be new made when thou art old,
And see thy blood warm when thou feel'st it cold.

17 OCTOBER

*The death in 1849 of composer Frédéric Chopin, who once played
a benefit concert with Franz Liszt for the wife of Hector Berlioz,
Shakespearean actress Harriet Smithson*

*Smithson's performance as Juliet in 1827 is said to have
elevated the role to equal status with Romeo for the
first time.*

JULIET
O Romeo, Romeo! wherefore art thou Romeo?
Deny thy father and refuse thy name;
Or, if thou wilt not, be but sworn my love,
And I'll no longer be a Capulet.

ROMEO
[Aside] Shall I hear more, or shall I speak at this?

JULIET
'Tis but thy name that is my enemy;
Thou art thyself, though not a Montague.
What's Montague? it is nor hand, nor foot,
Nor arm, nor face, nor any other part
Belonging to a man. O, be some other name!
What's in a name? that which we call a rose
By any other name would smell as sweet;
So Romeo would, were he not Romeo call'd,
Retain that dear perfection which he owes
Without that title. Romeo, doff thy name,
And for that name which is no part of thee
Take all myself.

Romeo and Juliet | **Act II, scene 2**

18 OCTOBER

The birthday in 1616 of the English herbalist Nicholas Culpeper

Villainous Iago takes full responsibility for his character, as he does for his herb garden.

IAGO
Virtue! a fig! 'tis in ourselves that we are thus
or thus. Our bodies are our gardens, to the which
our wills are gardeners: so that if we will plant
nettles, or sow lettuce, set hyssop and weed up
thyme, supply it with one gender of herbs, or
distract it with many, either to have it sterile
with idleness, or manured with industry, why, the
power and corrigible authority of this lies in our
wills. If the balance of our lives had not one
scale of reason to poise another of sensuality, the
blood and baseness of our natures would conduct us
to most preposterous conclusions: but we have
reason to cool our raging motions, our carnal
stings, our unbitted lusts, whereof I take this that
you call love to be a sect or scion.

Othello | Act I, scene 3

19 OCTOBER

Constitution Day in Niue, an island state which became a
self-governing colony of New Zealand in 1974

Prospero now rules the island of which enslaved and
resentful Caliban was once the only native.

CALIBAN

This island's mine, by Sycorax my mother,
Which thou takest from me. When thou camest first,
Thou strokedst me and madest much of me, wouldst give me
Water with berries in't, and teach me how
To name the bigger light, and how the less,
That burn by day and night: and then I loved thee
And show'd thee all the qualities o' the isle,
The fresh springs, brine-pits, barren place and fertile:
Cursed be I that did so! All the charms
Of Sycorax, toads, beetles, bats, light on you!
For I am all the subjects that you have,
Which first was mine own king: and here you sty me
In this hard rock, whiles you do keep from me
The rest o' the island.

The Tempest | Act I, scene 2

20 OCTOBER

The death in 1870 of Michael William Balfe, who wrote an opera called Falstaff *based on* The Merry Wives of Windsor

The tragedy of Falstaff, often seen as a comic character, is that he believes his partner in crime, Prince Hal, will remain a partner in crime after he becomes Henry V.

FALSTAFF
Marry, then, sweet wag, when thou art king, let not us that are squires of the night's body be called thieves of the day's beauty: let us be Diana's foresters, gentlemen of the shade, minions of the moon; and let men say we be men of good government, being governed, as the sea is, by our noble and chaste mistress the moon, under whose countenance we steal.

PRINCE HAL
Thou sayest well, and it holds well too; for the fortune of us that are the moon's men doth ebb and flow like the sea, being governed, as the sea is, by the moon. As, for proof, now: a purse of gold most resolutely snatched on Monday night and most dissolutely spent on Tuesday morning; got with swearing 'Lay by' and spent with crying 'Bring in;' now in as low an ebb as the foot of the ladder and by and by in as high a flow as the ridge of the gallows.

Henry IV, Part 1 | Act I, scene 2

21 OCTOBER

Thomas Edison applies for a patent for the incandescent lightbulb. It is granted three months later in 1879

Flickering candles are often metaphors for precarious life in Shakespeare's plays. Macbeth is beginning to realize that his time is up.

[A cry of women within]

MACBETH
[...] What is that noise?

SEYTON
It is the cry of women, my good lord. *[Exit]*

MACBETH
I have almost forgot the taste of fears;
The time has been, my senses would have cool'd
To hear a night-shriek; and my fell of hair
Would at a dismal treatise rouse and stir
As life were in't: I have supp'd full with horrors;
Direness, familiar to my slaughterous thoughts
Cannot once start me.
[Re-enter Seyton]
Wherefore was that cry?

SEYTON
The queen, my lord, is dead.

MACBETH
She should have died hereafter;
There would have been a time for such a word.
To-morrow, and to-morrow, and to-morrow,
Creeps in this petty pace from day to day

To the last syllable of recorded time,
And all our yesterdays have lighted fools
The way to dusty death. Out, out, brief candle!
Life's but a walking shadow, a poor player
That struts and frets his hour upon the stage
And then is heard no more: it is a tale
Told by an idiot, full of sound and fury,
Signifying nothing.

Macbeth | Act V, scene 5

22 OCTOBER

The Great Disappointment, when in 1844 the Doomsday foretold by Millerite Christians failed to appear

Antipholus' servant Dromio is in love with a kitchen maid of questionable hygiene.

DROMIO OF SYRACUSE
Marry, sir, besides myself, I am due to a woman; one that claims me, one that haunts me, one that will have me.

ANTIPHOLUS OF SYRACUSE
What claim lays she to thee?

DROMIO OF SYRACUSE
Marry sir, such claim as you would lay to your horse; and she would have me as a beast: not that, I being a beast, she would have me; but that she, being a very beastly creature, lays claim to me.

ANTIPHOLUS OF SYRACUSE
What is she?

DROMIO OF SYRACUSE
A very reverent body; ay, such a one as a man may not speak of without he say 'Sir-reverence.' I have but lean luck in the match, and yet is she a wondrous fat marriage.

ANTIPHOLUS OF SYRACUSE
How dost thou mean a fat marriage?

DROMIO OF SYRACUSE
Marry, sir, she's the kitchen wench and all grease; and I know not what use to put her to but to make a lamp of her and run from her by her own light. I warrant, her

rags and the tallow in them will burn a Poland winter:
if she lives till doomsday, she'll burn a week longer than
the whole world.

ANTIPHOLUS OF SYRACUSE
What complexion is she of?

DROMIO OF SYRACUSE
Swart, like my shoe, but her face nothing half so clean
kept: for why, she sweats; a man may go over shoes in the
grime of it.

ANTIPHOLUS OF SYRACUSE
That's a fault that water will mend.

DROMIO OF SYRACUSE
No, sir, 'tis in grain; Noah's flood could not do it.

The Comedy of Errors | Act III, scene 2

23 OCTOBER

Scotland and France sign the Treaty of Paris in 1295, forming an alliance against their common enemy, England

The Auld Alliance, as it is called today, persists as an affectionate description of the relationship between the two countries. An earl warns of the danger of being too distracted by war with France.

EARL OF WESTMORELAND
But there's a saying very old and true,
'If that you will France win,
Then with Scotland first begin:'
For once the eagle England being in prey,
To her unguarded nest the weasel Scot
Comes sneaking and so sucks her princely eggs,
Playing the mouse in absence of the cat,
To tear and havoc more than she can eat.

Henry V | Act I, scene 2

24 OCTOBER

In 1901, on her sixty-third birthday, Annie Taylor becomes the first woman to go over the Niagara Falls in a barrel

Clarence is to be murdered. A costard is a slang word for a head; a butt is a large barrel; malmsey is a wine.

FIRST MURDERER
Take him over the costard with the hilts of thy sword, and then we will chop him in the malmsey-butt in the next room.

SECOND MURDERER
O excellent devise! make a sop of him.

FIRST MURDERER
Hark! he stirs: shall I strike?

SECOND MURDERER
No, first let's reason with him.

DUKE OF CLARENCE
Where art thou, keeper? give me a cup of wine.

SECOND MURDERER
You shall have wine enough, my lord, anon.

DUKE OF CLARENCE
In God's name, what art thou?

SECOND MURDERER
A man, as you are.

DUKE OF CLARENCE
But not, as I am, royal.

SECOND MURDERER
Nor you, as we are, loyal.
[...]

DUKE OF CLARENCE
Wherefore do you come? [...] To murder me?

BOTH MURDERERS
Ay, ay.
[...]

DUKE OF CLARENCE
Relent, and save your souls.

FIRST MURDERER
Relent! 'tis cowardly and womanish.

DUKE OF CLARENCE
Not to relent is beastly, savage, devilish.
Which of you, if you were a prince's son,
Being pent from liberty, as I am now,
If two such murderers as yourselves came to you,
Would not entreat for life?
My friend, I spy some pity in thy looks:
O, if thine eye be not a flatterer,
Come thou on my side, and entreat for me,
As you would beg, were you in my distress
A begging prince what beggar pities not?
[...]

FIRST MURDERER
Take that, and that: [*Stabs him*] if all this will not do, I'll
drown you in the malmsey-butt within.

Richard III | Act I, scene 4

25 OCTOBER

The birthday in 1908 of Carmen Dillon, who won an Oscar as art director on Laurence Olivier's film version of Hamlet

Ophelia complains to her father about Hamlet's appearance in her room in a state of undress.

OPHELIA
O my lord, my lord, I have been so affrighted!

POLONIUS
With what, i' th' name of God?

OPHELIA
My lord, as I was sewing in my closet,
Lord Hamlet, with his doublet all unbrac'd,
No hat upon his head, his stockings foul'd,
Ungart'red, and down-gyved to his ankle;
Pale as his shirt, his knees knocking each other,
And with a look so piteous in purport
As if he had been loosed out of hell
To speak of horrors – he comes before me.
[...]
He took me by the wrist and held me hard;
Then goes he to the length of all his arm,
And, with his other hand thus o'er his brow,
He falls to such perusal of my face
As he would draw it. Long stay'd he so.
At last, a little shaking of mine arm,
And thrice his head thus waving up and down,
He rais'd a sigh so piteous and profound
As it did seem to shatter all his bulk
And end his being. That done, he lets me go,

And with his head over his shoulder turn'd
He seem'd to find his way without his eyes,
For out o' doors he went without their help
And to the last bended their light on me.

Hamlet | **Act II, scene 1**

26 OCTOBER

The death in 1952 of Hattie McDaniel, who was the first black actor to win an Oscar, for her role in Gone with the Wind; *she could not attend the film's premiere in a whites-only movie theatre*

The next black woman to win an Oscar was Whoopi Goldberg, fifty years later, for her role in Ghost. *The Earl of Warwick inspects the Earl of Gloucester's body for signs of murder.*

EARL OF WARWICK
See how the blood is settled in his face.
Oft have I seen a timely-parted ghost,
Of ashy semblance, meagre, pale and bloodless,
Being all descended to the labouring heart;
Who, in the conflict that it holds with death,
Attracts the same for aidance 'gainst the enemy;
Which with the heart there cools and ne'er returneth
To blush and beautify the cheek again.
But see, his face is black and full of blood,
His eye-balls further out than when he lived,
Staring full ghastly like a strangled man;
His hair uprear'd, his nostrils stretched with struggling;
His hands abroad display'd, as one that grasp'd
And tugg'd for life and was by strength subdued:
Look, on the sheets his hair you see, is sticking;
His well-proportion'd beard made rough and rugged,
Like to the summer's corn by tempest lodged.
It cannot be but he was murder'd here;
The least of all these signs were probable.

Henry VI, Part 2 | Act III, scene 2

27 OCTOBER

The death in 1553 of Michael Servetus, burnt as a heretic on a pile of his own books, which contained the evidence of his discovery of the pulmonary system

Caliban, enslaved by wizard Prospero's magic, seeks Stephano's help to free him from the spell.

CALIBAN
As I told thee before, I am subject to a tyrant, a sorcerer,
that by his cunning hath cheated me of the island.
[...]

STEPHANO
Now, forward with your tale.
[...] Come, proceed.

CALIBAN
Why, as I told thee, 'tis a custom with him,
I' th' afternoon to sleep: there thou mayst brain him,
Having first seized his books, or with a log
Batter his skull, or paunch him with a stake,
Or cut his wezand with thy knife. Remember
First to possess his books; for without them
He's but a sot, as I am, nor hath not
One spirit to command: they all do hate him
As rootedly as I. Burn but his books.
[...]

STEPHANO
Monster, I will kill this man.

The Tempest | Act III, scene 2

28 OCTOBER

The launch in 1971 of Prospero, the only British satellite launched from a British rocket

Prospero the magician invokes one final spell.

PROSPERO

Ye elves of hills, brooks, standing lakes and groves,
And ye that on the sands with printless foot
Do chase the ebbing Neptune and do fly him
When he comes back; you demi-puppets that
By moonshine do the green sour ringlets make,
Whereof the ewe not bites, and you whose pastime
Is to make midnight mushrooms, that rejoice
To hear the solemn curfew; by whose aid,
Weak masters though ye be, I have bedimm'd
The noontide sun, call'd forth the mutinous winds,
And 'twixt the green sea and the azured vault
Set roaring war: to the dread rattling thunder
Have I given fire and rifted Jove's stout oak
With his own bolt; the strong-based promontory
Have I made shake and by the spurs pluck'd up
The pine and cedar: graves at my command
Have waked their sleepers, oped, and let 'em forth
By my so potent art. But this rough magic
I here abjure, and, when I have required
Some heavenly music, which even now I do,
To work mine end upon their senses that
This airy charm is for, I'll break my staff,
Bury it certain fathoms in the earth,
And deeper than did ever plummet sound
I'll drown my book.
[Solemn music]

The Tempest | Act V, scene 1

29 OCTOBER

The birthday in 1883 of the French swimmer Victor Hochepied, who was eliminated in the first round of the 200m obstacle swimming race in the 1900 Olympic Games in Paris

Cassius attempts to enlist Brutus in the plot to assassinate Julius Caesar.

CASSIUS
I was born free as Caesar; so were you:
We both have fed as well, and we can both
Endure the winter's cold as well as he:
For once, upon a raw and gusty day,
The troubled Tiber chafing with her shores,
Caesar said to me 'Darest thou, Cassius, now
Leap in with me into this angry flood,
And swim to yonder point?' Upon the word,
Accoutred as I was, I plunged in
And bade him follow; so indeed he did.
The torrent roar'd, and we did buffet it
With lusty sinews, throwing it aside
And stemming it with hearts of controversy;
But ere we could arrive the point proposed,
Caesar cried 'Help me, Cassius, or I sink!'
I, as Aeneas, our great ancestor,
Did from the flames of Troy upon his shoulder
The old Anchises bear, so from the waves of Tiber
Did I the tired Caesar. And this man
Is now become a god, and Cassius is
A wretched creature and must bend his body,
If Caesar carelessly but nod on him.

Julius Caesar | Act I, scene 2

30 OCTOBER

The birthday in 1728 of shipping magnate Mary Hayley, whose ships supplied the tea involved in the Boston Tea Party

Shylock is deciding whether Antonio will make a good guarantor for a loan to Bassanio. An argosy is a fleet of trading ships.

SHYLOCK
Antonio is a good man.

BASSANIO
Have you heard any imputation to the contrary?

SHYLOCK
Oh, no, no, no, no: my meaning in saying he is a good man is to have you understand me that he is sufficient. Yet his means are in supposition: he hath an argosy bound to Tripolis, another to the Indies; I understand moreover, upon the Rialto, he hath a third at Mexico, a fourth for England, and other ventures he hath, squandered abroad. But ships are but boards, sailors but men: there be land-rats and water-rats, water-thieves and land-thieves, I mean pirates, and then there is the peril of waters, winds and rocks. The man is, notwithstanding, sufficient. Three thousand ducats; I think I may take his bond.

The Merchant of Venice | Act I, scene 3

31 OCTOBER

Halloween, or All Saints' Eve, traditionally a time when ghosts of the dead walk among us

As dawn approaches, Oberon, lord of the fairies, has ordered the goblin Puck to make some mischief.

PUCK

My fairy lord, this must be done with haste,
For night's swift dragons cut the clouds full fast,
And yonder shines Aurora's harbinger;
At whose approach, ghosts, wandering here and there,
Troop home to churchyards: damned spirits all,
That in crossways and floods have burial,
Already to their wormy beds are gone;
For fear lest day should look their shames upon,
They willfully themselves exile from light
And must for aye consort with black-brow'd night.

OBERON

But we are spirits of another sort:
I with the morning's love have oft made sport,
And, like a forester, the groves may tread,
Even till the eastern gate, all fiery-red,
Opening on Neptune with fair blessed beams,
Turns into yellow gold his salt green streams.
But, notwithstanding, haste; make no delay:
We may effect this business yet ere day.
[Exit]

PUCK

Up and down, up and down,
I will lead them up and down:
I am fear'd in field and town:
Goblin, lead them up and down.

A Midsummer Night's Dream | Act III, scene 2

NOVEMBER

All that glitters is not gold;
Often have you heard that told:
Many a man his life hath sold
But my outside to behold:
Gilded tombs do worms enfold.

The Merchant of Venice | Act II, scene 7

1 NOVEMBER

Chavang Kut, a harvest festival celebrated in northeastern India

*In the autumn a shepherdess refuses to grow gillyvors
– dianthus flowers – because they are pollinated by
humans, not by nature.*

POLIXENES
Shepherdess,
A fair one are you – well you fit our ages
With flowers of winter.

PERDITA
Sir, the year growing ancient,
Not yet on summer's death, nor on the birth
Of trembling winter, the fairest flowers o' the season
Are our carnations and streak'd gillyvors,
Which some call nature's bastards: of that kind
Our rustic garden's barren; and I care not
To get slips of them.

POLIXENES
Wherefore, gentle maiden,
Do you neglect them?

PERDITA
For I have heard it said
There is an art which in their piedness shares
With great creating nature.

POLIXENES
Say there be;
Yet nature is made better by no mean
But nature makes that mean: so, over that art
Which you say adds to nature, is an art

That nature makes. You see, sweet maid, we marry
A gentler scion to the wildest stock,
And make conceive a bark of baser kind
By bud of nobler race: this is an art
Which does mend nature, change it rather, but
The art itself is nature.

PERDITA
So it is.

POLIXENES
Then make your garden rich in gillyvors,
And do not call them bastards.

The Winter's Tale | Act IV, scene 4

2 NOVEMBER

The death in 1961 of actress Harriet Bosse, third wife of the Swedish playwright August Strindberg, who made her stage debut as Shakespeare's Juliet

Juliet and Romeo share their first kiss.

ROMEO
If I profane with my unworthiest hand
This holy shrine, the gentle fine is this:
My lips, two blushing pilgrims, ready stand
To smooth that rough touch with a tender kiss.

JULIET
Good pilgrim, you do wrong your hand too much,
Which mannerly devotion shows in this;
For saints have hands that pilgrims' hands do touch,
And palm to palm is holy palmers' kiss.

ROMEO
Have not saints lips, and holy palmers too?

JULIET
Ay, pilgrim, lips that they must use in prayer.

ROMEO
O, then, dear saint, let lips do what hands do;
They pray, grant thou, lest faith turn to despair.

JULIET
Saints do not move, though grant for prayers' sake.

ROMEO
Then move not, while my prayer's effect I take.
Thus from my lips, by yours, my sin is purged.

JULIET

Then have my lips the sin that they have took.

ROMEO

Sin from thy lips? O trespass sweetly urged!

Give me my sin again.

Romeo and Juliet | Act I, scene 5

3 NOVEMBER

The birthday in 1900 of the German cobbler Adolf Dassler, who founded, and gave his name to, the sportswear company Adidas

In Rome the common people are celebrating. Marullus and Flavius disapprove.

MARULLUS
[...] You, sir, what trade are you?

SECOND COMMONER
Truly, sir, in respect of a fine workman, I am but,
as you would say, a cobbler.

MARULLUS
But what trade art thou? answer me directly.

SECOND COMMONER
A trade, sir, that, I hope, I may use with a safe
conscience; which is, indeed, sir, a mender of bad soles.

MARULLUS
What trade, thou knave? thou naughty knave, what trade?

SECOND COMMONER
Nay, I beseech you, sir, be not out with me: yet,
if you be out, sir, I can mend you.

MARULLUS
What meanest thou by that? mend me, thou saucy fellow!

SECOND COMMONER
Why, sir, cobble you.

FLAVIUS
Thou art a cobbler, art thou?

SECOND COMMONER
Truly, sir, all that I live by is with the awl: I
meddle with no tradesman's matters, nor women's
matters, but with awl. I am, indeed, sir, a surgeon
to old shoes; when they are in great danger, I
recover them. As proper men as ever trod upon
neat's leather have gone upon my handiwork.

FLAVIUS
But wherefore art not in thy shop today?
Why dost thou lead these men about the streets?

SECOND COMMONER
Truly, sir, to wear out their shoes, to get myself
into more work. But, indeed, sir, we make holiday,
to see Caesar and to rejoice in his triumph.

Julius Caesar | Act I, scene 1

4 NOVEMBER

The oldest continuously operating theatre in the world, Teatro di San Carlo, opens in Naples in 1737, with the opera Achilles in Sciro

Good Hector of Troy, having spared the unarmed and arrogant Achilles of Greece earlier in battle, is sick of fighting.

HECTOR
Most putrefied core, so fair without,
Thy goodly armour thus hath cost thy life.
Now is my day's work done; I'll take good breath:
Rest, sword; thou hast thy fill of blood and death.
[Puts off his helmet and hangs his shield behind him]
[Enter Achilles and Myrmidons]

ACHILLES
Look, Hector, how the sun begins to set;
How ugly night comes breathing at his heels:
Even with the vail and darking of the sun,
To close the day up, Hector's life is done.

HECTOR
I am unarm'd; forego this vantage, Greek.

ACHILLES
Strike, fellows, strike; this is the man I seek.
[Hector falls]
So, Ilion, fall thou next! now, Troy, sink down!
Here lies thy heart, thy sinews, and thy bone.
On, Myrmidons, and cry you all amain,
'Achilles hath the mighty Hector slain.'
[A retreat is sounded]
[...]
The dragon wing of night o'erspreads the earth,

And, stickler-like, the armies separates.
My half-supp'd sword, that frankly would have fed,
Pleased with this dainty bait, thus goes to bed.
[Sheathes his sword]
Come, tie his body to my horse's tail;
Along the field I will the Trojan trail.

Troilus and Cressida | Act V, scene 8

5 NOVEMBER

The Gunpowder Plot to blow up the English Parliament, and with it King James VI & I, is foiled in 1605; Shakespeare drank in the Mermaid pub where the plotters also met to plan

The future Richard III plans to seize the crown now worn by his twelve-year-old nephew Edward V.

RICHARD, DUKE OF GLOUCESTER
[...] And yet I know not how to get the crown,
For many lives stand between me and home:
And I – like one lost in a thorny wood,
That rends the thorns and is rent with the thorns,
Seeking a way and straying from the way;
Not knowing how to find the open air,
But toiling desperately to find it out –
Torment myself to catch the English crown:
And from that torment I will free myself,
Or hew my way out with a bloody axe.
Why, I can smile, and murder whiles I smile,
And cry 'Content' to that which grieves my heart,
And wet my cheeks with artificial tears,
And frame my face to all occasions.
I'll drown more sailors than the mermaid shall;
I'll slay more gazers than the basilisk;
I'll play the orator as well as Nestor,
Deceive more slily than Ulysses could,
And, like a Sinon, take another Troy.
I can add colours to the chameleon,
Change shapes with Proteus for advantages,
And set the murderous Machiavel to school.
Can I do this, and cannot get a crown?
Tut, were it farther off, I'll pluck it down.

Henry VI, Part 3 | Act III, scene 2

6 NOVEMBER

The death in 1893 of the composer Tchaikovsky, who wrote orchestral works based on Hamlet, The Tempest, *and* Romeo and Juliet

The lines written for Juliet's nurse convey her character as well as her news, much to Juliet's frustration.

JULIET

Now, good sweet nurse – O Lord, why look'st thou sad?
Though news be sad, yet tell them merrily;
If good, thou shamest the music of sweet news
By playing it to me with so sour a face.

NURSE

I am a-weary, give me leave awhile:
Fie, how my bones ache! what a jaunt have I had!

JULIET

I would thou hadst my bones, and I thy news:
Nay, come, I pray thee, speak; good, good nurse, speak.

NURSE

Jesu, what haste? can you not stay awhile?
Do you not see that I am out of breath?

JULIET

How art thou out of breath, when thou hast breath
To say to me that thou art out of breath?
Is thy news good, or bad? answer to that;
Say either, and I'll stay the circumstance:
Let me be satisfied, is't good or bad?

NURSE

Well, you have made a simple choice; you know not
how to choose a man: Romeo! no, not he; though his

face be better than any man's, yet his leg excels
all men's; and for a hand, and a foot, and a body,
though they be not to be talked on, yet they are
past compare: he is not the flower of courtesy,
but, I'll warrant him, as gentle as a lamb. Go thy
ways, wench; serve God. What, have you dined at home?

JULIET
No, no: but all this did I know before.
What says he of our marriage? what of that?

NURSE
Lord, how my head aches! what a head have I!
It beats as it would fall in twenty pieces. [...]

JULIET
I' faith, I am sorry that thou art not well.
Sweet, sweet, sweet nurse, tell me, what says my love?

Romeo and Juliet | Act II, scene 5

7 NOVEMBER

October 25th by the old Julian calendar, when Russia's October Revolution began with the storming of the Winter Palace in St Petersburg, in 1917

Two brothers prepare to bury their fallen half-brother Cloten.

GUIDERIUS
Come on then, and remove him.

ARVIRAGUS
So. Begin.
[SONG]

GUIDERIUS
Fear no more the heat o' the sun,
Nor the furious winter's rages;
Thou thy worldly task hast done,
Home art gone, and ta'en thy wages:
Golden lads and girls all must,
As chimney-sweepers, come to dust.

ARVIRAGUS
Fear no more the frown o' the great;
Thou art past the tyrant's stroke;
Care no more to clothe and eat;
To thee the reed is as the oak:
The sceptre, learning, physic, must
All follow this, and come to dust.

GUIDERIUS
Fear no more the lightning flash,

ARVIRAGUS
Nor the all-dreaded thunder-stone;

GUIDERIUS
Fear not slander, censure rash;

ARVIRAGUS
Thou hast finish'd joy and moan:

BOTH
All lovers young, all lovers must
Consign to thee, and come to dust.

GUIDERIUS
No exorciser harm thee!

ARVIRAGUS
Nor no witchcraft charm thee!

GUIDERIUS
Ghost unlaid forbear thee!

ARVIRAGUS
Nothing ill come near thee!

BOTH
Quiet consummation have;
And renowned be thy grave!

Cymbeline | Act IV, scene 2

8 NOVEMBER

International Radiology Day, celebrating Wilhelm Röntgen's discovery of X-rays in 1895

Sherry (sherris-sack) benefits various organs of the body, unlike other weaker drinks.

FALSTAFF
[...] There's never none of these demure boys to any proof; for thin drink doth so over-cool their blood, making many fish-meals, that they fall into a kind of male green-sickness; and then, when they marry, they get wenches. They are generally fools and cowards – which some of us should be but for inflammation.

A good sherris-sack hath a two-fold operation in it. It ascends me into the brain; dries me there the foolish and dull and crudy vapours which environ it; makes it apprehensive, quick, forgetive, full of nimble, fiery, and delectable shapes; which delivered o'er to the voice, which is the birth, becomes excellent wit.

The second property of your excellent sherris is the warming of the blood; which cold and settled, left the liver white and pale, which is the badge of pusillanimity and cowardice; but the sherris warms and makes it course from the inwards to the parts extremes, illumineth the face, which, as a beacon, gives warning to all the rest of this little kingdom, man, to arm; and then the vital commoners and inland petty spirits muster me all to their captain, the heart, who, great and puff'd up with this doth any deed of courage – and this valour comes of sherris.

That skill in the weapon is nothing without sack, for
that it a-work; and learning, a mere hoard of gold kept
by a devil till sack commences it and sets it in act and
use. Hereof comes it that Prince Harry is valiant; for
the cold blood he did naturally inherit of his father, he
hath, like lean, sterile, bare land, manured, husbanded,
and till'd, with excellent endeavour of drinking good and
good store of fertile sherris, that he is become very hot
and valiant. If I had a thousand sons, the first humane
principle I would teach them should be to forswear thin
potations and to addict themselves to sack.

Henry IV, Part 2 | Act IV, scene 3

9 NOVEMBER

Day of the Skulls in Bolivia

A bishop objects to Henry Bolingbroke ascending the throne that was his cousin's, Richard II.

HENRY IV
In God's name, I'll ascend the regal throne.

BISHOP OF CARLISLE
Marry. God forbid!
[...] O, forfend it, God,
That in a Christian climate souls refined
Should show so heinous, black, obscene a deed!
[...]
And if you crown him, let me prophesy:
The blood of English shall manure the ground,
And future ages groan for this foul act;
Peace shall go sleep with Turks and infidels,
And in this seat of peace tumultuous wars
Shall kin with kin and kind with kind confound;
Disorder, horror, fear and mutiny
Shall here inhabit, and this land be call'd
The field of Golgotha and dead men's skulls.
O, if you raise this house against this house,
It will the woefullest division prove
That ever fell upon this cursed earth.
Prevent it, resist it, let it not be so,
Lest child, child's children, cry against you woe!

Richard II | Act IV, scene 1

455

10 NOVEMBER

In 1793 French revolutionaries replace Catholicism with a new atheistic religion, worshipping the Goddess of Reason

Reason was replaced within a year by the Cult of the Supreme Being.

HAMLET

[...] What a piece of work is a man! how noble in reason! how infinite in faculties! in form and moving how express and admirable! In action how like an angel! in apprehension how like a god! The beauty of the world, the paragon of animals! And yet to me what is this quintessence of dust? Man delights not me – no, nor woman neither, though by your smiling you seem to say so.

Hamlet | Act II, scene 2

11 NOVEMBER

Highwayman Joseph 'Blueskin' Blake is hanged in London in 1724

Shakespeare accuses the flowers of robbery.

SONNET 99

The forward violet thus did I chide:
Sweet thief, whence didst thou steal thy sweet that smells,
If not from my love's breath? The purple pride
Which on thy soft cheek for complexion dwells
In my love's veins thou hast too grossly dyed.
The lily I condemned for thy hand,
And buds of marjoram had stol'n thy hair:
The roses fearfully on thorns did stand,
One blushing shame, another white despair;
A third, nor red nor white, had stol'n of both
And to his robbery had annex'd thy breath;
But, for his theft, in pride of all his growth
A vengeful canker eat him up to death.
More flowers I noted, yet I none could see
But sweet or colour it had stol'n from thee.

12 NOVEMBER

The birthday in 1929 of beloved actress Grace Kelly, the future Princess Grace of Monaco

Helena loves Demetrius. Demetrius is more interested in Hermia. Hermia and Lysander are in love. Mischievous Puck has cast a spell on Demetrius so that he will fall in love with Helena.

DEMETRIUS
O Helena, goddess, nymph, perfect, divine!
To what, my love, shall I compare thine eyne?
Crystal is muddy. O, how ripe in show
Thy lips, those kissing cherries, tempting grow!
That pure congealed white, high Taurus snow,
Fann'd with the eastern wind, turns to a crow
When thou hold'st up thy hand: O, let me kiss
This princess of pure white, this seal of bliss!

A Midsummer Night's Dream | Act III, scene 2

13 NOVEMBER

The first showing, in 1940, of Walt Disney's animated orchestral film Fantasia

Brutus' servant Lucius is asleep.

BRUTUS
Boy! Lucius! Fast asleep? It is no matter;
Enjoy the honey-heavy dew of slumber:
Thou hast no figures nor no fantasies,
Which busy care draws in the brains of men;
Therefore thou sleep'st so sound.

Julius Caesar | **Act II, scene 1**

14 NOVEMBER

The death in 1687 of comic actress Nell Gwyn, one of the first to appear on the English stage after King Charles II – coincidentally her lover – made it legal for women to perform

Mistresses Page and Ford have received exactly the same love letter from the rogue Sir John Falstaff.

MISTRESS FORD
Why, this is the very same; the very hand, the very words. What doth he think of us?

MISTRESS PAGE
Nay, I know not: it makes me almost ready to wrangle with mine own honesty. I'll entertain myself like one that I am not acquainted withal; for, sure, unless he know some strain in me, that I know not myself, he would never have boarded me in this fury.

MISTRESS FORD
'Boarding,' call you it? I'll be sure to keep him above deck.

MISTRESS PAGE
So will I. If he come under my hatches, I'll never to sea again. Let's be revenged on him: let's appoint him a meeting; give him a show of comfort in his suit and lead him on with a fine-baited delay, till he hath pawned his horses to mine host of the Garter.

MISTRESS FORD
Nay, I will consent to act any villany against him, that may not sully the chariness of our honesty. O, that my husband saw this letter! it would give eternal food to his jealousy.

MISTRESS PAGE

Why, look where he comes; and my good man too: he's as far from jealousy as I am from giving him cause; and that I hope is an unmeasurable distance.

MISTRESS FORD

You are the happier woman.

MISTRESS PAGE

Let's consult together against this greasy knight.

The Merry Wives of Windsor | Act II, scene 1

15 NOVEMBER

The launch in 2001 of Microsoft's Xbox console, and in 2013 of Sony's Playstation 4

A fortune teller warns Antony to keep his distance from Julius Caesar, a worse man but a luckier gambler.

ANTONY
Say to me,
Whose fortunes shall rise higher, Caesar's or mine?

SOOTHSAYER
Caesar's.
Therefore, O Antony, stay not by his side:
Thy demon, that's thy spirit which keeps thee, is
Noble, courageous high, unmatchable,
Where Caesar's is not; but, near him, thy angel
Becomes a fear, as being o'erpower'd: therefore
Make space enough between you.

ANTONY
Speak this no more.

SOOTHSAYER
To none but thee; no more, but when to thee.
If thou dost play with him at any game,
Thou art sure to lose; and, of that natural luck,
He beats thee 'gainst the odds: thy lustre thickens,
When he shines by: I say again, thy spirit
Is all afraid to govern thee near him;
But, he away, 'tis noble.

Antony and Cleopatra | Act II, scene 3

16 NOVEMBER

The birthday in 1900 of Eliška Junková, Czech racing driver, the first woman to win a Grand Prix event

No need for a horse, when a lover can outrun any beast in their enthusiasm to reach their loved one.

SONNET 51

Thus can my love excuse the slow offence
Of my dull bearer when from thee I speed:
From where thou art why should I haste me thence?
Till I return, of posting is no need.
O, what excuse will my poor beast then find,
When swift extremity can seem but slow?
Then should I spur, though mounted on the wind;
In winged speed no motion shall I know:
Then can no horse with my desire keep pace;
Therefore desire of perfect'st love being made,
Shall neigh – no dull flesh – in his fiery race;
But love, for love, thus shall excuse my jade;
Since from thee going he went wilful-slow,
Towards thee I'll run, and give him leave to go.

17 NOVEMBER

The day in 1558 when Shakespeare's patron Queen Elizabeth ascended the throne of England

Coriolanus's mother has succeeded in dissuading him from attacking Rome with the Volscian army.

SICINIUS VELUTUS
What's the news?

SECOND MESSENGER
Good news, good news; the ladies have prevail'd,
The Volscians are dislodged, and Coriolanus gone:
A merrier day did never yet greet Rome.
[...]

MENENIUS AGRIPPA
This is good news:
I will go meet the ladies. This Volumnia
Is worth of consuls, senators, patricians,
A city full; of tribunes, such as you,
A sea and land full. You have pray'd well to-day:
This morning for ten thousand of your throats
I'd not have given a doit. Hark, how they joy!
[...]

SICINIUS VELUTUS
They are near the city?

SECOND MESSENGER
Almost at point to enter.

SICINIUS VELUTUS
We will meet them,
And help the joy.

[Enter two Senators with Volumnia, Virgilia and Valeria, passing over the stage]

FIRST SENATOR
Behold our patroness, the life of Rome!
Call all your tribes together, praise the gods,
And make triumphant fires; strew flowers before them:
Unshout the noise that banish'd Coriolanus,
Repeal him with the welcome of his mother;
Cry 'Welcome, ladies, welcome!'

Coriolanus | Act V, scenes 4 and 5

18 NOVEMBER

Mickey Mouse's official birthday, the day in 1928 when his first talkie,
Steamboat Willie, was released

Everyone has gone to bed.

PUCK
Now the hungry lion roars,
And the wolf behowls the moon;
Whilst the heavy ploughman snores,
All with weary task fordone.
Now the wasted brands do glow,
Whilst the screech-owl, screeching loud,
Puts the wretch that lies in woe
In remembrance of a shroud.
Now it is the time of night
That the graves all gaping wide,
Every one lets forth his sprite,
In the church-way paths to glide:
And we fairies, that do run
By the triple Hecate's team,
From the presence of the sun,
Following darkness like a dream,
Now are frolic: not a mouse
Shall disturb this hallow'd house:
I am sent with broom before,
To sweep the dust behind the door.

A Midsummer Night's Dream | **Act V, scene 1**

19 NOVEMBER

The death in 1703 in the Bastille of the unidentified Man in the Iron Mask, whose mask was actually made of black velvet

The men are coming, disguised as Russians, intent on wooing the women they love. The Princess of France has a plan to have some fun at their expense.

PRINCESS OF FRANCE
But what, but what, come they to visit us?

BOYET
They do, they do: and are apparell'd thus.
Like Muscovites or Russians, as I guess.
Their purpose is to parle, to court and dance;
And every one his love-feat will advance
Unto his several mistress, which they'll know
By favours several which they did bestow.

PRINCESS OF FRANCE
And will they so? the gallants shall be task'd;
For, ladies, we shall every one be mask'd;
And not a man of them shall have the grace,
Despite of suit, to see a lady's face.
Hold, Rosaline, this favour thou shalt wear,
And then the king will court thee for his dear;
Hold, take thou this, my sweet, and give me thine,
So shall Berowne take me for Rosaline.
And change your favours too; so shall your loves
Woo contrary, deceived by these removes.

Love's Labour's Lost | Act V, scene 2

20 NOVEMBER

The death in 1606 of playwright John Lyly, whom contemporaries considered the equal of Shakespeare for comedy

Shakespeare frequently uses the lily as a metaphor for purest white. Why try to improve on perfection?

SALISBURY
Therefore, to be possess'd with double pomp,
To guard a title that was rich before,
To gild refined gold, to paint the lily,
To throw a perfume on the violet,
To smooth the ice, or add another hue
Unto the rainbow, or with taper-light
To seek the beauteous eye of heaven to garnish,
Is wasteful and ridiculous excess.

King John | Act IV, scene 2

21 NOVEMBER

The birthday in 1897 of the anarchist Mollie Steimer, who has the rare distinction of having been deported from both the USA and Soviet Russia for her activities

Celia appeals to Frederick against the banishment of her cousin Rosalind.

FREDERICK
Mistress, dispatch you with your safest haste,
And get you from our court.

ROSALIND
Me, uncle?

FREDERICK
You, cousin.
Within these ten days if that thou beest found
So near our public court as twenty miles,
Thou diest for it.

ROSALIND
I do beseech your Grace,
Let me the knowledge of my fault bear with me.
[...]

FREDERICK
Thou art thy father's daughter; there's enough.

ROSALIND
So was I when your Highness took his dukedom;
So was I when your Highness banish'd him.
Treason is not inherited, my lord.
[...]

CELIA

Dear sovereign, hear me speak.

FREDERICK

Ay, Celia; we stay'd her for your sake,
Else had she with her father rang'd along.

CELIA

I did not then entreat to have her stay;
It was your pleasure, and your own remorse;
I was too young that time to value her,
But now I know her. If she be a traitor,
Why so am I: we still have slept together,
Rose at an instant, learn'd, play'd, eat together;
And wheresoe'er we went, like Juno's swans,
Still we went coupled and inseparable.

FREDERICK

She is too subtle for thee; and her smoothness,
Her very silence and her patience,
Speak to the people, and they pity her.
Thou art a fool. She robs thee of thy name;
And thou wilt show more bright and seem more virtuous
When she is gone. Then open not thy lips.
Firm and irrevocable is my doom
Which I have pass'd upon her; she is banish'd.

As You Like It | **Act I, scene 3**

22 NOVEMBER

The death in 1963 of novelist Aldous Huxley, author of the dystopian vision Brave New World

Huxley is one of many authors to borrow Shakespearean phrases for their titles. Miranda, accustomed to a solitary life, meets the survivors of a shipwreck for the first time.

MIRANDA
O, wonder!
How many goodly creatures are there here!
How beauteous mankind is! O brave new world,
That has such people in't!

The Tempest | Act V, scene 1

23 NOVEMBER

The death in 1585 of English composer Thomas Tallis, a master of polyphonic choral music

There's a songsmith at the door.

SERVANT

O master, if you did but hear the pedlar at the door, you would never dance again after a tabour and pipe; no, the bagpipe could not move you: he sings several tunes faster than you'll tell money; he utters them as he had eaten ballads and all men's ears grew to his tunes.

CLOWN

He could never come better; he shall come in. I love a ballad but even too well, if it be doleful matter merrily set down, or a very pleasant thing indeed and sung lamentably.

SERVANT

He hath songs for man or woman, of all sizes; no milliner can so fit his customers with gloves: he has the prettiest love-songs for maids; so without bawdry, which is strange; with such delicate burthens of dildos and fadings, 'jump her and thump her;' and where some stretch-mouthed rascal would, as it were, mean mischief and break a foul gap into the matter, he makes the maid to answer 'Whoop, do me no harm, good man;' puts him off, slights him, with 'Whoop, do me no harm, good man.'

The Winter's Tale | Act IV, scene 4

24 NOVEMBER

The day that the FBI Crime Lab was formally opened in 1932

A father urges his son to avenge his murder.

FATHER'S GHOST
I am thy father's spirit,
Doom'd for a certain term to walk the night,
And for the day confin'd to fast in fires,
Till the foul crimes done in my days of nature
Are burnt and purg'd away. But that I am forbid
To tell the secrets of my prison house,
I could a tale unfold whose lightest word
Would harrow up thy soul, freeze thy young blood,
Make thy two eyes, like stars, start from their spheres,
Thy knotted and combined locks to part,
And each particular hair to stand on end
Like quills upon the fretful porcupine.
But this eternal blazon must not be
To ears of flesh and blood. List, list, O, list!
If thou didst ever thy dear father love—

HAMLET
O God!

FATHER'S GHOST
Revenge his foul and most unnatural murder.

HAMLET
Murder?

FATHER'S GHOST
Murder most foul, as in the best it is;
But this most foul, strange, and unnatural.

HAMLET

Haste me to know't, that I, with wings as swift

As meditation or the thoughts of love,

May sweep to my revenge.

Hamlet | Act I, scene 5

25 NOVEMBER

The Feast Day of St Catherine of Alexandria, who survived many forms of torture including the Breaking Wheel, from which the name of the Catherine Wheel firework derives

Paulina berates the king for his cruelty in accusing the queen of infidelity. The queen has collapsed under the strain.

PAULINA
Woe the while!
O, cut my lace, lest my heart, cracking it,
Break too.

FIRST LORD
What fit is this, good lady?

PAULINA
What studied torments, tyrant, hast for me?
What wheels? racks? fires? what flaying? boiling?
In leads or oils? what old or newer torture
Must I receive, whose every word deserves
To taste of thy most worst? Thy tyranny
Together working with thy jealousies,
Fancies too weak for boys, too green and idle
For girls of nine, O, think what they have done
And then run mad indeed, stark mad! for all
Thy by-gone fooleries were but spices of it.
[...]
When I have said, cry 'woe!' the queen, the queen,
The sweet'st, dear'st creature's dead.

The Winter's Tale | **Act III, scene 2**

26 NOVEMBER

Day of the Brink's-Mat robbery in London, in 1983, when £26 million in gold bars was stolen from a vault

Portia asks her suitor, the Prince of Morocco, to choose one of three caskets.

PORTIA
[...] Now make your choice.

PRINCE OF MOROCCO
The first, of gold, who this inscription bears,
'Who chooseth me shall gain what many men desire;'
The second, silver, which this promise carries,
'Who chooseth me shall get as much as he deserves;'
This third, dull lead, with warning all as blunt,
'Who chooseth me must give and hazard all he hath.'
How shall I know if I do choose the right?

PORTIA
The one of them contains my picture, prince:
If you choose that, then I am yours withal.

PRINCE OF MOROCCO
Some god direct my judgment! Let me see;
I will survey the inscriptions back again.
[...]
Let's see once more this saying graved in gold
'Who chooseth me shall gain what many men desire.'
Why, that's the lady; all the world desires her.
[...]
They have in England
A coin that bears the figure of an angel
Stamped in gold, but that's insculp'd upon;
But here an angel in a golden bed

476

Lies all within. Deliver me the key:
Here do I choose, and thrive I as I may!

PORTIA
There, take it, prince; and if my form lie there,
Then I am yours.
[He unlocks the golden casket]

PRINCE OF MOROCCO
O hell! what have we here?
A carrion Death, within whose empty eye
There is a written scroll! I'll read the writing.
[Reads]
> All that glitters is not gold;
> Often have you heard that told:
> Many a man his life hath sold
> But my outside to behold:
> Gilded tombs do worms enfold.
> Had you been as wise as bold,
> Young in limbs, in judgment old,
> Your answer had not been inscroll'd:
> Fare you well; your suit is cold.
> Cold, indeed; and labour lost:
> Then, farewell, heat, and welcome, frost!
> Portia, adieu. I have too grieved a heart
> To take a tedious leave: thus losers part.

The Merchant of Venice | **Act II, scene 7**

27 NOVEMBER

The birthday in 1809 of actress, playwright, poet and travel writer Fanny Kemble, whose journal of life on her husband's plantation reflected her support for the abolition of slavery

Kemble's marriage failed when her husband forbade her to publish her journal. Helena's husband, a prince, has left her because she is low-born. His mother is disappointed in him.

COUNTESS
What angel shall
Bless this unworthy husband? he cannot thrive,
Unless her prayers, whom heaven delights to hear
And loves to grant, reprieve him from the wrath
Of greatest justice. Write, write, Rinaldo,
To this unworthy husband of his wife;
Let every word weigh heavy of her worth
That he does weigh too light: my greatest grief.
Though little he do feel it, set down sharply.
Dispatch the most convenient messenger:
When haply he shall hear that she is gone,
He will return; and hope I may that she,
Hearing so much, will speed her foot again,
Led hither by pure love: which of them both
Is dearest to me. I have no skill in sense
To make distinction: provide this messenger:
My heart is heavy and mine age is weak;
Grief would have tears, and sorrow bids me speak.

All's Well That Ends Well | **Act III, scene 4**

28 NOVEMBER

In 1582, in Stratford-upon-Avon, William Shakespeare and Anne Hathaway get married

In his will, Will famously left Anne his second-best bed.

SONNET 116

Let me not to the marriage of true minds
Admit impediments. Love is not love
Which alters when it alteration finds,
Or bends with the remover to remove:
O no! it is an ever-fixed mark
That looks on tempests and is never shaken;
It is the star to every wandering bark,
Whose worth's unknown, although his height be taken.
Love's not Time's fool, though rosy lips and cheeks
Within his bending sickle's compass come:
Love alters not with his brief hours and weeks,
But bears it out even to the edge of doom.
If this be error and upon me proved,
I never writ, nor no man ever loved.

29 NOVEMBER

The death in 1530 of Cardinal Thomas Wolsey, Lord Chancellor to Henry VIII

Henry has discovered the extent to which Wolsey has been lining his own pockets, thanks to a paper which Wolsey sent the king by mistake.

HENRY VIII
[...] Read o'er this [*Giving him papers*];
And after, this: and then to breakfast with
What appetite you have.
[*Exit Henry VIII, frowning upon Cardinal Wolsey*]

CARDINAL WOLSEY
What should this mean?
What sudden anger's this? how have I reap'd it?
He parted frowning from me, as if ruin
Leap'd from his eyes: so looks the chafed lion
Upon the daring huntsman that has gall'd him;
Then makes him nothing. I must read this paper;
I fear, the story of his anger. 'Tis so;
This paper has undone me: 'tis the account
Of all that world of wealth I have drawn together
For mine own ends; indeed, to gain the popedom,
And fee my friends in Rome. O negligence!
Fit for a fool to fall by: what cross devil
Made me put this main secret in the packet
I sent the king? Is there no way to cure this?
No new device to beat this from his brains?
I know 'twill stir him strongly; yet I know
A way, if it take right, in spite of fortune
Will bring me off again. What's this? 'To the Pope!'
The letter, as I live, with all the business
I writ to's holiness. Nay then, farewell!

I have touch'd the highest point of all my greatness;
And, from that full meridian of my glory,
I haste now to my setting: I shall fall
Like a bright exhalation in the evening,
And no man see me more.

Henry VIII | Act III, scene 2

30 NOVEMBER

The Feast of St Andrew, patron saint of Scotland; in 1872 the first ever international soccer match is played on St Andrew's Day, between Scotland and England, a goalless draw

French and English armies besiege Angiers, each headed by a rival claimant to the English throne. Heralds from each side hope to enlist the support of the city's citizens.

FIRST CITIZEN
Heralds, from off our towers we might behold,
From first to last, the onset and retire
Of both your armies; whose equality
By our best eyes cannot be censured:
Blood hath bought blood and blows have answered blows;
Strength match'd with strength, and power confronted power:
Both are alike; and both alike we like.
One must prove greatest: while they weigh so even,
We hold our town for neither, yet for both.

King John | Act II, scene 1

DECEMBER

The barge she sat in, like a burnish'd throne,
Burn'd on the water: the poop was beaten gold;
Purple the sails, and so perfumed that
The winds were love-sick with them...

Antony and Cleopatra | Act II, scene 2

1 DECEMBER

The birth in 1761 of wax sculptor Marie Tussaud

Leontes believes that Hermione has been dead for sixteen years. In fact she is alive and well and sheltering with her friend Paulina who tries to pass her off as a statue of herself.

LEONTES
O Paulina,
We honour you with trouble: but we came
To see the statue of our queen.
[...]

PAULINA
O, patience!
The statue is but newly fix'd, the colour's not dry.
[...]

LEONTES
Would I were dead, but that, methinks, already –
What was he that did make it? See, my lord,
Would you not deem it breathed? and that those veins
Did verily bear blood?

POLIXENES
Masterly done:
The very life seems warm upon her lip.

LEONTES
The fixture of her eye has motion in't,
As we are mock'd with art.
[...] Still, methinks,
There is an air comes from her: what fine chisel

Could ever yet cut breath? Let no man mock me,
For I will kiss her.

PAULINA
Good my lord, forbear:
The ruddiness upon her lip is wet;
You'll mar it if you kiss it, stain your own
With oily painting. Shall I draw the curtain?

LEONTES
No, not these twenty years.

The Winter's Tale | Act V, scene 3

2 DECEMBER

The death in 1814 of the Marquis de Sade, to whom the word 'sadism' refers

Ferdinand derives some pleasure from the pain of the task he has been ordered to complete.

FERDINAND
There be some sports are painful, and their labour
Delight in them sets off: some kinds of baseness
Are nobly undergone and most poor matters
Point to rich ends. This my mean task
Would be as heavy to me as odious, but
The mistress which I serve quickens what's dead
And makes my labours pleasures: O, she is
Ten times more gentle than her father's crabbed,
And he's composed of harshness. I must remove
Some thousands of these logs and pile them up,
Upon a sore injunction: my sweet mistress
Weeps when she sees me work, and says, such baseness
Had never like executor. I forget:
But these sweet thoughts do even refresh my labours,
Most busy lest, when I do it.

The Tempest | Act III, scene 1

3 DECEMBER

Doctors Day in Cuba

*Dr Cornelius suspects the queen's motives in requesting
some fatal poisons from him.*

QUEEN
Now, master doctor, have you brought those drugs?

CORNELIUS
Pleaseth your highness, ay: here they are, madam:
[*Presenting a small box*]
But I beseech your grace, without offence –
My conscience bids me ask – wherefore you have
Commanded of me those most poisonous compounds,
Which are the movers of a languishing death;
But though slow, deadly?

QUEEN
I wonder, doctor,
Thou ask'st me such a question. Have I not been
Thy pupil long? Hast thou not learn'd me how
To make perfumes? distil? preserve? yea, so
That our great king himself doth woo me oft
For my confections? Having thus far proceeded –
Unless thou think'st me devilish – is't not meet
That I did amplify my judgment in
Other conclusions? I will try the forces
Of these thy compounds on such creatures as
We count not worth the hanging, but none human,
To try the vigour of them and apply
Allayments to their act, and by them gather
Their several virtues and effects.
[...]

CORNELIUS

[Aside] I do not like her. She doth think she has
Strange lingering poisons: I do know her spirit,
And will not trust one of her malice with
A drug of such damn'd nature. Those she has
Will stupefy and dull the sense awhile;
Which first, perchance, she'll prove on cats and dogs,
Then afterward up higher: but there is
No danger in what show of death it makes,
More than the locking-up the spirits a time,
To be more fresh, reviving. She is fool'd
With a most false effect; and I the truer,
So to be false with her.

QUEEN

No further service, doctor,
Until I send for thee.

CORNELIUS

I humbly take my leave.

Cymbeline | Act I, scene 5

4 DECEMBER

In 1956 four musicians gather in a recording studio – they are rock-n-roll giants Elvis Presley, Johnny Cash, Jerry Lee Lewis and Carl Perkins, the so-called Million Dollar Quartet

Lord Capulet, in expansive mood, is holding a masked ball, and defies anyone not to dance.

CAPULET
Welcome, gentlemen! ladies that have their toes
Unplagued with corns will have a bout with you.
Ah ha, my mistresses! which of you all
Will now deny to dance? she that makes dainty,
She, I'll swear, hath corns; am I come near ye now?
Welcome, gentlemen! I have seen the day
That I have worn a visor and could tell
A whispering tale in a fair lady's ear,
Such as would please: 'tis gone, 'tis gone, 'tis gone:
You are welcome, gentlemen! come, musicians, play.
A hall, a hall! give room! and foot it, girls.
[Music plays, and they dance]
More light, you knaves; and turn the tables up,
And quench the fire, the room is grown too hot.
Ah, sirrah, this unlook'd-for sport comes well.
Nay, sit, nay, sit, good cousin Capulet;
For you and I are past our dancing days:
How long is't now since last yourself and I
Were in a mask?

Romeo and Juliet | **Act I, scene 5**

5 DECEMBER

The birthday in 1830 of author Christina Rossetti, who wrote the poem Remember, *often read at funerals*

Laertes, about to depart, receives advice from his father, Polonius, which we would all do well to remember.

POLONIUS
Yet here, Laertes? Aboard, aboard, for shame!
The wind sits in the shoulder of your sail,
And you are stay'd for. There – my blessing with thee!
And these few precepts in thy memory
Look thou character. Give thy thoughts no tongue,
Nor any unproportion'd thought his act.
Be thou familiar, but by no means vulgar:
Those friends thou hast, and their adoption tried,
Grapple them unto thy soul with hoops of steel;
But do not dull thy palm with entertainment
Of each new-hatch'd, unfledg'd comrade. Beware
Of entrance to a quarrel; but being in,
Bear't that th' opposed may beware of thee.
Give every man thine ear, but few thy voice;
Take each man's censure, but reserve thy judgment.
Costly thy habit as thy purse can buy,
But not express'd in fancy; rich, not gaudy;
For the apparel oft proclaims the man,
And they in France of the best rank and station
Are most select and generous, chief in that.
Neither a borrower nor a lender be;
For loan oft loses both itself and friend,
And borrowing dulls the edge of husbandry.
This above all – to thine own self be true,
And it must follow, as the night the day,

Thou canst not then be false to any man.
Farewell. My blessing season this in thee!

Hamlet | **Act I, scene 3**

6 DECEMBER

The birth in 1421 of Henry VI, who succeeded to the English throne at only nine months old and to the French throne a month later

Dissatisfied nobles rebelled against Henry VI in 1455, precipitating civil war known as the Wars of the Roses.

HENRY VI
Why, Warwick, hath thy knee forgot to bow?
Old Salisbury, shame to thy silver hair,
Thou mad misleader of thy brain-sick son!
What, wilt thou on thy death-bed play the ruffian,
And seek for sorrow with thy spectacles?
O, where is faith? O, where is loyalty?
If it be banish'd from the frosty head,
Where shall it find a harbour in the earth?
Wilt thou go dig a grave to find out war,
And shame thine honourable age with blood?
Why art thou old, and want'st experience?
Or wherefore dost abuse it, if thou hast it?
For shame! in duty bend thy knee to me
That bows unto the grave with mickle age.

Henry VI, Part 2 | Act V, scene 1

7 DECEMBER

The death in 1962 of Norwegian opera singer Kirsten Flagstad, known as the Voice of the Century

Early in her career Flagstad took on the role of Desdemona in Verdi's Otello. *Here, Desdemona is unaware that wicked Iago has engineered her husband's rejection of her love.*

DESDEMONA
O good Iago,
What shall I do to win my lord again?
Good friend, go to him; for, by this light of heaven,
I know not how I lost him. Here I kneel:
If e'er my will did trespass 'gainst his love,
Either in discourse of thought or actual deed,
Or that mine eyes, mine ears, or any sense,
Delighted them in any other form;
Or that I do not yet, and ever did.
And ever will – though he do shake me off
To beggarly divorcement – love him dearly,
Comfort forswear me! Unkindness may do much;
And his unkindness may defeat my life,
But never taint my love. I cannot say 'whore:'
It does abhor me now I speak the word;
To do the act that might the addition earn
Not the world's mass of vanity could make me.

Othello | Act IV, scene 2

8 DECEMBER

In 1660, after a change in the law, a woman – either Anne Marshall or Margaret Hughes – appears on an English stage for the first time, playing the part of Desdemona

Lying Iago plants the seed of doubt in the mind of Desdemona's loving husband, Othello.

OTHELLO
Give me a living reason she's disloyal.

IAGO
I do not like the office:
But, sith I am enter'd in this cause so far,
Prick'd to't by foolish honesty and love,
I will go on. I lay with Cassio lately;
And, being troubled with a raging tooth,
I could not sleep.
There are a kind of men so loose of soul,
That in their sleeps will mutter their affairs:
One of this kind is Cassio:
In sleep I heard him say 'Sweet Desdemona,
Let us be wary, let us hide our loves;'
And then, sir, would he gripe and wring my hand,
Cry 'O sweet creature!' and then kiss me hard,
As if he pluck'd up kisses by the roots
That grew upon my lips: then laid his leg
Over my thigh, and sigh'd, and kiss'd; and then
Cried 'Cursed fate that gave thee to the Moor!'

Othello | Act III, scene 3

9 DECEMBER

Birthday in 1779 of Tabitha Babbitt, inventor of a process for making false teeth

Brothers Oliver and Orlando are fighting, much to the distress of old family servant Adam.

OLIVER
What, boy! *[Strikes him]*

ORLANDO
Come, come, elder brother, you are too young in this.

OLIVER
Wilt thou lay hands on me, villain?

ORLANDO
[...] Wert thou not my brother, I would not take this hand from thy throat till this other had pull'd out thy tongue for saying so. Thou has rail'd on thyself.

ADAM
[Coming forward] Sweet masters, be patient; for your father's remembrance, be at accord.
[...]

OLIVER
Get you with him, you old dog.

ADAM
Is 'old dog' my reward? Most true, I have lost my teeth in your service. God be with my old master! He would not have spoke such a word.

As You Like It | Act I, scene 1

10 DECEMBER

The first edition of the Encyclopaedia Britannica *is published in 1768*

Leontes has discovered a plot against him and believes his friend to be implicated in it. Ignorance, he feels, would have been bliss. There are some things that, once learned, you cannot unknow.

LEONTES
How blest am I
In my just censure, in my true opinion!
Alack, for lesser knowledge! how accursed
In being so blest! There may be in the cup
A spider steep'd, and one may drink, depart,
And yet partake no venom, for his knowledge
Is not infected: but if one present
The abhorr'd ingredient to his eye, make known
How he hath drunk, he cracks his gorge, his sides,
With violent hefts. I have drunk,
and seen the spider.

The Winter's Tale | Act II, scene 1

11 DECEMBER

In 1913 Leonardo da Vinci's painting the Mona Lisa is recovered in Florence, two years after it was stolen from the Louvre in Paris

Misanthropic Timon of Athens rails against the robbers who want to steal his gold.

TIMON
[...] Yet thanks I must you con
That you are thieves profess'd, that you work not
In holier shapes: for there is boundless theft
In limited professions. Rascal thieves,
Here's gold. Go, suck the subtle blood o' the grape,
Till the high fever seethe your blood to froth,
And so 'scape hanging: trust not the physician;
His antidotes are poison, and he slays
More than you rob: take wealth and lives together;
Do villany, do, since you protest to do't,
Like workmen. I'll example you with thievery.
The sun's a thief, and with his great attraction
Robs the vast sea: the moon's an arrant thief,
And her pale fire she snatches from the sun:
The sea's a thief, whose liquid surge resolves
The moon into salt tears: the earth's a thief,
That feeds and breeds by a composture stolen
From general excrement: each thing's a thief:
The laws, your curb and whip, in their rough power
Have uncheque'd theft. Love not yourselves: away,
Rob one another. There's more gold. Cut throats:
All that you meet are thieves: to Athens go,
Break open shops; nothing can you steal,
But thieves do lose it: steal no less for this
I give you; and gold confound you howsoe'er! Amen.

Timon of Athens | Act IV, scene 3

12 DECEMBER

The death in 1968 of wise-cracking actress Tallulah Bankhead,
whose performance in Antony and Cleopatra *was reviewed thus:*
'Bankhead barged down the Nile – and sank'

Cleopatra, informed that the man she admires is
already married, reacts as Bankhead might have
done to a bad review.

CLEOPATRA
Rogue, thou hast lived too long.
[Draws a knife]

MESSENGER
Nay, then I'll run.
What mean you, madam? I have made no fault.
[Exit]

CHARMIAN
Good madam, keep yourself within yourself:
The man is innocent.

CLEOPATRA
Some innocents 'scape not the thunderbolt.
Melt Egypt into Nile! and kindly creatures
Turn all to serpents! Call the slave again:
Though I am mad, I will not bite him: call.

Antony and Cleopatra | Act II, scene 5

13 DECEMBER

The birthday in 1913 of the illustrator Susanne Suba, among whose credits were illustrations for two books by Noel Streatfeild: The Theatre Cat, *and* Osbert, *a story about a dog*

Romeo, banished from Verona, envies the luck of dogs, cats and flies.

ROMEO
'Tis torture, and not mercy: heaven is here,
Where Juliet lives; and every cat and dog
And little mouse, every unworthy thing,
Live here in heaven and may look on her;
But Romeo may not: more validity,
More honourable state, more courtship lives
In carrion-flies than Romeo: they may seize
On the white wonder of dear Juliet's hand
And steal immortal blessing from her lips,
Who even in pure and vestal modesty,
Still blush, as thinking their own kisses sin;
But Romeo may not; he is banished:
Flies may do this, but I from this must fly:
They are free men, but I am banished.
And say'st thou yet that exile is not death?
Hadst thou no poison mix'd, no sharp-ground knife,
No sudden mean of death, though ne'er so mean,
But 'banished' to kill me? – 'banished'?
O friar, the damned use that word in hell;
Howlings attend it: how hast thou the heart,
Being a divine, a ghostly confessor,
A sin-absolver, and my friend profess'd,
To mangle me with that word 'banished'?

Romeo and Juliet | Act III, scene 3

14 DECEMBER

In 1542 the six-day-old daughter of James V becomes Mary Queen of Scots, conspicuously absent from Shakespeare's histories because it was Queen Elizabeth who had Mary executed

The Scots are usually the enemy in Shakespeare, as here in a report of an English victory at the Battle of Homildon Hill in 1402.

HENRY IV
Here is a dear, a true industrious friend,
Sir Walter Blunt, new lighted from his horse.
Stain'd with the variation of each soil
Betwixt that Holmedon and this seat of ours;
And he hath brought us smooth and welcome news.
The Earl of Douglas is discomfited:
Ten thousand bold Scots, two and twenty knights,
Balk'd in their own blood did Sir Walter see
On Holmedon's plains. Of prisoners, Hotspur took
Mordake the Earl of Fife, and eldest son
To beaten Douglas; and the Earl of Athol,
Of Murray, Angus, and Menteith:
And is not this an honourable spoil?
A gallant prize? ha, cousin, is it not?

Henry IV, Part 1 | Act I, scene 1

15 DECEMBER

*The birthday in 1859 of L.L. Zamenhof, the inventor of the
Esperanto language*

*Holofernes and Sir Nathaniel, speaking in both Latin
and English, are critical of the accent of a Spanish
visitor, Don Adriano.*

HOLOFERNES
Satis quod sufficit.

SIR NATHANIEL
I praise God for you, sir: your reasons at dinner have
been sharp and sententious; pleasant without scurrility,
witty without affection, audacious without impudency,
learned without opinion, and strange without heresy. I
did converse this quondam day with a companion of the
king's, who is intituled, nominated, or called, Don Adriano
de Armado.

HOLOFERNES
Novi hominem tanquam te: his humour is lofty, his
discourse peremptory, his tongue filed, his eye ambitious,
his gait majestical, and his general behavior vain, ridiculous,
and thrasonical. He is too picked, too spruce, too affected,
too odd, as it were, too peregrinate, as I may call it.

SIR NATHANIEL
A most singular and choice epithet.

HOLOFERNES
He draweth out the thread of his verbosity finer than the
staple of his argument. I abhor such fanatical phantasimes,
such insociable and point-devise companions; such rackers
of orthography, as to speak dout, fine, when he should say
doubt; det, when he should pronounce debt – d, e, b, t,

not d, e, t: he clepeth a calf, cauf; half, hauf; neighbour
vocatur nebor; neigh abbreviated ne. This is abhominable
– which he would call abbominable: it insinuateth me of
insanie: anne intelligis, domine? to make frantic, lunatic.

SIR NATHANIEL
Laus Deo, bene intelligo.

HOLOFERNES
Bon, bon, fort bon, Priscian! a little scratch'd, 'twill serve.

SIR NATHANIEL
Videsne quis venit?

HOLOFERNES
Video, et gaudeo.
[Enter Don Adriano, Moth and Costard]

DON ADRIANO
Chirrah!

HOLOFERNES
[To Moth] Quare chirrah, not sirrah?

DON ADRIANO
Men of peace, well encountered.

HOLOFERNES
Most military sir, salutation.

MOTH
[Aside to Costard] They have been at a great feast of
languages, and stolen the scraps.

16 DECEMBER

The birthday in 1775 of novelist Jane Austen, who learned satire through watching and writing comedy drama, and whose wit was favourably compared in her lifetime to Shakespeare's

At least twelve sonnets by Shakespeare address the sin of pride, a subject of Austen's best-loved novel.

SONNET 144

Two loves I have of comfort and despair,
Which like two spirits do suggest me still:
The better angel is a man right fair,
The worser spirit a woman colour'd ill.
To win me soon to hell, my female evil
Tempteth my better angel from my side,
And would corrupt my saint to be a devil,
Wooing his purity with her foul pride.
And whether that my angel be turn'd fiend
Suspect I may, but not directly tell;
But being both from me, both to each friend,
I guess one angel in another's hell:
Yet this shall I ne'er know, but live in doubt,
Till my bad angel fire my good one out.

17 DECEMBER

A giant circular stone carving is discovered in 1790 while digging drains in Mexico City, known today as the Aztec Calendar Stone

Theatre director Quince is presented with some staging problems during rehearsals.

QUINCE
[...] But there is two hard things; that is, to bring the moonlight into a chamber; for, you know, Pyramus and Thisby meet by moonlight.

SNOUT
Doth the moon shine that night we play our play?

BOTTOM
A calendar, a calendar! look in the almanac; find out moonshine, find out moonshine.

QUINCE
Yes, it doth shine that night.

BOTTOM
Why, then may you leave a casement of the great chamber window, where we play, open, and the moon may shine in at the casement.

QUINCE
Ay; or else one must come in with a bush of thorns and a lanthorn, and say he comes to disfigure, or to present, the person of Moonshine. Then, there is another thing: we must have a wall in the great chamber; for Pyramus and Thisby says the story, did talk through the chink of a wall.

SNOUT
You can never bring in a wall. What say you, Bottom?

BOTTOM
Some man or other must present Wall: and let him have some plaster, or some loam, or some rough-cast about him, to signify wall; and let him hold his fingers thus, and through that cranny shall Pyramus and Thisby whisper.

QUINCE
If that may be, then all is well. [...]

A Midsummer Night's Dream | Act III, scene 1

18 DECEMBER

In 1898 the first official land speed record is set, by French aristocrat Gaston de Chasseloup-Laubat, who drives a Jeantaud electric car at a breakneck 63.13 km/h, or 39.23 mph

After a hard day's travails, where do the weary traveller's thoughts turn?

SONNET 27

Weary with toil, I haste me to my bed,
The dear repose for limbs with travel tired;
But then begins a journey in my head,
To work my mind, when body's work's expired:
For then my thoughts, from far where I abide,
Intend a zealous pilgrimage to thee,
And keep my drooping eyelids open wide,
Looking on darkness which the blind do see
Save that my soul's imaginary sight
Presents thy shadow to my sightless view,
Which, like a jewel hung in ghastly night,
Makes black night beauteous and her old face new.
Lo! thus, by day my limbs, by night my mind,
For thee and for myself no quiet find.

19 DECEMBER

The birthday in 1902 of the great Shakespearean actor Ralph Richardson, who was inspired to take to the stage after seeing a performance of Hamlet

Hamlet, chatting with an actor, has trouble remembering his lines.

HAMLET

I heard thee speak me a speech once, but it was never acted; or if it was, not above once; for the play, I remember, pleas'd not the million, 'twas caviary to the general; but it was (as I receiv'd it, and others, whose judgments in such matters cried in the top of mine) an excellent play, well digested in the scenes, set down with as much modesty as cunning. I remember one said there were no sallets in the lines to make the matter savoury, nor no matter in the phrase that might indict the author of affectation; but call'd it an honest method, as wholesome as sweet, and by very much more handsome than fine. One speech in't I chiefly lov'd. 'Twas Aeneas' tale to Dido, and thereabout of it especially where he speaks of Priam's slaughter. If it live in your memory, begin at this line – let me see, let me see:

    The rugged Pyrrhus, like th' Hyrcanian beast—

'Tis not so; it begins with Pyrrhus:

    The rugged Pyrrhus, he whose sable arms,
    Black as his purpose, did the night resemble
    When he lay couched in the ominous horse,
    Hath now this dread and black complexion smear'd
    With heraldry more dismal. Head to foot
    Now is he total gules, horridly trick'd
    With blood of fathers, mothers, daughters, sons,
    Bak'd and impasted with the parching streets,
    That lend a tyrannous and a damned light

> To their lord's murder. Roasted in wrath and fire,
> And thus o'ersized with coagulate gore,
> With eyes like carbuncles, the hellish Pyrrhus
> Old grandsire Priam seeks.

So, proceed you.

Hamlet | Act II, scene 2

20 DECEMBER

The death in 1862 of Scottish surgeon Robert Knox, for whose anatomical dissections the murderers Burke and Hare procured corpses

Two of Titus Andronicus's sons are being framed with a forged letter for the murder of Saturninus's brother.

SATURNINUS
[To Titus] Two of thy whelps, fell curs of bloody kind,
Have here bereft my brother of his life.
Sirs, drag them from the pit unto the prison:
There let them bide until we have devised
Some never-heard-of torturing pain for them.
[...]

TITUS ANDRONICUS
High emperor, upon my feeble knee
I beg this boon, with tears not lightly shed,
That this fell fault of my accursed sons,
Accursed if the fault be proved in them—

SATURNINUS
If it be proved! you see it is apparent.
[...]
Thou shalt not bail them: see thou follow me.
Some bring the murder'd body, some the murderers:
Let them not speak a word; the guilt is plain;
For, by my soul, were there worse end than death,
That end upon them should be executed.

Titus Andronicus | Act II, scene 3

21 DECEMBER

The Winter Solstice, the shortest day in the Northern Hemisphere

Several composers have arranged music for Under the Greenwood Tree, *including Thomas Arne (who wrote 'Rule Britannia') and Donovan (who wrote 'Mellow Yellow').*

AMIENS
[Sings]
Under the greenwood tree
Who loves to lie with me,
And turn his merry note
Unto the sweet bird's throat,
Come hither, come hither, come hither.
Here shall he see
No enemy
But winter and rough weather.

JAQUES (LORD)
[SONG]
Who doth ambition shun,
And loves to live i' th' sun,
Seeking the food he eats,
And pleas'd with what he gets,
Come hither, come hither, come hither.
Here shall he see
No enemy
But winter and rough weather.

As You Like It | Act II, scerne 5

22 DECEMBER

The Feast Day of St Anastasia of Sirmium, known as the Pharmakolytria, the Deliverer from Potions

Macbeth seeks a cure for his wife, who is suffering mental torment induced by her guilt.

MACBETH
[...] How does your patient, doctor?

DOCTOR
Not so sick, my lord,
As she is troubled with thick coming fancies,
That keep her from her rest.

MACBETH
Cure her of that.
Canst thou not minister to a mind diseased,
Pluck from the memory a rooted sorrow,
Raze out the written troubles of the brain
And with some sweet oblivious antidote
Cleanse the stuff'd bosom of that perilous stuff
Which weighs upon the heart?

DOCTOR
Therein the patient
Must minister to himself.

MACBETH
Throw physic to the dogs; I'll none of it.
[...]

Macbeth | Act V, scene 3

23 DECEMBER

Tom Bawcock's Eve, celebrated in the Cornish village of Mousehole with Stargazy Pie – Bawcock saved the village from famine by going out to fish in a storm

Trinculo finds shelter from a storm – but has to share it with the monster Caliban.

TRINCULO

Here's neither bush nor shrub, to bear off any weather at all, and another storm brewing; I hear it sing i' the wind: yond same black cloud, yond huge one, looks like a foul bombard that would shed his liquor. If it should thunder as it did before, I know not where to hide my head: yond same cloud cannot choose but fall by pailfuls.

What have we here? a man or a fish? dead or alive? A fish: he smells like a fish; a very ancient and fish-like smell; a kind of not of the newest Poor-John. A strange fish! Were I in England now, as once I was, and had but this fish painted, not a holiday fool there but would give a piece of silver: there would this monster make a man; any strange beast there makes a man: when they will not give a doit to relieve a lame beggar, they will lazy out ten to see a dead Indian. Legged like a man and his fins like arms! Warm o' my troth! I do now let loose my opinion; hold it no longer: this is no fish, but an islander, that hath lately suffered by a thunderbolt. *[Thunder]*

Alas, the storm is come again! my best way is to creep under his gaberdine; there is no other shelter hereabouts: misery acquaints a man with strange bed-fellows. I will here shroud till the dregs of the storm be past.

The Tempest | **Act II, scene 2**

24 DECEMBER

Christmas Eve

A theatrical company has arrived, and Sly the drunkard is not in the mood for slapstick comedy – or 'comonty', as he mispronounces it. Luckily the play will prove to be The Taming of the Shrew.

MESSENGER
Your honour's players, hearing your amendment,
Are come to play a pleasant comedy;
For so your doctors hold it very meet,
Seeing too much sadness hath congeal'd your blood,
And melancholy is the nurse of frenzy.
Therefore they thought it good you hear a play
And frame your mind to mirth and merriment,
Which bars a thousand harms and lengthens life.

CHRISTOPHER SLY
Marry, I will; let them play it. Is not a comonty, a
Christmas gambold or a tumbling-trick?

PAGE
No, my good lord, it is more pleasing stuff.

CHRISTOPHER SLY
What, household stuff?

PAGE
It is a kind of history.

CHRISTOPHER SLY
Well, we'll see't. Come, madam wife, sit by my side and
let the world slip; – we shall ne'er be younger.

The Taming of the Shrew | Prologue

25 DECEMBER

Christmas Day

A Christmas stocking full of Shakespeare on gifts.

CELIA
Let us sit and mock the good housewife Fortune from her wheel, that her gifts may henceforth be bestowed equally.

As You Like It | Act I, scene 2

OPHELIA
Rich gifts wax poor when givers prove unkind.

Hamlet | Act III, scene 1

BEROWNE
At Christmas I no more desire a rose
Than wish a snow in May's new-fangled mirth.

Love's Labour's Lost | Act I, scene 1

TIMON
Is not thy kindness subtle, covetous,
If not a usuring kindness, and, as rich men deal gifts,
Expecting in return twenty for one?

Timon of Athens | Act IV, scene 3

VALENTINE
Win her with gifts, if she respect not words:
Dumb jewels often in their silent kind
More than quick words do move a woman's mind.

The Two Gentlemen of Verona | Act III, scene 1

FLORIZEL
Old sir, I know
She prizes not such trifles as these are:
The gifts she looks from me are pack'd and lock'd
Up in my heart; which I have given already,
But not deliver'd.

The Winter's Tale | Act IV, scene 4

26 DECEMBER

The Feast Day of St Stephen, when – according to the song – Good King Wenceslas looked out and saw snow lying all about, deep and crisp and even

A beggar hawks his wares. Lawn is an old word for linen; cyprus is cotton; a bugle bracelet is made of beads; quoifs are hairpieces; stomachers are belts or girdles.

AUTOLYCUS
Lawn as white as driven snow;
Cyprus black as e'er was crow;
Gloves as sweet as damask roses;
Masks for faces and for noses;
Bugle bracelet, necklace amber,
Perfume for a lady's chamber;
Golden quoifs and stomachers,
For my lads to give their dears:
Pins and poking-sticks of steel,
What maids lack from head to heel:
Come buy of me, come; come buy, come buy;
Buy lads, or else your lasses cry: Come buy.

The Winter's Tale | Act IV, scene 4

27 DECEMBER

The birthday in 1888 of Thea von Harbou, who wrote the screenplay for her husband's pioneering silent science-fiction film Metropolis

The film's final caption declares that 'the mediator between the head and the hands must be the heart'. Here evil Tarquin enters Lucretia's bedroom, intent on a dark deed.

Into the chamber wickedly he stalks,
And gazeth on her yet unstained bed.
The curtains being close, about he walks,
Rolling his greedy eyeballs in his head:
By their high treason is his heart misled;
Which gives the watch-word to his hand full soon
To draw the cloud that hides the silver moon.

From The Rape of Lucrece

28 DECEMBER

The death in 1924 of brilliant Russian stage designer Léon Bakst who worked with Sergei Diaghilev and the Ballets Russes

One of his first commissions was the costumes for Mikhail Fokine's Cléopâtre *(1909), which were considered scandalously revealing at the time. Antony's general describes Cleopatra's arrival.*

DOMITIUS ENOBARUS
The barge she sat in, like a burnish'd throne,
Burn'd on the water: the poop was beaten gold;
Purple the sails, and so perfumed that
The winds were love-sick with them; the oars were silver,
Which to the tune of flutes kept stroke, and made
The water which they beat to follow faster,
As amorous of their strokes. For her own person,
It beggar'd all description: she did lie
In her pavilion – cloth-of-gold of tissue –
O'er-picturing that Venus where we see
The fancy outwork nature: on each side her
Stood pretty dimpled boys, like smiling Cupids,
With divers-colour'd fans, whose wind did seem
To glow the delicate cheeks which they did cool,
And what they undid did.

Antony and Cleopatra | Act II, scene 2

29 DECEMBER

The birthday in 1914 of jazz musician Billy Tipton, who lived his life as a man, and whose birth as a woman was unsuspected by his band members, his friends and all of the five Mrs Tiptons

Orsino loves Olivia, who loves Cesario (Viola, disguised as a man), who loves Orsino. Viola and Sebastian, Viola's identical twin, thought each other had drowned.

ORSINO
One face, one voice, one habit, and two persons,
A natural perspective, that is and is not! [...]

ANTONIO
Sebastian are you? [...]
How have you made division of yourself?
An apple, cleft in two, is not more twin
Than these two creatures. Which is Sebastian?

OLIVIA
Most wonderful!

SEBASTIAN
[seeing Cesario] Do I stand there? I never had a brother;
Nor can there be that deity in my nature,
Of here and every where. I had a sister,
Whom the blind waves and surges have devour'd.
Of charity, what kin are you to me?
What countryman? what name? what parentage?

VIOLA
Of Messaline: Sebastian was my father;
Such a Sebastian was my brother too,
So went he suited to his watery tomb.
[...]

SEBASTIAN

[...] Were you a woman, as the rest goes even,

I should my tears let fall upon your cheek,

And say 'Thrice-welcome, drowned Viola!'

VIOLA

My father had a mole upon his brow.

SEBASTIAN

And so had mine.

VIOLA

And died that day when Viola from her birth

Had number'd thirteen years.

SEBASTIAN

O, that record is lively in my soul!

He finished indeed his mortal act

That day that made my sister thirteen years.

VIOLA

If nothing lets to make us happy both

But this my masculine usurp'd attire,

Do not embrace me till each circumstance

Of place, time, fortune, do cohere and jump

That I am Viola. [...]

SEBASTIAN

[To Olivia] So comes it, lady, you have been mistook:

But nature to her bias drew in that.

You would have been contracted to a maid;

Nor are you therein, by my life, deceived,

You are betroth'd both to a maid and man.

Twelfth Night | **Act V, scene 1**

30 DECEMBER

The birthday in 1911 of actress Jeanette Nolan, who played Lady Macbeth in her debut screen role, opposite Orson Welles

Macbeth returns home to his Lady after an encounter with three witches who predict that he will be king. They both know, without having to say it, that King Duncan's fate is sealed.

MACBETH
My dearest love,
Duncan comes here to-night.

LADY MACBETH
And when goes hence?

MACBETH
To-morrow, as he purposes.

LADY MACBETH
O, never
Shall sun that morrow see!
Your face, my thane, is as a book where men
May read strange matters. To beguile the time,
Look like the time; bear welcome in your eye,
Your hand, your tongue: look like the innocent flower,
But be the serpent under't. He that's coming
Must be provided for: and you shall put
This night's great business into my dispatch;
Which shall to all our nights and days to come
Give solely sovereign sway and masterdom.

MACBETH
We will speak further.

LADY MACBETH

Only look up clear;

To alter favour ever is to fear:

Leave all the rest to me.

Macbeth | **Act I, scene 5**

31 DECEMBER

New Year's Eve

Falstaff complains bitterly, having been the victim of a prank which saw him carried off in a laundry basket and thrown into the river.

FALSTAFF
Have I lived to be carried in a basket, like a barrow of butcher's offal, and to be thrown in the Thames? Well, if I be served such another trick, I'll have my brains ta'en out and buttered, and give them to a dog for a new-year's gift. The rogues slighted me into the river with as little remorse as they would have drowned a blind bitch's puppies, fifteen i' the litter: and you may know by my size that I have a kind of alacrity in sinking; if the bottom were as deep as hell, I should down. I had been drowned, but that the shore was shelvy and shallow – a death that I abhor; for the water swells a man; and what a thing should I have been when I had been swelled! I should have been a mountain of mummy.

The Merry Wives of Windsor | Act III, scene 5

INDEX OF PLAYS